"She's here"

This would be his date. He reminded himself to show the proper amount of surprise, so it would look natural on camera, but didn't end up having to fake it. He'd seen pictures of Aja Kermani, but they simply didn't do her justice, not in that stunning dress.

He came to his feet. "Wow! Hello, I'm Grady Amos."

"Aja Kermani."

Her hand felt small and cold when he shook it, and she glanced away with a blush, suggesting she was shy or self-conscious.

He moved around the table to hold her chair while she sat down, but she stepped on her dress and pitched forward. Fortunately, he caught her before she could crash into the table and send everything flying, and then she *really* blushed.

"Sorry," she mumbled.

"Don't be nervous," he said with a grin.

She claimed she wasn't, but he could tell that she was. He understood. He'd never had a camera pointed in his face when he was trying to get to know someone, either. But he had an advantage over her. He knew he was on the show for the duration— unless she refused to marry him, which was exactly what he hoped.

Dear Reader,

This is such a landmark year! It's been twenty-five years since I published my very first novel, marking a career spanning a quarter of a century! Almost all my books have been published by Harlequin, so it's fitting that I would have the privilege of writing a special novel for their big 75th anniversary. When I was in high school, their stories brought me so many hours of delicious escapism, and they've continued to bring me joy throughout my life.

This book is also special because it completes my popular Whiskey Creek series. There's one Amos brother who's been waiting to have his story told—Grady—so I'm excited to finally bring him his happily-ever-after. Although this book also stands alone, if you'd like to read the rest of the series, it goes like this: *When Lightning Strikes*, *When Snow Falls*, *When Summer Comes*, *Home to Whiskey Creek*, *Taking Me Home for Christmas*, *Come Home to Me*, *The Heart of Christmas*, *This Heart of Mine*, *A Winter Wedding* and *Discovering You*.

Thank you for celebrating this special milestone with me and with my publisher!

Brenda Novak

TYING THE KNOT

BRENDA NOVAK

SPECIAL EDITION

Harlequin®
SPECIAL EDITION™

Recycling programs for this product may not exist in your area.

ISBN-13: 978-1-335-40196-0

Tying the Knot
Copyright © 2024 by Brenda Novak, Inc.

When We Touch
First published in 2012. This edition published in 2024 with revised text.
Copyright © 2012 by Brenda Novak, Inc.
Copyright © 2024 by Brenda Novak, Inc., revised text edition

Harlequin Enterprises ULC
22 Adelaide St. West, 41st Floor
Toronto, Ontario M5H 4E3, Canada
www.Harlequin.com

Printed in Lithuania

MIX
Paper | Supporting responsible forestry
FSC® C021394

Author **Brenda Novak** is a *New York Times* and *USA TODAY* bestselling author with more than ten million books in print, translated into twenty different languages. She also runs Brenda Novak for the Cure, a charity to raise money for diabetes research (her youngest son has this disease). To date, she's raised $2.7 million. For more about Brenda, please visit brendanovak.com.

Books by Brenda Novak

Harlequin Special Edition

Whiskey Creek

When Lightning Strikes
When Snow Falls
When Summer Comes
Home to Whiskey Creek
Taking Me Home for Christmas
Come Home to Me
The Heart of Christmas
This Heart of Mine
A Winter Wedding
Discovering You

Visit the Author Profile page
at Harlequin.com for more titles.

To Janet Costanzo Robel

I love your zest for life!
Thanks for infusing my online book group
on Facebook with your positive energy and for
all you do to support me as a friend and a reader.
The bookish community I look forward to interacting
with every day wouldn't be the same without you.

CONTENTS

TYING THE KNOT

Chapter One

"You want me to do *what*?" Grady Amos had been leaning toward the woman he'd just met—Winnie…something. He couldn't remember her last name. But he liked her. She was attractive in a polished, fashionable way, wearing a long straight skirt and a sleeveless blouse—obviously designer clothes that fit her trim figure to perfection—with her blond hair pulled back in a sleek ponytail at her nape. A woman in high heels who smelled like the perfume counter at Macy's wasn't something he ran into very often in the small Gold Country town in Northern California where he'd been raised. Folks were pretty casual in Whiskey Creek. So when he'd walked into Sexy Sadie's to relax after a long day at work, she'd stood out—enough that he'd veered over to the bar to claim the empty seat next to her.

But what she'd just said had him scooting back by a foot at least.

"You'd make a great contestant on the dating show I'm producing," she repeated.

He made a face to show he wasn't excited by that idea. She'd said she was in town for two days visiting a friend on her way to Los Angeles. She was coming through after spending the weekend in Lake Tahoe at her parents' cabin. But she was obviously recruiting along the way. She was probably always recruiting. She seemed ambitious, the type to take her work very seriously.

"You're making a reality TV show?" he said. She'd told him she was a producer, but she hadn't gotten specific until she'd learned that he was unattached. When she'd started to probe to find out his status, he'd assumed she was asking because she was interested in him the same way he was interested in her, so that was part of his disappointment.

She looked a bit crestfallen herself. Most people probably showed a great deal more interest when she mentioned what she did for a living. "We're in our third season. You've never seen *Tying the Knot*?"

"I'm afraid not." He'd never been interested in reality TV... other than *Survivor*. He made an exception for that show because it was freaking amazing. And maybe *Naked and Afraid*. He considered the dating ones—*The Bachelor*, *The Bachelorette* and all the others—to be for women.

She adjusted the straw on the Moscow mule he'd bought her. "You should give it a try, see what you think."

He doubted it would be anything he'd enjoy, but he liked talking to her and was hoping to get her to go out with him even if it meant he had to drive six or seven hours to LA. "What's the show about, exactly?"

"It's a study of first impressions—whether human beings can choose a mate based on looks and instant chemistry, or if they need time to get to know each other in order to have a successful relationship."

"Oh, it's like that show my sister-in-law was talking about the other night." He cast about in his mind for the name. "What's it called? The one where they meet at their own wedding?"

"*Married at First Sight*? Not really," she said with a shake of her head. "On my show, you'd get to choose your bride."

He finished his beer and signaled for the bartender to bring him another. "How does it work?"

"Our contestants take a battery of personality tests. Then they're sent on three dates, each with a different woman—" she selected a peanut out of the bowl in front of them "—all of whom have been vetted and handpicked by psychologists as being compatible. And then they get to choose one of the three."

"To continue dating?"

"To marry."

Of course. He knew there'd be a catch. The show had to have a shocking premise. That was what gave it word of mouth, made it worth tuning in. "Sounds like whoever does this is asking for trouble."

Her eyes widened at his response. "Not really. If the marriage doesn't work out, they can always have it annulled," she said as if it was no big deal. "It's not that different from dating in the real world. There are connections and breakups. Some relationships work and others don't."

If it was that similar to real life, they wouldn't be making a show out of it. But he didn't say so. "The women don't get to choose?" He grinned. "Isn't that a little misogynistic?"

She arched her eyebrows. "The men chose in season one, the women chose in season two."

So it was the men's turn…

He rubbed the beard growth on his chin. He wanted to find a good woman with whom he could start a family. He'd wanted that for a long time. And yet, here he was staring down his fortieth birthday and he hadn't yet found love.

He was beginning to worry he'd be single for the rest of his life, which was why, for a brief moment, a small part of him was tempted to try something this unconventional. At least it would put him in close proximity to Winnie, whom he considered the real prize. He didn't want to spend the rest of his life alone. But with all the posturing and deceit on those matchmaking sites, online dating was already out of his comfort zone. Why would he take an even bigger risk? "Meeting someone on the internet is about as wild as I get."

"You've tried that, then?"

"I have, here and there." He'd pulled down his profile probably four years ago, after one of the women he'd met began to stalk him, so it'd been some time.

She popped another peanut into her mouth. "And how has that worked out for you?"

He gave her a dirty look. "It hasn't, but there's no guarantee this would, either." There had to be a lot of heartache involved in something like this. Embarrassment, too, since so much of what happened would be made public. He wasn't one to seek the limelight, even if he could leave Whiskey Creek for as long as it would take to shoot the various episodes…which he couldn't. "Would my odds be any better going onto a reality TV show?" he challenged.

"Maybe. We have three couples from seasons one and two who are still married," she said proudly. "I plan to incorporate them—in a small way—in this year's show."

He straightened. "Three out of how many?"

"Eight."

Nearly 50 percent wasn't bad. "I'm shocked to hear the success ratio is that high."

"We do a lot of testing before we even get started," she said with a measure of satisfaction. "We want people to be happy."

He began to peel the label on his locally brewed IPA. "How do you find your contestants?"

"People apply online. We've nearly finished casting this season. I just need one more guy. Actually, I need two guys. There's one person I'd like to replace." She grimaced. "I'm not totally sure about him."

"What do I have that he doesn't?" Grady asked.

"You're not vying for attention, not already applying for every other show on TV or looking for a way to break into showbiz. That alone will give you more sincerity, make you more convincing and appealing in general."

He'd suspected reality shows weren't actually "real." They were well-choreographed, and this proved it. But he supposed that was the only way they'd ever work, so he couldn't get too upset about it. Most people understood they weren't completely unscripted. "I doubt I'll be any good on TV. I've never been on before. And there has to be drama, or it'll be boring. You won't get much drama out of me."

"Trust me, the situation brings its own drama," she said with an appealing laugh. "I don't need you or any other contestant to be difficult. The odds are already stacked against us—against the survival of long-term relationships in general—and yet that's exactly what we're striving for. Our viewers are rooting for our contestants to fall in love."

"I think I'm too private of a person."

"You'd be well compensated."

"I have a job," he pointed out. She'd asked him what he did when he sat down, so she already knew that.

She took another sip of her drink. "You said you work at an auto body shop?"

Clearly, she wasn't dazzled by his vocation, but he made a good living. Money wasn't one of his problems. "I don't just work there, I own it," he clarified. He wanted to impress her, or he would've added that he didn't own Amos Auto Body entirely on his own. He and his four brothers were partners, but they'd grown the business a great deal since they'd taken over from their father. They had three locations now—the original shop here in Whiskey Creek and two others, one run by his second oldest brother in Reno, Nevada, and the other by his younger brother, the baby of the family, in Silver Springs, California, which wasn't too far from Los Angeles.

"But this could make you a star," she said as if it was the ultimate enticement.

He didn't want to be a star. He just wanted to find a good woman. "There's no way I could take that much time away from my business even if I wanted to."

He assumed she'd let it go at that, but she didn't. "If you're the boss, don't you have employees who can take care of things while you're gone?"

Since Aaron and Mack had moved away, he, Dylan and Rod had taken on a couple of guys to fill their slots, plus one more to give them some breathing room. Dylan and Rod had families and couldn't work the kind of hours they'd put in before. But *he* was still there all day, every day. Although they split the money evenly, it made sense that he should carry more of the load since he didn't have quite so many demands on his time. "I have a few."

"Then do something unexpected, something wild." She lowered her voice. "It could change your life."

"We'll see." It was hard to turn down such a beautiful, earnest face. But he simply wasn't the type to go after something like this. She'd said that three of the couples who'd been on the show were still together, but that didn't mean they'd withstand the test of time. This was only the third season!

Maybe once they'd passed their tenth anniversary, he'd believe they had a fighting chance.

"Don't you want to get married?" she pressed.

He craved the committed and hectic but happy lives his brothers were living. But he doubted this was the way to get it. "I'd like to find someone," he admitted. "But it would need to be the right woman, and I can't imagine meeting my wife in such a way."

"Don't knock it 'til you've tried it," she said. "Best-case scenario, you find the woman of your dreams. Worst case, you come back here and do what you've always done."

When she put it that way, staying in Whiskey Creek didn't sound all that appealing. Just lonely.

But a reality TV show? No way. "I'll think about it."

She checked her phone, seemed startled by the time and slid off her stool. "I've got a conference call. But here's my card." She winked as he accepted it, and her smile hit him right in the gut. "Give me a call if you change your mind."

He slid the card in his pocket as she walked out. He wanted to give her a call, but it wasn't because he wished to be on her TV show.

Chapter Two

She was going to disappoint her mother. There was no way around that now.

Aja Kermani frowned at the latest text she'd received from Esther. A picture of another wedding dress. Last night, her mother had sent color schemes, suggesting black and ivory would be "lovely." And yesterday morning? Ideas for the cake. Esther didn't know that there would be no wedding. Aja had broken up with Arman four days ago, the night he proposed. She couldn't continue the relationship; it gave him false hope, led him to believe she felt something she didn't.

Bottom line, she wasn't interested in living the life her parents had carefully choreographed for her, didn't want to become an exact replica of them.

There was nothing wrong with them, of course. She loved them dearly, had tried to please them as far back as she could remember. She understood the sacrifices they'd made to immigrate to the United States, hoping to build a better life, and the opportunities that provided for her and her brother, and she was grateful.

But Aja wanted something more. Or something else, she thought, quickly correcting herself. As much as she kept trying to follow what her parents insisted would be the best course for her, she was no longer interested in forcing herself into a mold she clearly didn't fit. As time went by, the vague lack of fulfillment she'd battled through the years was turning into a deep dissatisfaction. She wanted to be free to dream her own dreams and then try to accomplish them, and the hunger to do so had been growing for years…since all the way back in middle school.

Do you like this? It's nearly $7,000, but I think you'd look stunning in it.

Aja read her mother's follow-up message twice. Her parents would be willing to spend seven thousand dollars *on a dress*?

That was a lot of money. But they had it. Her father was an ophthalmologist, and her mother an orthodontist—both professionals. They lived in a beautiful home in Newport Beach, an expensive part of Orange County, and spent a lot on vacations, cars and other things. It didn't surprise her *too* much that they'd go all out for her wedding.

So…what were they going to say when she told them that she couldn't bring herself to marry their best friends' son?

She sank into the soft leather chair behind her desk in the small office of her dental practice and sighed as she gazed at her diplomas, pictures of her family and various friends hanging on the walls. She'd been a dentist for eight years, had built a solid practice in a relatively short amount of time.

But it was getting more and more difficult to make herself come to work each day. It was her parents who'd really wanted her to become a dentist. She'd done it to please them, and because she didn't have a clear alternative—knew they'd be mortified if she told them what she really wanted to do—she'd fallen in line.

But how much longer could she continue slogging through each day? She was feeling cornered and claustrophobic, needed to break out of the same old routine.

She just didn't know how, or if she'd regret it later.

It was the fear of regret—and dashing her parents' hopes for something that wouldn't turn out to be successful—that had held her firmly in place. But then Arman had proposed, and she'd realized that marrying him would set the rest of her life in cement. The fear that'd swamped her in that moment had chilled her to the bone.

Knowing she couldn't continue to ignore her mother's texts, she gathered her resolve and called Esther.

"There you are!" her mother chirped. "Are you still at the office?"

Aja worked long hours. Too long. That was part of the problem. She didn't have much of a life outside of her practice. She'd had very little time to work on her pottery, hadn't been in the studio for months. And before she got her degree, it'd taken everything she had just to make it through dental school. Biology, anatomy and physiology had been such difficult subjects for her, especially because all she'd wanted to do was create. "I am."

"What do you think of that wedding dress I sent you? Isn't it absolutely stunning?"

Her mother had good taste; Aja had to give her that. "It is."

"So? Do you want to try it on? Tomorrow's Saturday. We could have lunch and spend the afternoon shopping."

Aja squeezed her eyes closed. *Here goes...* "I'm afraid not." She opened her mouth to continue, but Esther filled every break in any conversation and spoke before she could.

"If tomorrow won't work, we could go Sunday before dinner. Your father could grill, and I could arrange the sides in advance."

They had family dinner every Sunday. It was a tradition, and a weekly opportunity for her parents to make sure their children were still on track. "No, Mom. It—it's not the day that's the problem. I need to tell you something."

"What is it?" she asked, obviously surprised by the serious tone of Aja's voice.

"There isn't going to be a wedding."

Silence. Then her mother said, in a panic, "Arman told his parents that he was going to propose on Monday. Did I blow it? Jump the gun? Oh, my God! Has he not asked you yet? I'm *so* sorry! Now I know why you didn't call to tell us. He hasn't followed through quite yet."

Wincing, she cleared her throat. "Actually, he *did* ask, but I said no."

"Why would you do that?" her mother snapped.

Aja squeezed her forehead with one hand. "Because I'm not in love with him."

"Arman's a good boy. He'll make a wonderful husband and father."

"I'm sure that's true. He's a nice person. The problem is...I don't love him," she explained.

There was another long stretch of silence. Her mother had to be stunned. Her parents and Arman's parents had believed for years that they'd one day be celebrating the union of their children, thereby bringing the two families even closer. "So...*that's* why we haven't heard from the Kahns," she said as she processed what Aja had just told her. "They must be heartbroken for their son and—and angry with us."

"I hope not," Aja said. "It wasn't my intent to...hurt anyone or cause problems in your relationship with them."

"Your father and I believed... Well, we obviously thought marriage and a family was what you wanted."

"It *is* what I want, Mom. Just not with Arman."

"With who, then?" she asked, as if he was the only logical choice.

"I don't know! I haven't been free to find someone who excites me, who makes me feel...how I should feel before committing myself for the rest of my life."

"You're not interested in Ali, are you?" she asked suspiciously. "I know he's shown a great deal of interest in you. But Arman is a heart surgeon, Aja! Ali is...well, he's nice, but..."

But Ali was a dance instructor. His earning potential couldn't match Arman's. It wouldn't be nearly as advantageous of a match.

"I wouldn't recommend a man like him," her mother said.

Aja had circulated within the Persian community in Los Angeles her whole life. She wanted to expand beyond the people she already knew, but saying so would only upset her mother. Her father, too, when he heard. They'd wanted to come to America for safety and upward mobility but didn't really want their children to be *American*. They clung to the old world, the one they'd left.

But she'd been born here. To her, living in the United States meant embracing change—looking forward, not back. Almost everyone in America had originally come from somewhere else. It was the world's great melting pot, and yet her parents didn't want her to conform. "I don't plan on dating Ali, Mom. We're just friends." That was true and yet she admired him. He'd stood up to his own parents, was being who and what he most wanted to be.

"Who then?" her mother asked.

She remembered some of the young men she'd met at UCLA. There'd been several she'd found attractive, and yet she'd turned down those who'd asked her out. Some had even been in dental school with her, meaning they'd also be professionals, but they weren't Persian, which meant she'd have to cope with upset and disappointment—and possibly downright antagonism—at home. Since she'd already been struggling just to get through school, she hadn't dared take on that fight at the same time.

But now… She was thirty-four. She'd lived her parents' way long enough to know, deep in her soul, that it wasn't *her* way. As well-intentioned as they were, as much as they loved her and thought they were doing what was best for her, she had to insist on more free-dom and autonomy—had to be able to, like Ali, forge her own path.

Better late than never, she thought. But… She frowned as her eyes once again circled her tiny cubicle of an office. Did that mean selling her practice? Or bringing in another dentist so she could have time to focus on her pottery?

Either was a risk. She didn't have the financial security of her parents, couldn't withstand a serious mistake…

Could she dare take action?

This was the question that always drove her back into the same old corral.

"I don't have anyone in mind," she told her mother. "I just… know it wouldn't be right to marry Arman."

Aja could feel her mother's disapproval coming through the phone; it washed over her like a tidal wave. "I think you might live to regret that," her mother said.

"I know."

"Arman is handsome and smart—"

"But I'm not in love with him," she said adamantly, breaking in. "I've now said that two other times."

"Love grows from respect, Aja. And that head-over-heels feeling isn't all it's cracked up to be. Arman adores you. He treats you like a queen."

"I'd be doing him a disservice," she insisted. "I like him too well to saddle him with an unhappy wife."

"Unhappy…" her mother echoed.

"Yes—unhappy. I'd be unhappy if I married him," she said, and that was probably what finally convinced Esther to back off.

"Okay," she said. "Only you know what's best for you."

Exactly. Those words felt like a soothing balm, and yet Aja knew her mother didn't truly believe them, or she'd be in an entirely different situation.

"I'd better call Behar and try to explain."

Aja liked Behar and Behram, Arman's parents. She liked his brother, too. They'd been part of almost every holiday, several vacations and lots of Sunday dinners. It was going to be difficult to face them, given they probably no longer liked her. "I'm sorry for disappointing them," she said. "I'm sorry for disappointing you, too."

"It's fine," her mother said stiffly. "I just… I hope you're not making a terrible mistake."

So did Aja. Life was fluid. There were no guarantees.

She said goodbye and disconnected, then looked at her watch. It was six thirty on a Friday night. Her receptionist and hygienist had left at three thirty. They had families to go home to and enjoy the weekend with. She had no plans. Except on Sunday, of course. But showing up at her parents' house for dinner this week would not be easy.

She was just finishing annotating various patient charts and calling to check on a couple of people she'd given root canals earlier in the week when she received a text from her brother.

Oh, no, you didn't.

She frowned. Her mother must've called him about Arman. She'd essentially kicked the beehive that was their world, their status quo, and sent her parents and all their friends buzzing.

Oh, yes, I did.

Are you going to stick by it?

She knew *he'd* want her to. Any barriers she busted through left a hole for him.

I have no choice. I simply can't marry Arman.

How'd he take the news?

Not well. I'm guessing he thinks I might change my mind because he hasn't told his parents. Otherwise, they would've contacted Mom and Dad.

Or he *did* tell them, and they're mad.

That's what Mom thinks.

Damn. I didn't know you were such a troublemaker.

I wish I had an older sibling to knock down barriers for me. ;)

News flash. You've conformed for thirty-four years. That's not knocking down barriers. But now you're giving me a little hope.

Very funny. Have you told Mom and Dad that you don't want to be a lawyer? That you'd rather be an actor?

Not yet. I haven't received any great opportunities that would force my hand. But I have another audition coming up.

What is it for this time?

A reality TV show called Tying the Knot.

Aja googled the show and read the premise. Are you kidding me? You could wind up married!

I could also be discovered, Darius replied.

You don't care about the risks?

Not really. It's something for my résumé, a potential start. And it pays a decent amount.

But what about Mom and Dad?

They don't watch reality TV. They'll never know.

You'd just bring your wife home to meet them when it's all over? What are the chances she'll be Persian?

Admittedly, not great. But if I love her, it'd be worth fighting that fight. And if I don't? I'll get an annulment, and they'll never be the wiser.

You're so reckless. [rolling eyes emoji]

We have only one life. I plan to live mine.

Aja wanted to live hers, too, but it wasn't that simple. If you make them too mad, they could cut you off, quit paying for school.

Then I'll drop out. Unlike you, I can't be bought. ;)

Tough talk for someone who only does what he wants in secret. ;)

That's called being smart. Why make waves if I don't have to?

Aja chuckled. When's the audition?

Tomorrow. Want to go with me? We could grab lunch after.

That would certainly be more fun than laundry and housecleaning. Why not go and offer him some moral support? Seeing how auditions like that worked could be interesting...

Sure. What time?

Ten. But I'll pick you up at nine. You know what traffic can be like in this city.

I'll be ready.

Setting down her phone, Aja took a deep breath. She'd refused the marriage proposal of her parents' best friends' son and longed to quit dentistry so she could have her own pottery studio. Darius had no interest in becoming a lawyer, even though he was in law school. He hoped to become an actor, which was even riskier than being an artist. Almost everyone in LA wanted to be an actor...

She bit her lip as she considered the dark clouds gathering on the horizon. Her parents were soon going to realize that they didn't have either one of their children under control.

Chapter Three

They arrived twenty minutes early—traffic had been light—and waited in the lobby of an office on the fifteenth floor of a high-rise in Burbank. The office didn't seem to be fully staffed, and the receptionist was dressed casually, giving Aja the impression Saturdays weren't normal workdays. She assumed they were putting in extra hours to finish casting the show. From what Darius had said in the car, they were supposed to start shooting soon.

The receptionist looked up when they checked in, then motioned them to the leather couch and chairs surrounding a very modern-looking coffee table. They were reading the magazines they'd found on that table when the producer walked out ten minutes later.

She shook Darius's hand before turning to Aja. "And who is this?"

Darius explained that she was his sister and had just come along for the ride, but the producer, who'd told them to call her Winnie—invited them both back to her office.

Aja tried to beg off. She didn't want to intrude. But Winnie insisted it wouldn't be a problem, so she sent her brother an apologetic glance, in case her presence was hurting his chances of getting on the show, and he gave her a little shrug as if to say there was nothing they could do about it now.

One whole wall of the producer's office overlooked the busy street below. Aja wanted to walk over to it and sip the coffee she'd purchased on the ground floor while letting the two of them talk, but Winnie pulled an extra chair up to her desk and motioned for them both to sit down.

Wishing she'd waited in the car, Aja clung to her coffee as she complied.

"So… I've had a look at the application you filled out online," Winnie said to Darius, lifting a piece of paper that was probably a printout of that application. "You definitely look interesting to me. You're attractive, well-educated with great earning potential. And you scored well on the personality test. The only problem is…you're a little young."

"I'm almost twenty-six," he said.

She made a face that suggested his age might be a sticking point. "Most of our contestants are over thirty. The psychologists who help us with the show feel we'll have a better chance of success with those who are slightly older. They have more experience with relationships, tend to know more about what they want and are more likely to be content when they settle down." She dropped his application back on her desk. "What makes you want to be on a show like *Tying the Knot*?"

"I'm an adventurous person and think this might be an interesting way to meet someone. I also enjoy psychology, so the experiment aspect appeals to me."

Aja silently applauded the fact that he said nothing about becoming a star. But she could tell the beautiful, poised woman dressed in cream slacks and a matching blouse was no one's fool. Aja was willing to bet she saw right through him…

"You aren't currently in a relationship…" she said.

"No."

Her gaze shifted to Aja. "How old are you?"

Aja had just lifted her coffee to her mouth, so Darius answered for her. "Thirty-four."

"And…are you attached?" the producer asked.

Swallowing, Aja lowered her cup. "No, um, I'm not seeing anyone right now."

"What do you do for a living?"

Uncomfortable with the attention, she shifted in her seat. Wasn't this supposed to be Darius's interview? "I'm a dentist."

"Here in LA?"

She nodded. "I've been in practice for the past eight years."

"And you're not dating anyone?" she asked again, as if she couldn't quite believe it.

"I just broke up with my boyfriend. But… I'm not applying to be on the show." She gestured at her brother. "We're getting lunch afterward. I didn't mean to intrude on his audition...or interview," she corrected, since he wasn't actually running lines.

"You're not intruding," Winnie insisted. "I'm glad you're here. There's been some last-minute jockeying with the cast. Now, I need another female contestant, and I'm out of time to advertise. But you seem ideal. You're *very* attractive."

Aja was glad Winnie didn't mention the Disney princess Jasmine. So many of her patients asked if she worked for the park in her off hours. But then, Winnie probably knew better than to perpetuate racial stereotypes. "I appreciate the compliment. But—"

"If you'll come on the show, I'll take your brother, too," she said matter-of-factly, cutting off Aja.

Aja blinked. She could feel the heat of Darius's gaze—it seemed to be boring holes into her—as he willed her to accept. He believed this could be his big break. But she couldn't even imagine being part of a reality TV show. "Um, I'm not sure... I mean, I have patients I need to see."

"You could reschedule them," Darius said quickly. "You work too hard, could use some time off. You've told me that before. Why not grab hold of this? Challenge yourself in a different way?"

Hadn't she just been hankering for change? The idea of doing something daring appealed to her. She'd played it safe for so long. But she wasn't convinced this was her type of daring... "I'm just not...cut out for TV," she said with a laugh that sounded nervous even to her own ears.

Winnie cocked her head. "What makes you say that?"

"I've never aspired to be an actor, never even tried out for anything."

"I'm not looking for professional actors," she said. "Just solid contestants. Men and women who want to fall in love and would make good spouses, so that any couples who get together as a result of the show stand a good chance of lasting."

Aja had thought Darius was reckless for agreeing to find a

mate in such a way. *She* couldn't do it, too! And yet… She could sense him silently pleading with her. "Darius would be perfect—"

Winnie interrupted her again, this time with a skeptical expression. "He's a little young."

Damn. That wasn't just a statement. It'd come off like a decree. The woman was going to stick with her both-or-neither offer…

"Come on, Aja. Live a little," Darius murmured, and she couldn't bring herself to disappoint him. Why not throw away the rule book for a change? It'd be an adventure, an experience. Besides, she could be one of the contestants who got rejected after the first date. Then, she would've helped her brother without it even costing her much time away from her practice.

But just in case, she asked, "How long would it take to film the whole season?"

"A little over a month," Winnie told her. "But you'll be well-compensated. Even if you get kicked off the show, you make about three-fourths as much as those still on it for promotional support, in case we need you to come back for an episode here or there, or do a talk show or something. And we do our homework. The psychologists who work with our contestants are some of the best. They do an analysis on each person to establish an in-depth personality profile that takes into consideration their hopes and dreams."

"How long would I have to notify my patients and shift my schedule around?" Aja said.

"We start filming in three weeks," Winnie continued. "Before that, though, I'd need you to come back and meet the director, take some pictures and test video for promotional purposes, get a medical exam, which, just to warn you, includes some drug testing, and go through a pretty rigorous psychological exam."

"The psychological exam is different from the personality tests?" Darius asked.

"It is. This one's designed to weed out any fragile or dangerous people." She waved a hand as if to say it was just a formality. "I'm sure you'll both pass with flying colors, but I wanted to mention it so that you're prepared, and also to reassure you that the people you meet will have been put through the same safety precautions."

"Sounds like it'll be busy even before we start to film," Aja said.

Winnie tightened the ponytail at her nape. "There will be some appointments, for sure, but we can work around your schedule to give you the time you need."

"Will you do it?" Darius pressed.

Why not? This meant so much to him. Maybe it really would be his big opportunity. "Okay," she said.

"Yes!" Her brother pumped his fist and a smile spread over the producer's face. Winnie was obviously pleased to have gotten her way. Aja guessed she was rarely denied.

"Wonderful." The producer got to her feet. "Just give me a minute while I grab the contracts, and we can go over them together."

"So…you're really going to do this?" Mack asked skeptically. "This…producer woman is *that* gorgeous?"

Grady had driven six hours to Silver Springs, where he'd spent the night with his youngest brother and his wife, Natasha. He was now only two hours from LA and, after having breakfast with them and their three kids in their new home tucked back in the hills, he was just climbing into his truck to be able to make his lunch appointment with Winnie Bruckner. "She's *that* gorgeous."

Tasha stood next to Mack on the sidewalk, holding their youngest, a little girl who was about to turn one, in her arms while their oldest kicked a soccer ball in the front yard with his brother. "But you're going to be marrying someone else," she said, her forehead creasing in confusion.

"Winnie needs one more male contestant, and she's out of time. Filming starts in a week. I'm just doing her a favor…and hoping to get to know her in the process."

"In the process of marrying someone else," Mack responded, going right back to the point his wife had made.

"It's just a show!" he said in exasperation. "The marriage can be annulled."

Mack grimaced as he stretched his neck. "Doing this... It... doesn't seem like you."

It *wasn't* like him. But he had an opportunity; he figured he might as well take it. All his brothers had wives and families. So did his friends. It felt as though he was being left behind. And it wasn't as if he'd reached out to Winnie. A week after he met her, she'd gone to the trouble of looking him up and calling him at the auto body shop, and what she'd said made a lot of sense. "If you do what you've always done, you'll get what you've always got," she'd said. "So why not take a chance?"

Agreeing to participate could be a big mistake, something he'd live to regret. He was well aware of that. But playing it safe wasn't getting him what he wanted. At least this way he'd be in almost daily contact with her. "I'll just pick a contestant I'm completely incompatible with—who will refuse to marry me, so no one gets hurt—and see how it goes with Winnie in the time I'm there."

"No doubt she'll be grateful that you've made the effort to take so much time off work and drive to LA to save her show," Tasha said. "But...it's weird to think she'll be trying to pair you up with someone else."

"And even if it goes great, and you wind up seeing her instead, what happens if word gets out that you're dating the producer?" Mack asked. "Won't that cause a big PR fiasco? One that could ruin the show?"

Grady got in and buckled his seat belt, leaving the door open so they could continue to talk. "I guess if things go that well, we'd just wait until the show's over before we start to date."

"But it films before it airs," Tasha said. "You might be waiting a while."

"It'll air right after, and we can always talk behind the scenes."

"Okay, but..." Tasha adjusted the bow in baby Hazel's hair. "Are you sure she's not taking advantage of your interest in her?"

He lifted his hands. "I'm not sure of anything. But you know what they say—nothing ventured, nothing gained. We'll see how it goes."

He took the baby and gave her a kiss before handing her back. "I'll stay in touch." He yelled goodbye to the boys, who yelled back, almost in unison, "'Bye, Uncle Grady!"

Mack and Natasha exchanged a worried look, but he'd already arranged for the time off and come this far. He wasn't turning back now.

He closed the door and started the engine. Before he could drive off, however, he heard his phone ding with a text.

It was from Winnie: You're still coming, right?

I'll be there, he wrote back and waved as he pulled away from the curb.

Chapter Four

In just a few days, Grady had signed the contract setting out the rules of the show, including a nondisclosure agreement, been photographed, filmed, given a physical, taken a drug test and had a psych evaluation. He knew the show was doing a background check on him, too. And that was all before they'd started the personality tests, which had taken the better part of the past two days.

But because he'd come at the last minute just to help Winnie out, she'd agreed to make an important exception for him. Instead of having the psychologists employed by the show select the three women he would meet, he'd convinced her to give him the profiles of the female contestants so he could choose himself. After all, Winnie had the final word and had admitted to making changes after receiving recommendations in the past. She'd said that sometimes she had to make certain decisions for the good of the show, so he didn't feel too guilty about pressing her to bend the rules. Especially because, when looking through those profiles, it'd been easy to find the woman who was going to help him escape this sticky situation—the one who'd all but guarantee he'd be free to date Winnie when the show was over.

Her name was Aja Kermani. She was well-educated—a dentist—and had been born and raised in the big city. He was an auto body repairman whose mother had committed suicide and father had gone to prison when he was a kid, so he'd been raised by his oldest brother and had only a high school diploma. She'd had two loving parents who'd given her the benefit of everything money could buy. He'd had very little growing up, including supervision, and he lived in a Gold Country town that was so small it'd probably bore her to tears. She liked art and theater. He preferred action movies. She liked to read. He fell asleep whenever he opened a book and would rather spend his time outdoors.

They had absolutely nothing in common.

He stared down at her picture. She was beautiful, with large brown eyes, smooth, light brown skin and thick dark hair. And her mouth…what a smile! But there was no way someone like her would ever want to marry to him.

He chuckled as he leafed through the rest of her profile. This was turning out even better than he'd thought. Apparently, her younger brother was a contestant, too. Grady had found a hand-written note in her file saying Aja had only agreed to come on the show so that her brother, Darius, could participate. Whoever wrote that note, probably Winnie, felt that having siblings on the show would be an interesting twist, and Grady had to agree. He was curious to see how it would play out. And he was glad this Aja woman didn't have her heart set on coming out of the experience with a long-term relationship. That meant he couldn't disappoint her.

It was all so perfect, especially because he was getting to see the woman he *really* wanted almost every day.

His phone signaled a text. "Speaking of the devil," he mumbled. It was Winnie.

Are you coming down?

The show was putting him and the other men up in a huge mansion in Hollywood. He supposed the women were in a similar situation, just somewhere else. Tonight was the big kickoff of the show, where they were going to film a meet-and-greet, first with the women and then with the men. They had to do it separately, since the two sexes couldn't meet until they had their "dates."

He checked his watch. I was told seven. Are we doing it earlier?

I'm not talking about filming. I need to get those files back before someone finds out I gave them to you.

I thought you were the boss. ;)

Very funny. I am the boss, but breaking the rules could damage the image of the show, especially if someone leaked it to the press.

A good scandal might actually help her. She could use the headlines to boost ratings. Her show hadn't taken off quite like she'd hoped—at least not yet. But he was glad she wasn't out to get that kind of attention, because this time it would involve him.

Understood. Just putting on my shoes. Where do you want to meet?

Everyone's getting ready, so it's quiet down here. Have you been to the pool house out back?

No, but he'd seen the pool from his window. I can certainly find it.

After he hustled through the corridors of the house, through the kitchen and out onto the deck, she was waiting for him with a satchel when he finally reached the pool.

"Do you want to go inside the pool house?" he asked.

"No. That might look even more odd," she replied. "No one's out here. Just give them to me."

He handed her the files, and she immediately stuffed them in her satchel.

"Did you find someone?" she asked.

"I did. Aja Kermani."

"The Persian woman? Why?"

He grinned. "Her personality test, of course."

She rolled her eyes. "Just so you know, that isn't one of the women our panel of psychologists recommended for you."

Somehow, that didn't surprise him. No doubt they'd seen exactly what he'd seen—there was no way they'd be compatible. "Who do they think I'll have a better chance with?"

"I'm not going to tell you, so at least it'll be a surprise when you meet the other two."

"I guess I can go along with that," he said with a shrug. "Just out of curiosity, can you tell me who they paired her with?"

"Omar Hussan."

"Because he has a similar ethnicity?"

She looked alarmed. "You've already met him? You were supposed to be kept separate from each other until tonight."

"Don't worry. The security guards are doing their job. I guessed from the name."

"Oh, of course," she said, visibly relaxing. "We're playing the odds here. For something like this, we have to. Two people often find it easier to get along when they share the same cultural heritage, religious beliefs, political beliefs and so on."

He gave her a funny look. "You've read her file, right? She's not Muslim."

"No, but he is. And I'm guessing she'll be more familiar with his religion than any of our other contestants. I certainly can't see her with you. You probably won't even be able to agree on the type of food you want to eat when you go out."

Grady wasn't worried about that. He could be flexible since it wouldn't really matter in the end. "I'm sure we can compromise. Thanks for letting me have the profiles."

"You're welcome." She glanced at the house and lowered her voice. "But we're even now, okay? You have to play by the rules from here on out. I can't be granting you any more favors."

"No problem."

She smiled up at him. "God, you're handsome. I just know you're going to be a favorite on the show." Her smile turned slightly devilish. "I hope you're ready for the attention and publicity."

He liked the first thing she'd said. He wasn't so thrilled about the second. "Did I forget to tell you I'm a private person?" he asked.

She glanced over her shoulder as she walked away, her heels

clicking on the cement. "The psychologists have filled me in—I know all your dark secrets," she said with a wink.

Last night, after the meet-and-greet that would serve as the first part of episode one, the director—a man named Jim Kline—and Winnie had debated for almost fifteen minutes on whether to take Aja's cell phone away so that she couldn't communicate with her brother during the month they were filming. They didn't want the two of them passing information back and forth—what certain people were saying at the girls' house and what certain people were saying at the boys' house.

Fortunately, in the end, they'd let her keep it, but only because of the possibility that what she and Darius said to each other would create more drama.

Witnessing that conversation had made Aja more than a little uneasy. She knew she'd signed a contract that gave them a lot of power over her life—even down to what she could say about the show for five years after it aired—but she'd never really thought she'd be at risk of losing her cell phone. She was a dentist. Her office should be able to get hold of her if one of her patients had an emergency. Her receptionist and hygienist were still working, doing cleanings and the like. And she'd arranged to have a colleague handle the appointments she hadn't been able to reschedule as well as be on-call in case of an emergency. But she cared about her patients, wanted to know what was happening with them.

Besides, she and Darius had told their parents they were taking a month off to travel to Italy together, but Esther and Cyrus would still expect to hear from them on occasion.

"You look a little lost."

She turned away from the kitchen window, where she'd been staring out into the backyard since they got up from the breakfast table a few minutes earlier, to see that she'd been approached by one of the other eleven contestants—Barbie LaFaver, who looked remarkably similar to her namesake, even down to the way she dressed. The rest of the women were standing around the room talking as they waited to film the final segment of the opening show, which would involve receiving the name of their potential groom.

"I didn't sleep well," Aja said, which was true. She'd tossed and turned for hours, wondering why she'd allowed her brother to get her involved in something like this.

Barbie lowered her voice. "Don't tell me you're having second thoughts…"

"Maybe a few," she admitted.

"I understand. I don't like that they're watching our cell phones so carefully. But filming won't last forever—only a month, right? This is a great opportunity. Even if we don't find love, the notoriety that comes with it can open so many doors that would remain closed to us otherwise."

Aja nodded. She'd heard that some reality TV stars were able to parlay their start into something that made a lot more money.

"Are you nervous about your date?" Barbie asked.

Aja was actually eager for it. If she was eliminated from the show, she wouldn't have to worry so much about how she was going to survive a whole month of being micromanaged—where other people limited her cell-phone use and denied her access to the internet, television, even books. She hadn't truly understood how demanding and confining it would be. But she was quickly learning that those running the show planned to test them in various ways; reality TV wasn't any good without an abundance of emotion and people were more likely to exhibit emotion if they were under a great deal of stress. "Maybe a little," she said.

Barbie gripped her hands tightly in front of her. "I'm *super* nervous."

"Since we aren't the ones choosing, I wish they'd let us watch the segment they filmed last night, introducing the men."

"I do, too, but they want it to be a 'cold meeting' on both sides so they can film our faces when we first see each other."

Before Aja could respond, the director came into the room with a film crew. "We're starting in five," he barked out.

They were about to hand out the envelopes. The men would get three names in theirs, of course; the women, this year, only one.

The people in charge of makeup scurried forward to blot the shine from their foreheads and slick back or tuck away any strands of hair that weren't fully cooperating, while the sound crew performed mic checks.

A few minutes later, when all was in place, the host, a man named Danny Schular, smiled and said, "Everyone ready?"

The director looked around and seemed comfortable with what he saw, so he lifted his hand to signal for silence. "Action!"

"As you know, this is the day when you get the envelope containing the name of the man who might soon be your husband," Danny said as the cameras rolled. "It won't mean much to you, since you haven't even seen a picture of those who are participating this season, but since we've just introduced them to our viewers, it'll mean something to them." He grinned for the cameras' sake. "So, tell me, are you eager to meet the man you could spend the rest of your life with? Or are you a little anxious you won't advance beyond the first date?"

Barbie spoke first. "I'm not super confident, but I can't wait to see how I do. I've never been lucky in love. To have a psychologist pick someone who is compatible with me? That sounds awesome."

Another one of the women, Vana Kozlowski, talked about how traumatized she was from past relationships, and how she was working on overcoming her fear of intimacy to be able to give the relationship she hoped would come from the show a fighting chance. Another woman, Sheila Golding, shared some of her not-so-pleasant experiences with online dating, including one relationship with a narcissist that had just about destroyed her.

Several of the others chimed in, too. Some of the footage would probably be cut during editing—only the best sound bites would air—and plenty of people responded, so Aja thought she was off the hook, until Danny looked at her.

"What about you?"

Aja froze for a second. She couldn't tell the truth—that she was longing to break out of the mold her parents had created for her despite the love and gratitude she felt for them. If they ever saw the show, it would break their hearts. So she said something about being so busy as a dentist that she hadn't had time to focus on her love life, and now that she was approaching thirty-five, she was feeling her biological clock ticking and decided the show might be able to help her find the man of her dreams.

She was happy about her response but surprised when she was the only one to get a follow-up question.

"How do you feel about your brother being matched with one of the women you've just met?" Danny asked, gesturing good-naturedly toward her fellow participants.

Several of the women straightened, others leaned forward to hear her response, but all seemed duly surprised. This was, of course, the first they'd heard of her having a sibling on the show, and she couldn't help wondering if they were pleased or put off by the idea.

She couldn't see her brother with any of them, but she couldn't say that. What if Darius married one? They'd soon be sisters-in-law. "He's my baby brother, only twenty-five. Of course, I feel protective of him. But he, too, has been very busy. He's in law school at UCLA and will be taking the bar soon, so, like me, he hasn't had a lot of time to date. If he could find someone special… I can't imagine that wouldn't be a good thing for him."

Danny leaned in close. "But which one of these women would you choose for him?" he asked.

She laughed as if she wasn't uncomfortable, even though she was. He was hoping she'd make either an ally or an enemy, get the intrigue started right away. "I haven't had the chance to see what they're really like."

"Well, you know this is a show about first impressions…" he persisted.

"*My brother's* first impression, not mine," she quipped and was relieved when he simply chuckled and let it go.

"Then we'd best get on with it and see who will be going out to dinner with him," he said as he handed out the envelopes he'd just taken from his jacket pocket. "As soon as you open your envelope, be sure to get together with the participants who have the same potential groom so the three of you can draw a number from the buckets we'll be passing around. That's how we will determine who'll go first, second and third when it comes to the dating sequence."

The cameras came forward to get close-ups as they opened the envelopes and pulled out the slips inside.

"Darius Kermani!" Barbie exclaimed, reading hers aloud. "That has to be your brother. Kermani's your last name, right?"

Aja's heart pounded as she nodded—she wasn't sure why. Probably because she was afraid Darius had also made a mistake coming on the show. Although she liked Barbie, she couldn't see how any self-respecting psychologist would pair her with Darius— she was nothing like the girls Aja had seen him date before—so she was losing confidence in a system that'd once sounded fairly logical.

"Neal Kirkpatrick," a woman named Liz called out. "I like his name," she added with a laugh.

Cindy—Aja couldn't remember her last name—held up her slip. "I've got Omar Hussan! So if you've got him, too, watch out. I'm bringing my A game, complete with six-inch stilettos on our first date."

Everyone started laughing and connecting with those who had the same potential groom, as instructed. Aja was the only one standing alone when the exclamations and random comments died down.

"Who do you have?" Danny asked as everyone looked at her.

She read her slip again before holding it up. "Grady Amos."

"Taylor and I have him, too," a woman named Genevieve said and motioned her over.

It was the first time Aja had really considered the competition aspect of the show. Until this moment, she'd simply told herself she didn't care if she was eliminated. But when she saw that Winnie and Jim—or the psychologists behind the scenes—had put her up against two of the most beautiful, confident women on the show, she had a feeling Grady was their prize catch.

Chapter Five

Aja had texted her brother to learn more about Grady, but Darius hadn't been much help. In typical Darius fashion, he summarized everything in one general statement. Seems like a cool dude.

Unsatisfied, she tried to draw out more detail. Do you think we'd be a good match?

Depends. Does it bother you that he's white?

Their parents would not be pleased, but Aja wanted to be blind to race, to entertain the possibility of growing close to any nice man she was attracted to. Not at all. What does he look like?

He's tall, fit. I guess most women would consider him handsome. I don't know. You'll have to judge for yourself.

She sighed. Again, that didn't tell her much. But at least she wouldn't have to wait long to see Grady for herself. She was first in the lineup for the dating portion of the show, which was starting in just a few hours.

She got another text from her brother: What about the women who've been chosen for me? Which one do you think I'll like best?

Now she could understand why he'd been so vague. She didn't know them very well, so she couldn't share much about their lives or personalities. And she thought one was prettier than the others but wasn't sure he'd agree. The last thing she wanted to do was criticize the woman he ended up marrying. Barbie's super friendly, she told him.

What does that mean? Pick her?

A text came in from the director. A driver will be there in thirty. Make sure you're downstairs.

I don't know, she wrote to her brother. I guess you'll have to judge for yourself, too. I have to get ready. I'm first.

Good luck.

She was determined not to get swept up in the competitive spirit that'd taken hold of the participants earlier—changing the sisterhood they'd all felt last night for making the show and being in the same challenging situation to adversaries for fear of being eliminated—and simply be who she really was. But taking something so unusual in stride was easier said than done. She grew more and more nervous as the time drew closer to her departure.

When her alarm went off five minutes before she was supposed to be downstairs, she took one last look in the mirror. They'd been directed to wear evening gowns, so she was dressed in a burnt orange mermaid-style dress that fell off the shoulders, and she was wearing her hair down, brushed until it was gleaming and curled. A professional had helped with her makeup, so she'd look good despite the bright lights necessary for filming, and had painted her nails to match her dress.

A ball of nervous energy sat in the pit of her stomach as she descended the stairs. The rest of the contestants were waiting in the entryway to see her off and looked up when they heard the rustle of her dress.

A gratifying murmur went through the crowd, and Barbie met her as she stepped onto the slate floor to tell her that the color of her dress was absolutely perfect for her. "And it contrasts so nicely with your gorgeous white teeth," she added.

There was a sweetness in Barbie, a sincerity, that was making Aja hope Darius *would* choose her. "Thank you," she murmured, and was immediately ushered outside and into a limousine with darkened windows.

Winnie and Jim had insisted Grady wear a suit, which meant he'd had to go buy one. The last time he'd gotten this dressed up was over two decades ago, for prom.

The support crew and gaffers had set up tables and cameras with the appropriate lighting on the veranda, in the dining room, in the kitchen and in a wine cellar, so they could film all four dates one right after the other, two hours apart. He was up first, which meant he had to have dinner with his date in the wine cellar, where they could control the lighting to make it look later, as if it was dark outside.

He was stationed at a candlelit table for two, set with linen, silverware and fine china, as well as a bottle of champagne on ice. He was no expert in the finer things of life, but everything looked classy to him. He liked the brick walls and floor, the wooden casks and wine racks to one side, the stylish lights that hung from the ceiling and the general ambience. It was a cool place to have dinner.

Hearing footsteps on the stairs, he scooted his chair back and looked up as the cameraman entered the room.

"She's here," he announced and got into position as someone else started to descend the stairs.

This would be his date. Grady didn't know which of the "choices" he'd meet first, but he'd seen all their pictures because he'd had the files. He just had to be careful not to let on that he knew more than he should about whomever showed up.

He reminded himself to show the proper amount of surprise, so it would look natural on camera, but didn't end up having to fake it. He'd seen pictures of Aja Kermani, but they simply didn't do her justice, not in that stunning dress.

He came to his feet. "Wow! Hello, I'm Grady Amos."

"Aja Kermani."

Her hand felt small and cold when he shook it, and she glanced away with a blush, suggesting she was shy or self-conscious.

He moved around the table to hold her chair while she sat down, but she stepped on her dress and pitched forward. Fortunately, he caught her before she could crash into the table and send everything flying, and then she *really* blushed.

"Sorry," she mumbled.

"Don't be nervous," he said with a grin.

She claimed she wasn't, but he could tell that she was. He understood. He'd never had a camera pointed in his face when he was trying to get to know someone, either. But he had an advantage over her. He wasn't taking the show seriously, so it was probably easier for him to ignore the unusual circumstances. He also wasn't competing against the other guys the way she was against two other women, so he didn't have anything to lose. He knew he was on the show for the duration…unless she refused to marry him, which was exactly what he hoped.

He popped the champagne and poured them each a glass. "So I guess we should start with the basics," he said. He needed to have her tell him the information he already knew—like the fact that she was a dentist—so he couldn't blow it by mentioning any of those details before she did. "Where are you from?"

"I was born and raised in Newport Beach."

"Is that where you'd like to settle?"

"I can't go too far from the area. I'm a dentist, and my practice is here in LA."

Bingo. He smiled. "Of course. It'd be difficult to rebuild a practice."

"What about you?" she asked.

"I'm from a small town in Northern California with only about two thousand people called Whiskey Creek."

"I've never heard of it." She took a sip of her champagne. "What do you do there?"

"Auto body work."

She cleared her throat. "You fix cars?"

"Not the engine. The body, after a collision."

To her credit, other than that slight pause while she cleared her throat, she didn't act as if a man with a blue-collar job was totally out of the realm of possibility for her. Given that she was so educated, he would've thought she'd be a little more put off. But the camera could have something to do with her tempered response. Maybe she didn't want to come off as arrogant or stuck-up…or do anything to make him choose someone else, which would mean she'd be eliminated from the show. "And do you like it?" she asked.

"I do."

She put down her glass. "Were you born in Whiskey Creek? Is that where you'd like to spend the rest of your life?"

"I really like it there, but…" He thought of Winnie, who would be watching this. She probably wouldn't be any more eager to leave the Los Angeles area than Aja. "Nothing's set in stone. I could always open a franchise here."

She sat back. "Oh, so you own the shop."

"In partnership with my brothers. We own three—one in Whiskey Creek, one in Reno and one just two hours from here in Silver Springs."

She put her napkin in her lap as someone entered with a crab cake appetizer. "How'd you get into that line of work?"

He settled his napkin in his lap, too, and leaned back as the plates were put in front of them. "My father started the business. But he went to prison when I was only twelve, so my oldest brother had to take over and try to provide for the rest of us. Otherwise, we would've been put into foster care and likely split up."

Her eyes widened. "Where was your mother?"

"I didn't have one at that time. She suffered from depression and overdosed on her meds not too long before my father went to prison. So it was just Dylan taking care of the rest of us."

Her fork hung in the air with her first bite. She glanced at the camera and quickly lowered it. "I'm so sorry. How many siblings do you have?"

"Four—all brothers. And Dylan had to finish raising us. Can you imagine?"

"I can't. That means your father must've been in prison for…a while."

"Almost twenty years." This information would come up with each date—and Winnie probably already knew about it because of his background check—so he figured he might as well state it up front, get it out of the way. Plus, with Aja, scaring her away was part of his strategy. "He wasn't usually violent, but he started drinking after my mother died and knifed a man in a bar for taunting him about her death."

Aja's jaw dropped. This was obviously completely foreign to anything she'd experienced. Grady almost started to laugh. He didn't find any part of his childhood funny, but he was shocking the hell out of her—that was the funny part. This was going down exactly as he'd expected. Winnie would have to be pleased with the drama.

"That must've been terrible," she murmured. "How old was... Dylan, did you say his name is?"

"Eighteen. He had to drop out before graduating and take over at the auto body shop."

She blinked several times. "Wow, that is young. He must be an amazing person."

"He is." Grady had nothing but love and respect for his oldest brother, who'd taken on a task few people could. Dylan hadn't been a perfect substitute father, but he'd done his damnedest, and he'd turned the business around, too.

She finally took a bite of her crab cake. "Where do you fall in the family?" she asked.

He cut into his food, too. "Right in the middle."

"So...you have two older brothers and two younger ones. Five boys wouldn't be easy for anyone to raise, let alone someone only eighteen."

"You got that right. We were such hooligans that we had quite a reputation. People in town called us the Fearsome Five," he said with a chuckle, "because we were always in some sort of trouble. Fortunately, we've cleaned up our act since then."

"I get the impression your father's out of...prison now. How's he doing?"

There was a lot he could say about JT but he figured he'd stick with the facts, which were bound to come out, anyway, because of being on this show. "Better," he said. "He's come a long way."

She took another drink of champagne, and he couldn't help

noticing that her manners were impeccable. "Do you have a relationship with him?" she asked.

"I do. He works at the shop with me these days and comes to the house now and then."

"I'm happy to hear that."

He put more sauce on his crab cake. "There's a guy on the show with the same last name you have and looks a great deal like you. Could it be that he's your brother?"

Her chest lifted as she drew a breath, and her smile grew less strained. "Yes. He's my only sibling, younger by eight years."

"And what do your parents do?"

"My father's an ophthalmologist. My mother's an orthodontist."

"And your brother's in law school. You're a family of professionals."

"My parents really pushed us in school."

The same person who'd brought the appetizer returned with two plates filled with garlic-encrusted filet mignon, au gratin potatoes and asparagus spears.

"What made you decide you wanted to do a show like this?" he asked as the person waiting on their table cleared away what was left of the crab cakes.

"I, um, I had a couple of reasons, actually."

He started to cut into his steak, but when she paused, he looked up.

"I've been too busy to date in the traditional way and was… looking to introduce a bit of daring into my life, I guess."

He felt his eyebrows go up. "You've always played it safe?"

"I guess I have."

She was the classic "good girl." And he was the classic "bad boy." This reminded him of the movie *Grease*. "And? What do you think? Are you glad you did it?"

"So far?" She gave him a sweet smile. "I go back and forth."

Perfect answer, he thought. She couldn't be completely honest on camera, but he got the impression "no" was what she wanted to say—and that was reassuring, at least as far as he was concerned.

Chapter Six

Aja felt like crying. She'd done terribly on the date. Although Grady seemed like a nice person—and he certainly wasn't bad looking—she didn't think he'd be a good fit for her so she tried to console herself with that. But it was hard to fail at anything—she'd been taught failure wasn't an option—and was willing to bet, after tonight, he wouldn't hesitate to choose someone else. No doubt both of the poised women who were next in line would perform better than she had. Before signing up for this show, she should've given more weight to the fact that she was an introvert, and this setting would be extremely stressful for her. She would have if she hadn't been trying to make her brother happy.

Oh, well, I wasn't really expecting anything to come from it, anyway, she told herself as the limousine drove her back.

Still, she felt overly emotional, so maybe that wasn't true. Maybe she just wasn't willing to admit that she actually found Grady quite attractive and *did* have her hopes up that this would be the start of something new and exciting—a breath of fresh air as she burst out of the box that'd confined her since she could remember. She'd broken up with someone she'd known her whole life and now missed—not in a romantic sense but as a friend—and couldn't even call him without him thinking there might be a chance at reconciliation. And she'd done it—and upset her parents and threatened their relationship with Behar and Behram, who were like an aunt and uncle to her—because she desperately craved *something else.*

She managed to hold in her emotions and smile for the other girls, who were waiting for her, eager to hear all about the experience, when she walked into the mansion. She told them Grady was charming and the food was delicious and the camera wasn't too intrusive, even though she'd been far too nervous to be able to taste the food and she'd been so self-conscious about the camera she'd tripped and nearly fallen...and not much had improved from there. She couldn't understand why they'd been paired in the first place. They didn't seem to have *anything* in common.

Genevieve and Taylor, the other two women who'd also been selected to meet Grady, watched her closely. She could feel the difference in the way they looked at her versus anyone else and got the feeling they were sizing her up, trying to determine just how high the bar had been set. They were also trying to pick up any nuggets of information that might prove helpful to them.

Everyone else congratulated her, complimented her dress and speculated on the men they'd meet.

She stayed in the living room with them long enough to make her response to the date seem convincing. She didn't want to tip off the assistant producer, or anyone else who worked for the show, that there was anything deeper going on, or the cameras would follow her to her room.

But as soon as she felt she could get away, she told them she had a headache and went up to change and go to bed. She needed a few minutes of privacy—something they didn't like to allow on the show because they were afraid the contestants would decompress and thereby avoid an argument or something else that might prove interesting to viewers—and had just changed out of her gown when she heard a knock.

Holding her breath for fear it would be someone with a camera, she tightened the belt on her robe and hurried to the door. "Who is it?"

"Barbie."

Aja let her breath go. She really wanted to be alone. But Barbie was better than Winnie or Jim or any other *Tying the Knot* personnel. She opened the door and forced a smile, hoping the dim lighting in the hallway would hide the evidence of her tears.

"Is something wrong?" Barbie asked.

Aja stepped back to let her in as she shook her head. "Just the stress. I have a headache."

Barbie closed the door behind her. "That's why I came," she whispered. "When I got here, they took away all my meds, even my antihistamines, so I'm guessing they did the same to you and everyone else. They expect us to ask for a doctor if we need anything, so I wanted to see if you needed some painkillers."

"Do you have some?" Aja asked in surprise. "I thought you just said they took away all your meds…" They probably would've taken hers, too, but she didn't have any.

Barbie grinned conspiratorially. "They did, but they missed a small pack of ibuprofen."

"And you're willing to give that to me when it's all you have? You're *too* nice."

"We have to stick together. It'll make this experience so much more enjoyable."

"Even though most of us will be going home soon? They'll be done filming the first dates by tomorrow night, you know. They're starting first thing in the morning and going all day."

She handed Aja a small envelope containing two pills. "Well, I'm hoping you and I will still be around."

"Me, too," she said and was amazed to find it was true. As difficult as it was, she wasn't the type of person who liked to lose and didn't want to return to her practice to find she was in the same exact position she'd been in before taking this leap.

"I'll let you get some sleep." Barbie started to leave but turned back at the last second. "Aja?"

"What?"

"Do you think your brother will like me?"

"I don't know anyone who wouldn't," Aja said and meant it.

Barbie must've heard the sincerity in her voice because she impulsively hugged Aja. "Thank you."

"What time is your date?" Aja asked.

"I go right after lunch tomorrow—at one."

"I'll come help you get ready."

Barbie's face brightened. "Really?"

"Why not?" Since her date was over, she wouldn't have much else to do. She'd just be waiting for the big reveal, which wouldn't

happen until the day after. First, they had to film the guys rumi-
nating over their choices and struggling to make the right decision.

"Thanks," Barbie said and left.

Aja put the pills in her purse in case Barbie needed them later.
Just having a friend stop by to show some concern had made her
feel better.

She got in bed and texted Darius.

How was your date tonight?

Not that great. What about you?

I did terrible! It was so embarrassing.

What went wrong?

To start things off, I tripped on my dress and would've wiped
out the whole table if my date hadn't caught me.

[crying laughing emoji]

Stop! It's not funny.

Okay. Seriously, that's not a big deal.

It is to me!

I'm sure a guy can overlook that. What did you think of Grady?

She pictured the tall, dark-haired man she'd met. He had pierc-
ing hazel eyes and a five-o'clock shadow that covered a strong
jaw and chin. But it was his smile she liked best. His teeth weren't
perfectly straight, but the way one front tooth lapped slightly over
the other gave his smile a unique character. He's okay-looking,
I guess.

Would you say you're compatible?

One date really isn't enough to be able to tell. To be honest, if I were to get into a serious relationship with him, I'd be a little worried about his childhood. Anything terrible that could happen did.

Anything? Like what?

You'll see. Suicide. Prison. Five boys trying to raise themselves. He must carry some very deep scars, and who knows how that informs the man he is today.

That's concerning.

Right?

I gotta go. They're calling a meeting about tomorrow.

Just one more thing. Keep an open mind when it comes to Barbie.

You've picked a favorite for me, after all?

I guess so. She's got a very kind heart.

[thumbs-up emoji]

An hour later, Aja was just feeling better, more optimistic, when she got a text from the director.

Can you come down? I'd like a word with you.

Winnie held her wineglass loosely in one hand as she studied him. "How'd it go? Do you think you chose the right one?"

Grady leaned back as he considered the question. It was late. Everyone at the mansion was asleep. At least, all the lights were out over there. He and Winnie were sitting at the small kitchen table in the guesthouse, where she was staying so she could be on-site to take care of any problems that cropped up in their off hours, as well as oversee all the filming. "I haven't met the other two women yet," he said. "That's tomorrow, right?"

She poured him some more wine. "But you already picked Aja from the profiles. I'm asking if you think you'll stick with her after having met her."

"I don't see why not. She seems ideal." He took a drink of his chardonnay. "Well, ideal in that she's all wrong for me," he added.

Winnie grimaced at his response. "We've never had a participant sabotage their own journey on the show. You'll be able to capitalize on this opportunity much better if you can be one of its success stories. It'll keep you on the show longer, you'll be asked to return in future seasons, you'll have more interest from the press. You might even get booked on other shows—"

"Except I'm not here for the money, the fame or any more of the same kind of work," he interrupted.

She must've known where he was going with that comment because she narrowed her eyes in mock anger. "What *are* you here for?"

He met her gaze. The question was sort of a challenge, but he wasn't afraid of it. "I'm here for you."

"For *me*," she said, pressing a hand to her chest.

"That comes as a surprise?" He chuckled. "I tried picking you up at a bar. Obviously, I like what I see."

"Okay, maybe I'm not entirely surprised…" she said.

Grady resisted a yawn. He was dead tired. It'd been a long day doing things he definitely wasn't accustomed to doing. "So… are you going to go out with me when this whole thing is over?"

She got up and went to the window. "Grady, this show means a lot to me. I really want you to give it your best shot."

He crossed his legs in front of him. "I'm giving it my best shot. Didn't you like the footage from my date?"

She hesitated, then admitted, grudgingly, "That footage was pretty good."

"Lots of dirty laundry there," he pointed out. "Perfect for prime time, but it came at my expense. I had to talk about my past. That isn't something I like to do." In previous years, he wouldn't have done it no matter what the incentive. It was the passage of time and having a much better life in the years since that made it possible.

Winnie looked slightly abashed. "I can see why. I'm sorry. But you were using it on purpose, trying to make yourself unappealing to Aja."

"There's that," he admitted, then got up and walked over to her. He liked that she'd invited him over to "check in on how things were going for him on the show," as her text said, but he wasn't going to try to take it any further than a conversation she could have with any of the participants. There wasn't any reason to create a scandal that could threaten her hopes for the series…and her career in general. He only wanted to get close enough that she'd look up at him again. "You never answered my question."

"What question?"

"You know what question. Are you going to go out with me after this is all over?"

Continuing to stare out the window, probably because it allowed her to avoid his gaze, she didn't answer.

"I hope I'm not doing this for nothing…" he added.

She finally shot him a grudging smile. "Yes, I'll go out with you when the show's over. You have this—this thing about you. Charisma, charm or whatever. It sort of grows on people."

She didn't sound happy to admit it, which made it even more of a victory. He gave her a broad smile. He'd been wanting to find someone for a long time.

Maybe he finally had.

But first, he had to get through the show.

Chapter Seven

Jim had demanded Darius's phone and had taken screenshots of the texts Aja had sent for possible inclusion in the dating episode, which meant Grady would see them. She hated the idea of that, hadn't written them with that in mind. She'd argued against it, but the show's director had insisted people would love the vulnerability she felt, as well as her candid reaction to the trauma Grady suffered as a child. He also liked the guidance she'd offered her younger brother, which revealed her budding friendship with a fellow contestant.

"The women in the audience will definitely be able to identify with your concerns," he'd said. "Grady's background is something a potential wife *should* consider. This will allow everyone some insight on your decision—whatever that will be if he chooses you as his bride—and make them root for you. Bottom line, it's engaging stuff."

She'd asked if she could take out a few lines—censor it a bit to save her and Grady some embarrassment—but he'd refused. Those were the parts he found most valuable.

"This will make you popular among viewers, and that's never a bad thing," he'd said.

She was willing to bet he used that excuse with contestants whenever it served him. He didn't care about her. He didn't care about Grady, either. He cared about boosting the show's ratings.

"You didn't say anything *really* bad," Jim had insisted when she'd continued to argue.

At least that was true. But there were still things in that exchange that made her cringe when she imagined Grady reading them. She'd said he was "okay-looking," for one. And she'd basically said, with a background like his, he must be damaged goods.

Punching her pillow, she flopped onto her other side. She'd been tossing and turning ever since she'd gotten into bed. At this rate, it would be morning before she fell asleep, which meant she'd have even lower emotional reserves.

She knew one thing, though. If she stayed on the show, she'd be a lot more careful in the future, would never let Jim or Winnie or anyone else with *Tying the Knot* get one over on her ever again.

Grady's other two dates weren't very remarkable. He might've asked Genevieve out on his own, had he met her somewhere else, but he didn't feel strongly about her one way or the other, and he really wasn't attracted to Taylor. He couldn't say why. She was pretty enough and said all the right things. There was just no chemistry.

He was ready to be off camera as evening approached, but he knew they'd be filming the big "decision" tonight, where the men would meet to discuss the pros and cons of each woman they'd been matched with. They'd decide if they'd marry one, and if so, which one it would be.

He considered bowing out. This whole thing was beginning to seem too ridiculous. But he'd committed to it and couldn't hurt the show Winnie was trying so hard to make a success. So he figured he'd go ahead and leave it in the hands of Aja Kermani. Regardless of what she decided, at least he would've done his part. He couldn't imagine she'd ever agree to marry him, anyway.

He was in his room, getting changed for the final taping of the day, when he received a text from his brother Rod.

I haven't heard from you. Now that you're going to be famous, maybe you don't have time for those of us who are less important. But I wanted to see how you're doing. Have we lost you from auto body work for good?

His brothers constantly teased him, about anything. Actually, he did his share of the same sort of thing. This is an experience, but don't hire anyone to replace me. I'm not going anywhere.

Acting's not your thing?

Definitely not.

But are any of the women interesting to you?

There's one. With the way Jim, the director, was acting about cell phones—how carefully their behavior was being monitored—Grady wasn't about to get specific and tell his brother that the "one" wasn't even a contestant.

Are you going to marry her?

I announce my pick tomorrow. We'll see what she says, he wrote, switching back to Aja in his mind. But I'm fairly certain I can start packing my bags.

You don't think she'll say yes...

I think she'd be crazy to. [laughing emoji]

You don't seem too disappointed.

I'll be okay. Something might still come from the show later.

Mack told me about that. Nothing's changed there?

Nothing's changed.

Looking forward to watching the show.

Grady was not excited about having his friends and family watch, but he was reconciled to the fact that it was going to happen.

Someone knocked on his door.

"We're waiting for you downstairs," a voice called through the panel.

Surprised, he checked his watch. Sure enough, he was running late. "Be right there!"

* * *

Jim must've leaked the texts she'd sent her brother, because when Aja went to breakfast the morning of eliminations, everyone was talking about it.

"You don't think Grady's attractive?" Barbie whispered, seemingly shocked.

Aja nearly swallowed her tongue. She'd known those texts would be revealed at some point, but she assumed it would be when the show aired, and by then they'd all be off living their separate lives again. "I… It's not that I think he's *un*attractive. He has a great smile when he actually smiles. It's just that his appeal is more…intangible."

"Genevieve and Taylor claim you must be blind, that he's totally hot."

Aja tried to defend her position. "He's got sex appeal, for sure. But there's also a certain wariness inside him that can be seen in his eyes. He's not exactly open. He's defensive, and it makes sense that he would be."

Barbie gave her a pitying, sheepish look. "I hope it makes sense to him, or…"

Or she'd be off the show. Barbie didn't say it, but Aja understood what this would likely mean. The director had sabotaged her. Maybe he thought she wasn't turning out to be interesting enough, after all.

"What happens happens." She was doing this for her brother, anyway, she reminded herself. If she had to go back to her regular life, with nothing changed, she'd try to figure out a saner path toward finding contentment.

Barbie squeezed her hand under the table. "Okay. I'm glad you won't be disappointed."

"It'll be fine," Aja said stoically.

"I wonder who your brother's going to choose…"

Aja squeezed her hand back. They'd spent most of yesterday together, were quickly becoming close. Barbie was the opposite of Grady—totally open and trusting—and Aja knew she really liked Darius. Aja didn't want to see someone like Barbie get hurt. "If he's as smart as I think he is, he'll choose you."

"He hasn't told you?" she asked uncertainly. "You'd say so if he did, right?"

"He hasn't told me. I won't text with him anymore. Not after the show took screenshots of our last exchange," Aja said and looked up to see Genevieve watching her.

The other woman smiled like the Cheshire cat while eating her egg soufflé, and Taylor, who was sitting next to her, leaned in to whisper something. They knew they had an advantage over her now.

Winnie came into the room, trailed by Jim. "This is going to be a big day," the producer announced to the room at large. "It's always exciting to narrow the show down to our couples. But it's also hard to say goodbye to the people who will be leaving. I just wanted to thank you all for being part of the experience and to tell you that even if you're eliminated, we'll look for opportunities to bring you back on and include you when we can."

The women glanced at each other, no doubt wondering whom this would pertain to...and hoping it wouldn't be them.

"We've decided to shoot the reveal segment here," Winnie continued. "Since we'll be cutting the cast on the female side from twelve to four, we won't need this much space, so tomorrow we'll be moving to a different house. That way, we can capture people packing up and leaving and get their take on what going home feels like—if they believe they could've made a successful match with the man they met even though they weren't chosen, that sort of thing."

Aja was so certain she would be leaving that an hour later, when the men filed into the living room where the women were already waiting, and all the contestants were together for the first time, studying each other curiously, she sat in a chair in the back, behind the others, her bags packed in her room.

After the normal drama and preamble to pump up the suspense, Neal Kirkpatrick took the floor. He opened a ring case to show a gold band to the camera. Then he walked over to one of

.the women he'd met as if he was going to propose, moved on to another as if it was really her and finally got down on one knee to propose to the third.

"Will you marry me?" he asked Liz Cheyne.

The other two girls began to cry in disappointment as Liz beamed at him. "I will!" she exclaimed, and he got up to embrace her.

Omar Hussan went next. He opened his ring but didn't mess around with trying to mislead anyone. He walked directly to a woman named Mirabelle Lacey, who seemed shocked that he'd picked her, and a little uncertain, but ultimately agreed.

They had two of their couples…

Aja swallowed hard as Darius got up. He showed off his ring before dramatically moving toward one woman before changing direction and getting down on one knee in front of Barbie.

After a quick celebratory glance at Aja, Barbie threw her arms around him before he could even ask her to marry him.

Everyone laughed as the two of them fell over. Then the focus turned to Grady. Aja couldn't help wondering how he felt about the texts she'd sent Darius. She had little doubt he'd heard about them and wished she could completely disappear. But she had to gut it out until those who were eliminated were interviewed.

The other contestants kept craning their heads to look at her, even though everyone knew he was going to choose between Genevieve and Taylor.

Aja watched him walk over to Genevieve, saw the confident expectation on her face and assumed that was it. But all he did was tell her she was a beautiful woman who would, no doubt, make someone else a very happy man. He gestured at Taylor and said the same was true for her. Then he wove through the chairs to reach Aja…and got down on one knee.

Grady thought he was in the perfect position. Three other couples had agreed to marriages. Providing they didn't get cold feet and back out in the next few days, Winnie could make a season even if he wasn't on it. And after what Aja had texted to her brother, he knew she didn't even find him attractive. But he tried to shrug it off because then he had an even greater chance she'd say no when he proposed.

He grinned as he opened the ring and showed it to her. It was nothing special—just a gold band provided by the show.

"Aja Kermani, I know you might not have enjoyed our date as much as I did, so I understand the risk I'm taking here. But I think I could make you happy…and prove that love isn't all about looks," he added jokingly, referring to the texts she'd sent her brother, which made everyone else laugh.

Her eyes widened and she covered her mouth with both hands, obviously shocked, maybe overwhelmed and probably embarrassed.

"If you could see it in your heart to marry me, I think we could prove that relationships can be successful when they're built on kindness, honesty and mutual respect instead of more superficial things. And maybe you can help me overcome the parts of me that aren't quite right because of the difficulties I encountered early in life."

Several of the women said, "Aw," letting him know they were sympathetic and liked what he'd said.

He was just trying to make a good episode, never dreamed that would sway her. He was positive she was going to say something conciliatory to cover for her texts, but ultimately refuse. He wasn't even worried when the woman her brother was going to marry jumped up, came over and kneeled down on her other side.

"Do it, Aja!" she encouraged. "If you don't, you'll never know what could've been."

"Let loose and take a chance for once," Darius added from where he stood.

And the next thing Grady knew, everything he'd planned, orchestrated and expected went right out the window. Aja looked from her brother to her soon-to-be sister-in-law, then back again, licked her lips nervously and said, "Okay, I'll do it!"

Chapter Eight

She'd turned down Arman but accepted the proposal of a stranger? What'd gotten into her?

Aja felt numb as they went through the motions of taking pictures for promotional purposes, holding hands with her "fiancé," showing her ring and filming short segments to tease the upcoming wedding episode.

The rest of the evening felt like a dream. But in those moments when reality intruded, a sense of panic would well up and she almost bailed out.

Maybe she would have, except it seemed too late—as though she'd already gotten on the ride and was committed to its climbs and falls and crazy corkscrews until it came to a stop on its own. And she was too much of a "good girl" to cause problems.

"What made you do it?" Darius murmured when, exhausted, she hugged him before heading to bed.

"I have no idea," she muttered. She knew if she said much more, the mics they were forced to wear would alert Jim or someone else on the production team that there might be an opportunity to get some good "reaction" footage.

She didn't have a very good answer, anyway. She couldn't make Grady be the only groom who was refused. That was one thing. She'd also been excited for Barbie and Darius, and wanted to continue the journey with them instead of being kicked off and having to wait until they finished filming in a month to learn how things went.

And after how superior Genevieve and Taylor had acted, maybe it was also a little gratifying that she was the one who'd gotten the ring.

Of course, if marrying Grady turned out to be a bad thing, *they* would be the lucky ones. But when her brother said, "Let loose and take a chance," she'd simply closed her eyes and, metaphorically speaking, made the leap.

As she went over the evening in her mind after she was in bed that night, she was stunned by her own behavior. And she felt bad for their parents, who would be mortified when they eventually learned what had happened. She and Darius, their only two children, were marrying people they wouldn't approve of—not to mention they were doing it without including them in the *aroosi*, or wedding.

"Oh, my God," she muttered.

On the other hand, they were both adults and should be able to do what they wanted with their lives. And it was just a TV show. It couldn't *really* mean anything. It would probably be a memory they laughed at in later years, an experience worth having but nothing permanent.

She must've eventually fallen asleep because the next time she opened her eyes, sunlight was flooding the room, and she panicked, thinking she'd overslept. Grabbing her phone, she saw that she'd actually awakened just before her alarm and slumped back on the pillows in relief.

Today, they'd be filming the wedding-dress segment. Winnie had told them it was the most popular episode of each season. "Everyone loves to see the brides, with all their jitters and uncertainty, getting beautiful for the wedding," she'd told them. Then she'd pulled Aja aside to say she'd like to incorporate some Persian traditions into the ceremonies for her and Darius.

Aja wondered what Grady would think of that, especially burning *esfand* or incense to ward off the "evil eye" that might cause them harm, and the consent ritual, in which he would say "I do" immediately, but she wouldn't answer until she'd been asked three times. In Persian weddings, the crowd played a part in this ritual by yelling things like *"aroos rafteh gol behshineh!"* which translated to "the bride has gone to pick flowers!" It was all to symbolize the groom's journey of earning his wife's love, but it would probably seem strange to someone who'd never experienced it.

Her alarm went off. She silenced it, then dragged herself out of bed. Then she peeled off her clothes to get in the shower but paused in front of the mirror. What about the intimacy aspect of the wedding? Was she really going to have sex with Grady Amos on their wedding night?

At the rate they were filming, that would be in two days!

She might be able to go through with the wedding, she told herself, but she wasn't sure she could go through with *that*.

Grady hadn't slept much. He was getting the distinct impression that he'd let his attraction to Winnie lead him down a very dangerous path. The question was whether to go ahead and follow it to its conclusion, or pull out of the show and run for home.

Winnie had texted him last night after the proposals, as surprised as he was that Aja had agreed to marry him. He'd hoped she would be more disappointed, maybe encourage him to cancel the engagement and leave LA, for the time being.

But she hadn't. He'd gotten the impression she was kind of excited by this turn of events because it did such great things for the series. Now the siblings would remain on the show all season, and he knew that was a dynamic Winnie was eager to explore. Those texts Aja had sent Darius juxtaposed to her acceptance of his ring would certainly create a buzz, and she needed that buzz to make the show successful. Winnie had said everyone would be watching to learn why Aja had agreed and to see if they could overcome the gulf between them.

He'd pushed back, said the season would probably be interesting enough without him and Aja on the show. But Winnie had insisted he shouldn't be too rash. Let it run its course, she'd said. Who knows? Maybe you and Aja are meant to be. But if that's not the case, and you end up breaking up, then, when this is all over...

She hadn't finished that sentence. But he knew what went there. Then they'd be free to date and find out if they were "meant to be."

He wasn't convinced he was being wise not to take more control of his own destiny. Winnie cared so much about what she was trying to create, that she had ulterior motives. But so far, the control he'd tried to take hadn't worked out too well for him. Besides, according to the contract he'd signed, there'd be significant financial penalties for quitting early, and even if that wasn't the case, he'd committed himself. He hated going back on his word. Maybe he was old-fashioned, but to him it just wasn't honorable.

Darius, Neal and Omar were already at breakfast by the time he walked into the kitchen. Neal and Omar came off like the type of men who were often featured on *The Bachelor*—men who were hoping to get a start in Hollywood, make some good money and/or become America's current heartthrob. Aja's brother seemed less stereotypical—like a nice kid who was just eager to live the American dream. At twenty-five, he could be forgiven for getting involved in something like this.

But Grady was nearly forty. He should've known better…

He dished up a bowl of oatmeal from the food that'd been prepared for them and sat down at one end of the table, away from the others. He was hoping they'd leave him to his thoughts. The show schedule was so tight there wasn't a lot of downtime, and since his brothers had all married, he was used to living alone. He craved a few more minutes to himself.

But Darius broke the silence almost immediately. "You sleep okay?"

Omar and Neal glanced up but continued eating.

Grady'd had a hell of a night, but he couldn't say that to the brother of the woman he was engaged to marry. "Pretty good. You?"

"Tossed and turned a bit. This show is…stressful. Makes you second-guess everything. I mean… I can't believe what we're doing. But in case you're worried, I just wanted to let you know what you're getting into with Aja."

Now Darius had his full attention. "What am I getting into?" he asked.

"She's the nicest person you'll ever meet," he said as if it was simply a fact, then got up to take his dishes to the sink.

The nicest person he'd ever meet…and yet, so far, his heart and mind had been completely closed against her.

Putting down his spoon, Grady sat back while the others finished and then got to their feet. "In case you haven't heard, we leave in twenty minutes to be fitted for our tuxedos," Omar said, then turned right back and followed the others out.

Grady nodded, but his mind was a million miles away. Why was he so sure he and Aja could never be happy together? She was smart, pretty, accomplished. He couldn't even blame her for sending those texts about him. A lot of people would've felt the same way.

Besides, she'd thought she was speaking privately to her brother, in an emotionally safe space. She had the right to be totally honest.

Someone from the cooking staff came to clear away the food and the rest of the dishes, and he slid his chair back while the woman took his half-empty bowl.

He was in this thing now; he might as well make the most of it.

The next few days were incredibly busy—so busy Aja didn't have time for regrets or second thoughts. It helped that the wedding-dress segment was so enjoyable. They were taken to a small bridal boutique in Bel Air that had racks of stunning dresses, and a professional stylist helped them find a gown that was unique—so they'd each have their own "look"—and flattering.

Aja selected an ecru satin dress that reminded her of the A-line cocktail dresses from the '50s. She loved the classic simplicity of it—there was no lace, no sequins or patterns of any kind—and she thought it went perfectly with a waterfall veil in the same shade. She knew she'd found the right ensemble when the stylist gaped at her as she walked out of the dressing room. Aja was especially flattered when Winnie did a double take and said, "Wow!"

They spent the rest of the day at the spa having their hair trimmed and nails done and, of course, filmed part of it. But the fun ended when Mirabelle Lacey couldn't be found the morning of the weddings. Liz was the first to know. Like Aja and Barbie, Mirabelle and Liz had become close friends. She'd gone to Mirabelle's room as soon as she got up only to find it empty, her clothes and toiletries gone. Liz had started to freak out, which brought the rest of them to the landing of their new place, where they'd moved after the elimination round, to see what was wrong. The security guard of their house had told them she'd quit in the middle of the night. That meant they were down a couple, which was 25 percent of the show.

Not long afterward, Winnie called an emergency meeting in the living room to remind them that they were fortunate to have the opportunity to be on the show, that there'd been a lot of applicants and yet they'd been chosen, that the show could open up a world of other opportunities and when they'd accepted, they'd made a commitment. She'd clearly been upset, and probably worried, too. Maybe she was afraid that Liz would follow Mirabelle's lead.

"Can you believe she just…panicked?" Barbie said to Aja after the meeting as they walked upstairs to her room.

"I can't," Aja said. "Or…maybe I can." She thought it was more remarkable that the rest of them were going through with it…

Barbie shot her a worried glance. "You're not going to back out, are you? You heard Winnie. If we lose any more people, we might not be able to finish the season."

Aja had gotten into this for the sake of her brother. She wasn't going to ruin it for him—or Barbie—now. She wouldn't ruin it for Winnie, either, because she *had* made a commitment. Besides, if she did bail out, she'd have to pay for her wedding gown on top of the other penalties, and it'd been very expensive. "I'm going through with it," she said. "But we don't know how the men are feeling. There could be other surprises."

They hadn't been allowed to see or communicate with their grooms since the proposals, so she had no idea what Grady was feeling, whether he was getting cold feet or not.

"They'll show up," Barbie said. "I feel bad for Omar. He really wanted to do it."

"He might be able to come back next season. And the show should be okay. They can fill in a bit with the couples who are still together from previous seasons. Everyone will want to know how they're doing."

Fortunately, the shock of Mirabelle leaving—and the distraction it caused—didn't give Aja a lot of time to get nervous. Mirabelle was supposed to have been the one getting married first. Now that she was gone, they were moving the weddings up so they wouldn't have to film late, and Aja needed to get ready.

She was fully dressed in her gown, veil and a simple strand of pearls, and was waiting for the limousine that would take her to the wedding venue, before she started to feel shaky.

"You look gorgeous!" Barbie gushed.

Fortunately, Barbie hadn't left her side, even though she should probably be getting ready herself. "You think so?"

She smiled warmly. "There's no question."

Aja grabbed Barbie's arm. "Do you think we're doing the right thing?" She'd asked that question a million times, but she had to ask again.

"Something wonderful will come from this," her friend insisted.

A knock sounded at the door, and Barbie went to answer it. Aja heard her speaking to the security guard. "Is it time?" she asked.

"It's time," Barbie confirmed.

They'd been told they could invite their immediate family to the wedding, but Aja couldn't tell her parents what she was doing, which meant she couldn't tell anyone else, either. And her brother was on the show, so he and Barbie couldn't attend; they had to get ready for their own wedding, which was right after hers.

She wondered if anyone would come from Grady's side. She knew it would mean driving seven hours, so maybe not.

"Don't be nervous," Barbie added and gave her a quick hug before she could leave the room.

Aja tried to say she wasn't nervous, but she couldn't even bring the words to her lips. Her heart was pounding so loud she was certain it would give her away, regardless. "Thanks," she said and lifted her skirt to descend the stairs.

Chapter Nine

Grady's brothers had left their wives at home with the kids, but all four of them were sitting in the front row. Dylan was scowling. He obviously didn't think Grady knew what he was doing. Aaron, the second oldest, was grinning, because he loved that Dylan was disapproving of someone else for a change—since they were closest in age, there'd always been more conflict between them—and Rod and Mack, the two youngest, in that order, just looked nervous for him.

Winnie came into the venue and approached him just before the ceremony was to start to say that Aja had nixed a couple of Persian customs she'd been planning to include. Apparently, his bride didn't want her parents to see the episode on TV later and be upset by it. Winnie also wanted to let him know that she was going to surprise Aja by having Darius be available to not only attend the ceremony, but also to walk her down the aisle and give her away.

"Smart move," he muttered. He could see exactly how that would play out on TV. Winnie was definitely good at her job.

"You look a little stressed," she told him sheepishly, likely because he would've backed out if he wasn't afraid of ruining her show and she knew it.

"I'm terrified," he admitted, keeping his eye on the closed doors at the back for when his bride would appear.

"It's going to be fine," Winnie assured him. "Aja's lovely, and I know this seems super serious—it has to be for the cameras—but you'll just be getting to know each other. That's no big deal. Think of it like…being roommates for a while."

Really? Maybe he was old-fashioned, too traditional, but to him, marriage was not a commitment he could easily walk away from. Maybe he'd tried to tell himself that in the beginning, when he truly believed it never would have gotten this far.

But there was also a small voice in the back of his head saying chances were good he never would've married had he not done something drastic like this. As much as he'd hoped to find some-one, whenever he started getting serious with a woman he was dat-ing, he'd dredge up an excuse not to move forward. The problem hadn't been finding someone. The problem had been the fortress he'd built around his heart. He didn't want to risk losing someone he loved that much, not after losing his mother—didn't want to be destroyed the way his father had been destroyed.

So maybe this—because it allowed him some emotional distance—would be just the thing for someone as damaged as he was.

The music started, and he shot his brothers a nervous glance. Dylan looked as though he was on the verge of getting up to put a stop to the whole thing, but Aaron reached out to keep him in his seat. Dylan was so protective of them all; he always had been, or he wouldn't have done what he'd done at eighteen. But this was Grady's choice. This time, Aaron had the right of it.

Grady cleared his throat. He seemed to be having trouble breathing. He adjusted the bow tie on his black tux, but it didn't make any difference. Then he started to sweat, despite the air-conditioning blasting into the room. He probably would've passed out if they'd made him wait any longer—but, fortunately, the doors at the back of the room were opened with a grand flourish.

The most beautiful woman he'd ever seen stood there looking at him, her eyes riveted on him as if she was looking for some kind of reassurance, without which she'd bolt.

He smiled, willing her to come forward, and was surprised when she responded so readily. Her lips also curved into a smile, and she allowed Darius to lead her down the aisle.

In his peripheral vision, Grady saw his brothers twist around to get their first look at his bride. He couldn't take his eyes off Aja long enough to even glance in their direction but they had to be astonished by her beauty, at least. He felt like it was his steady gaze that centered her and kept her coming toward him.

When she and her brother reached the front, and Darius put Aja's hand in his, Grady felt a strange sense of protectiveness. Her hands were soft, delicate and freezing cold. As his fingers closed around them, he looked down into her eyes…and suddenly felt breathless all over again, but for a much better reason.

This had to be one of the strangest weddings on the planet, he thought. And yet, despite all the reasons it shouldn't have felt right, it seemed like a pretty good start.

When she'd met Grady, Aja hadn't thought he was *overly* attractive. He'd seemed nice—she'd had no specific complaints about his behavior or his appearance. But today he was different. There was a much warmer gleam in his eyes. And his smile seemed far more genuine. It felt almost as if he was seeing her—*really* seeing her—for the first time.

The officiant started the ceremony. He didn't do it strictly in the traditional sense. He spoke about how love could grow out of respect and offered advice on how to build a strong union by putting each other first. He probably said some other valuable things before starting the actual vows, but she wasn't really listening. For a change, she wasn't self-conscious about the filming. Although there were people shifting and moving all around them, and the venue looked like a movie set, what with the lights and cameras just outside their very small circle, she was focused on other things. The warmth and inherent strength of Grady's hands as they held hers, keeping her steady. The quizzical yet hopeful expression on his face. The way his mouth quirked slightly to the side, as if he was oddly happy and tempted to grin, when he said, "I do."

When she was asked if she promised to honor, cherish and sustain Grady, she paused only a moment before she said, "I do."

"Now…you may kiss the bride," the officiant proclaimed.

Somewhere in the back of her mind, Aja knew those who'd be watching the show would be waiting for this moment when two people who barely knew each other would kiss as man and wife. The fear that'd mysteriously left her when Grady caught her eye at the door suddenly returned, reminding her of what a giant step this was, especially with a stranger.

But he didn't do anything that made her want to pull away. Didn't embarrass her, either. She caught a twinkle in his eye before he bent his head and gave her a soft, chaste kiss on the lips.

Relieved that he'd handled it so perfectly, she smiled up at him afterward and got the impression he knew she'd been more terrified in that moment than any other, because he chuckled as he squeezed her hands and said, "Thanks for taking a chance on me."

The show had arranged for each of the couples to have a different type of honeymoon, which would appear to be longer for the sake of the show but would really only last three days. Aja was told Winnie had come up with the varied settings to give each couple a unique environment to interact with.

Fortunately, there were plenty of options in or around LA, which made it more affordable than sending each couple to a faraway destination. Darius and Barbie were going to a penthouse suite at a luxurious downtown hotel. Liz and Neal were traveling to Palm Springs. And Aja and Grady were off to a small beach house right on the ocean near San Diego.

The other couples were expected to leave on their honeymoons right after their wedding, but Aja was allowed to witness Darius and Barbie's vows first. And Winnie told Grady they could also go out to dinner with his brothers while his family was in town, so as soon as their ceremony was over, they hurried to change out of their wedding clothes so they could be ready for both events.

The participants of the show weren't supposed to have much contact with the outside world during filming, and so far, they'd been severely limited. But Aja got the impression Winnie was trying new things to see how both the cast and the audience would react, and given Grady's unusual background, she was betting people would be intrigued by the dynamic of having all five Amos brothers in LA. Although Winnie didn't say it, Aja was willing to bet she also guessed viewers would be interested in seeing how the brothers got on with his new bride and was a bit nervous as they entered Cecconi's, an Italian restaurant in West Hollywood that had fabulous reviews.

"I hope you know what you're getting into," Mack said, giving Aja a playful nudge as they were seated. "This guy might be strong as an ox, but he's also stubborn as a jackass."

"Don't scare her away already," Grady joked with a mock scowl as the others laughed.

Aja grinned. She liked the men. Dylan was a little more morose than the others, but she knew it probably didn't have anything to do with her personally. No doubt he was concerned about his brother making such a "reckless" decision. She could only imagine how her parents would have reacted if they'd been invited to the wedding.

"Marriage isn't easy," Dylan stated unequivocally. "Even when you know and love the person you're marrying." He peered over his menu at Grady, drilling him with a pointed look.

"I know it's not easy," Grady said. "But we're having dinner right now, Dyl. Maybe you can save the lecture until I get home."

Dylan's eyebrows snapped together. Aja could tell he didn't like being shut down, but Grady was right. Why not celebrate while they were happy? It wasn't as if they could change their minds now. That ship had already sailed. Besides, this was being filmed.

Dylan shot a disgruntled glance at the cameraman, who was, fortunately, using an iPhone so they wouldn't make a huge spectacle in the restaurant, and lifted his menu higher, hiding his face.

Grady rolled his eyes at Aja as if to say "don't worry about him," and squeezed her hand under the table.

Aja was wearing a pair of beige wool slacks with a sleeveless sweater of the same color and a brown leather jacket, and she'd left her hair down, just as it had been at the wedding. Grady was wearing chinos and a button-down shirt, like his brothers. The Amos boys weren't exactly on the cutting edge of fashion, but they each were such tall, good-looking men it didn't matter. Grady seemed to be growing more and more handsome to her by the minute. And because he was around his family he seemed much less guarded…and more trusting and fun.

"Dylan, I understand your concerns," she said. "It's a very odd situation, which is why no one from my family was at the wedding. My parents would definitely not approve."

Dylan dropped his menu so she could see his face. "So why did you do it?"

Because of the camera, she couldn't talk as freely as she wanted, but she said, "I was missing something in my life. I guess this was my way of—" she shrugged "—trying to fill that void."

He looked skeptical. "And you think Grady might be the answer?"

"I know the odds aren't in our favor. But the fear of getting caught in the life I was living and not being able to change it if I waited any longer was what drove me here."

He seemed to grow more thoughtful. "You're a dentist, right? Did you grow up wanting to be a dentist?"

She sat back as a waitress passed out glasses of water. "No. It was my parents who really wanted me to be a doctor or a dentist," she said.

"Your parents…" He put his menu on the table. "What would *you* rather be?"

"I've always wanted to open my own ceramics studio. But—" she drew a deep breath "—the odds of financial success with something like that are…very low."

"That doesn't mean you shouldn't do it," Rod pointed out. "My wife also does ceramics. She loves to create."

"She's probably much better than I am. I haven't had the time to develop my skills," she responded. "It wasn't easy to get into, or through, dental school. Then, of course, I needed to develop a practice and once you start down a certain path, it can be difficult to turn around, especially if you're not even sure you should."

"So do you just let that other dream fade away?" Rod asked.

Turning her attention his way, she smiled. "Maybe?"

Aaron spoke up. "What about your brother? Why do you think *he* wanted to do the show? For the same reasons?"

She couldn't say he was hoping to break into show business on camera, so she said, "I think he'd also prefer a different path."

"So…what types of things do you and Grady have in common?" Dylan asked.

Aja was at a complete loss. "I'm not sure, to be honest. But the psychologists who work for the show did extensive personality testing, so maybe it's the way we view the world more than our individual circumstances, which are, obviously, very different."

Dylan's gaze cut back to Grady. "Damn, she's smart," he said, as if he was impressed in spite of himself and started laughing. "I can't see where the compatibility is coming from—you have completely different backgrounds, completely different cultural experiences, completely different *lives*. But she's as sweet and beautiful as she is smart, so maybe you got lucky, kid."

They all laughed with Dylan, then Aja leaned over to Grady. "Why do *you* think we were paired together?" she asked.

Looking uncomfortable for the first time since he'd changed out of his tux, Grady cleared his throat. "Like you say, the psychologists who work for the show must've seen something deeper, something that isn't obvious at this stage of our relationship," he said. Then he looked away.

Chapter Ten

Grady had been having a great time at dinner—until Aja brought up the psychologists. He'd never dreamed she might've been relying on the personality tests they'd been given to help her find a mate. And he'd gone around those tests, paired her with himself even though the psychologists weren't going to. How could he explain that to her?

Regardless, now was not the time. The marriage was too new, and they had a cameraman in the back seat who'd been assigned to chronicle their honeymoon.

He swallowed a sigh as he navigated to the address where they would spend three days alone together—well, they'd be alone some of the time. They'd been instructed to take a certain amount of selfie footage, which wouldn't be too hard. But they'd also have someone else coming to film periodically. The cameraman who was with them now was supposed to take an Uber home after he documented their reaction to the beach house and to spending their first night together, and Grady couldn't wait for that moment—for the opportunity to be "off the show" for a bit.

"I'm glad we got the beach house and not one of the other options, aren't you?" Aja asked.

They hadn't seen it yet, but it sounded the most appealing to him, too. "I am."

Her lips curved into a faint smile. "Maybe that was one thing the psychologists knew we'd have in common."

Shit. Just when he was getting excited about the possibility of having a relationship with Aja—just when he was beginning to wonder if, maybe, by some weird miracle, this relationship would be just the thing for both of them—he had to face the fact that he'd gotten her to marry him under false pretenses.

He glanced over, trying to read her mood, and saw her cover a yawn with one hand. She was probably exhausted. She'd been quiet since they left the restaurant, but he was fairly certain she'd liked his brothers. She'd loosened up, and talked and laughed more than he'd expected. He could tell his brothers liked her, too—even Dylan.

The beach house was more private than he'd imagined. They had trouble finding it even with GPS. Then they had to leave the car parked on a paved road and carry their luggage down a dirt path at the foot of a cliff, where they finally found the cottage on the beach. He wondered who'd built it, and who owned it now. It looked like an artist's retreat, especially once he let them in and turned on the light. There were paintings, sculptures, photography and mixed media everywhere.

He remembered Aja saying she hoped to open her own ceramics studio one day and decided Winnie, or whoever had picked this particular honeymoon location for them, had nailed it.

"This is spectacular!" Aja gushed as she walked around and inspected the house. "It's so private and intimate—the perfect place for a honeymoon."

"I can't believe how close we are to the ocean," Grady said. "You can hear the surf."

The cameraman trailed them to the bedroom and leaned in to take a shot. There was only one bed in the whole house. A small kitchen and living-room area that featured a piano and a wall of framed sheet music took up most of the rest of the living space. Other than that, there was only the big bathroom off the bedroom. But the best part of the whole place was the covered deck that looked out toward the sea and had a telescope, as well as a small sofa and chair with pillows and a throw.

"So...what do you think?" Aja asked him.

He thought it was going to be damn uncomfortable to sleep anywhere other than the bed and yet he knew Aja wouldn't be ready for that. The sofa on the porch was the only viable option, but it was more like a love seat, so he wouldn't have room to straighten his legs. It wasn't as if he could sleep on the floor, either. "I like it," he said.

"We can go for a walk on the beach first thing in the morning.

Maybe get into the water if it's warm enough. Then we could find a tennis court and play some tennis."

She liked tennis? He didn't remember reading that in her file... "You play?"

"I do. I love it. What about you?"

"I enjoy almost any sport." He felt a measure of relief. Maybe they had a commonality or two, after all. Tennis was something they could build on, wasn't it?

At that point, the conversation faltered. It was late, they were tired, and no one knew what to say or do about the sleeping arrangements. He wasn't even sure there was extra bedding so that he'd have a blanket if he slept on the deck—just that one light throw he'd seen, which was mostly for decorating purposes— and it could get chilly by the ocean, even in Southern California.

He brought her overnight case into the bedroom. The Prada label suggested it'd cost a pretty penny, which once again reminded him of their many differences. She'd been born with a silver spoon in her mouth and had two parents who still doted on her; he'd had no parents for much of his childhood, had known nothing but poverty and hard work, and his father was still more of a liability than an asset.

"Would you like to take a bath or a shower?" he asked.

She looked up in surprise, and he realized she'd thought that maybe he meant *with him* and lifted his hands. "Sorry. I know you don't know me well enough for that. I was just...letting you go first."

The tension in her body eased. "Oh. Thank you."

"As a matter of fact, on second thought, I don't even need to take a shower tonight. So, assuming you won't mind if I steal one of the pillows from the bed, I'm just going to crash on the deck."

She seemed unsure of what to say. "I saw champagne on the coffee table..."

He lifted his eyebrows. "Would you like a glass?"

"If you're not too tired to stay up for a few more minutes."

It was their wedding night. He didn't want to disappoint her;

he'd simply suggested going to bed so she wouldn't feel any pressure to act in a way that felt unnatural to her. "I'm happy to stay up a little longer. I'll go pour it."

"Okay, I'll be out in a minute."

"Take your time," he said.

When the door closed, Greg—the cameraman—lowered his voice. "That's promising."

"She's probably just going to the bathroom," Grady responded.

Greg gave him a suggestive look. "Might be a little more than that…"

Grady shook his head. "Sorry to disappoint you, but that isn't happening tonight."

"How do you know?" he challenged.

"Because it's too soon. And because I wouldn't want her to do something she might regret later. So… I'm not hitting her up."

Greg dropped into a chair. "Seriously?"

"Seriously." Grady stepped closer to him so he wouldn't have to talk very loudly. "So…is there any way you'd give us the next few minutes alone?"

He frowned. "I'm guessing Winnie would want me to stay and try to get a bit more footage so viewers can at least see you drifting in that direction."

"We've done all the drifting we're going to do, bro. There's nothing more to capture. I promise."

With a sigh, he came to his feet. "Fine. If you're that determined, you'll just wait until I leave, anyway."

"Exactly." Grady reached into his wallet and handed the guy a hundred-dollar bill. "But thank you for not making it harder than it had to be."

"To…" he prompted.

"Get rid of you," he said and showed him out.

He and Aja were alone. At last. There were no cameras rolling. The biggest decisions had already been made. Now they had three days to relax, unwind and see if they could be happy together…or if they'd just made the biggest mistake of their lives.

Closing his eyes, he drew a deep breath before cracking open the champagne. He'd just walked to the French doors leading out to the deck when he heard the bedroom door open behind him and turned to see his new wife.

She was wearing a silky, black, sliplike dress that fell to midthigh with no shoes. He didn't think it was lingerie exactly. Or maybe it was. It wasn't transparent or suggestive, but, God, was it sexy.

She had such good taste, he decided. What she had on didn't invite him into her bed tonight. It wasn't that kind of nightgown. But it offered him hope for later, which was exciting enough…

He tried to think of Winnie but couldn't even conjure a good picture of her in his head.

He allowed his gaze to run down Aja's body, and when he finally lifted his eyes, she blushed and glanced away. "I hope that's a good sign," she said with a little laugh.

"You hope what's a good sign?" he asked.

"The way you just looked at me."

"If you're wondering if I want you, I do," he said and handed her a glass.

Her mouth dropped open.

"But tonight's too soon," he added with a wink. "Shall we toast?"

He saw her throat work as she swallowed. "Um…sure."

"I'll go first." He lifted his glass. "To the most beautiful bride I've ever seen."

Her eyes widened as he clinked his glass against hers. "Do you mean it?"

"I wouldn't say it if I didn't mean it," he replied.

"That's nice." She glanced around. "And you couldn't have said it for the sake of the show because there are no cameras. How'd you get Greg to leave?"

He smiled. "I simply suggested it. Well, maybe I strongly suggested it," he added.

She laughed with him. "Good job. And now for my toast…

Here's to unusual beginnings—and the hope that this one will lead to something better than we even imagined."

"I'll drink to that," he said.

They each took a sip of champagne. "You're not really going to sleep on the deck, are you?" she asked. "Because I'd feel too guilty taking the only bed. That sofa would be *so* uncomfortable for you."

He gestured around the room. "They haven't given me a lot of options."

"You can sleep on your half of the bed."

"If you'd feel comfortable having me that close…"

"Of course. If I didn't feel I could trust you, I wouldn't have married you."

"Great."

He held out his free hand to take hers. "Let's go sit out on the deck for a few minutes."

Her smile suggested she was pleasantly surprised as she accepted his hand and let him lead her out.

When they relaxed on the sofa, he slipped his arm around her to help ward off the chill wind that was coming in off the ocean while they looked out at the white-crested waves and the glimmer of moonlight on water.

"It's so beautiful here," she said as she put her glass on the table.

He nodded in agreement. Then they fell into a companionable silence. After several minutes, he was about to suggest they go inside and get some sleep when he realized she'd already dozed off.

Chuckling to himself, he set his own glass down then shifted carefully and stood.

"Is it time for bed?" she mumbled, trying to rouse herself.

"It is. But don't worry, I've got you," he replied and lifted her in his arms to carry her inside.

Chapter Eleven

When Aja woke up, she found that she'd gravitated to the warmth in the bed, which just so happened to be Grady's body. She was smashed up against him, but he didn't seem to mind. She could hear his steady breathing, knew he was still asleep. Good. She wanted to have a few moments to herself to think about how it felt to be in the same bed as this man, who was mostly a stranger. Did she regret what she'd done?

That was the big question. Memories of last night filtered through her brain, and she found that she liked Grady. She'd enjoyed his brothers—loved the dry humor between them and the way they mercilessly teased each other. Seeing him in that setting had shown her a lot about her husband. He was funny, wry at times, part of a close family whose bonds had been forged in fire. And he was respectful of her. She didn't think the men she'd met last night would've behaved the way they did if Grady wasn't what he appeared to be, and that gave her some reassurance.

She was also impressed by the way he'd acted about the issue of intimacy. He'd been interested. She could tell by the way he'd looked at her when she came out in the slip-dress she'd purchased for their wedding night. He'd freely admitted it, which had been gratifying. But he hadn't pressed her, hadn't demanded she do anything she was uncomfortable with. That suggested he cared about their union and whether they had a future together.

So…could he be serious about her as a mate? And, if so, was she going to like being his wife?

"You awake?" he mumbled.

She immediately slid away from him so he wouldn't think she was ready for a greater physical connection. "I am. I'm sorry that I—I crowded you last night."

A crooked smile slanted his lips. "Believe me, I didn't mind."

She chuckled as she righted the slip that'd become twisted around her body. "What's our filming schedule today?"

"Greg will be back at nine for breakfast, but it's only seven. Why don't we take that walk on the beach you mentioned last night?"

"That sounds good." She got out of bed and went into the bathroom. She didn't bother with makeup. She just brushed her teeth and pulled her thick hair into a messy bun before putting on some yoga pants and a tank top with flip-flops. She didn't dawdle. She was afraid Greg would show up before they were ready for him and didn't want to miss the chance to go out and see the beauty of an early morning on the beach with her new husband.

"Your turn," she said when she emerged. "I'll put on some coffee."

"Coffee is your first thought? See? We have a lot in common," he joked, and she grinned as she let him have the bathroom.

He came out a few minutes later in a pair of shorts, an Amos Auto Body T-shirt and flip-flops. "That's your business, right?" she said, indicating the emblem on his shirt.

He nodded.

"Great logo."

"Thanks."

"How do you take your coffee?"

"Black."

"That's easy." She poured it for him and handed him a mug that read The Adventure Begins…

"You found this mug in the cupboard?" he asked. "Because it couldn't be more apropos."

She winked. "I thought you might like it." She'd chosen one for herself that said Life is Better at the Beach.

"I feel like we should have a dog to walk," he said. "Considering all the animal lovers who probably watch the series, I'm surprised the show hasn't provided one."

She laughed but was surprised she'd failed to ask him about pets. They'd had their minds on so many other things… "Do you have a dog at home?"

"Not right now. Had to put my German shepherd down last year and haven't been able to bring myself to get another one. Apollo won't be easy to replace. He went everywhere with me, hung out at the body shop all day while I worked. I even trained him to fetch certain things I needed. He was the smartest dog."

"I'm sorry."

"It's sad they don't live as long as we do. What about you?" he asked as he opened the door to the deck. There was a stairway on one side that went down to the beach. "Do you have a pet?"

"My parents have a corkie I get to see when I go home. But I haven't gotten a pet of my own quite yet. I'm gone too much, and I don't feel it's appropriate to bring a dog to a dental office."

A gentle breeze ruffled their clothes and hair as they reached the beach. "I can see where that might be a problem."

She sipped her coffee. "It's beautiful out."

His chest lifted as he breathed deeply. "It is. I don't get to see the beach very often."

"What's it like where you live?"

He took her hand as they started to walk, and it made her feel warm and secure and oddly happy, especially because it felt natural—not strained in any way. "Whiskey Creek sprung up during the gold rush in the foothills of the Sierra Nevada mountains," he replied. "It's small and doesn't seem to grow much each year, but it's drawing more and more tourists, thanks to all the wineries that are coming into the region. And it's not far from Sacramento, so if I want something only the big city can provide, I can get it easily enough."

She looked down at the sand as they walked. "How small is small? You told me there are only two thousand people, but it's hard for me to conceptualize that number. Do you have a movie theater? A major grocery store? How many stoplights?"

"No theater. No major grocery store—not a chain, anyway. Just a few antique stores, a bed-and-breakfast, some gift shops, several restaurants, a couple of bars that I've probably visited way too many times over the years, a mansion where they perform weddings, a bike shop, a corner grocer, that sort of thing. Only two stoplights."

"What's your favorite thing to do there?"

"Raise hell, I guess," he replied. "Lord knows I've done enough of it over the years."

"That's ominous." She gave him a dubious look. "What kind of hell?"

"Nothing serious. I'm just messing around."

She stopped, kicked off her flip-flops and picked them up. She wanted to feel the give of the wet sand beneath her feet. "Have you ever been in trouble with the law?"

"Couple of times. For fighting. But that was years ago when we had to fight just to survive. We were going through so much we weren't willing to put up with abuse from anyone, and that probably made us a bit too defensive—although there were plenty of people who tried to get up in our business." He picked up a small seashell and tossed it back into the sea. "And we were probably a little wild to begin with. Does that scare you?"

She liked the endearing expression on his face when he asked that question. She could tell he was just playing with her. "Maybe it would if I hadn't met your brothers. They seem to have turned out all right."

"They've calmed down a lot. Getting married and having kids does that to a man."

"Kids..." she said and stopped walking so she could stand and look out to sea.

He stopped, too. "Are you interested in having a family?"

"I'd like to have children." She glanced over at him. "What about you?"

"Same."

"How many?"

He shrugged. "I don't have a set amount."

"More than one?"

"If that's what...you want," he said awkwardly. She got the impression he'd been about to say "if that's what my wife wants," and then realized she *was* his wife.

She laughed. "It's going to take some time to get used to the idea of…of being married to each other, let alone having kids together."

"I hope it doesn't take *too* long," he said jokingly. "I'm not getting any younger."

"You turn forty this year?"

"Yep. I'll soon be an old man."

She waded into the water, letting the surf foam up around her ankles before turning back to face him. "I'm not getting any younger, either, which means we shouldn't wait too long."

Their eyes met briefly before they both looked away.

"Do you think Whiskey Creek would be a good place to raise a family?" she asked.

"If I had my choice, it'd be there."

"You love it that much."

"I do."

"But…"

He shaded his eyes. "It's not only up to me, right?"

She tried to imagine leaving LA—her parents and her brother. That would be hard. And what about her practice? She supposed she could sell it and start over in Whiskey Creek. But that would also be hard. She wondered why the show hadn't paired her with someone in Los Angeles. There were millions of people in Southern California, most of whom were trying to get on TV or in a movie. They should've had more than enough to choose from.

And yet…maybe it wouldn't have been the same with anyone else; maybe she wouldn't have made it this far. "Have you ever been engaged?" she asked.

"I've gotten close to an engagement but never actually popped the question…before you."

"Why do you think that's the case?"

"The way I lost my mother, I guess. I don't want to love anyone quite that much."

"And *this* particular marriage didn't require love."

He didn't respond to her comment. They stood in silence for a few minutes, letting what had been said settle into their minds. Then he asked, "What about you? Have you ever been engaged?"

"No. But… I just broke off a long-term relationship that was definitely heading in that direction."

"Where did you meet him? Online?"

"I've known him most my life. His parents and my parents are best friends."

"Oh, damn. I can't imagine that went over very well."

"It didn't. I feel bad for putting my parents in the position they're in, but I couldn't go through with it. I didn't want to follow the script my parents have laid out for me, become just like them, if that makes sense."

"They're not happy?"

"Happy enough, I guess. But… I want something different, something of my own choosing."

"Because they've chosen everything else for you."

"Something like that."

"Is that why you came on the show? Was it some…big rebellion?"

"I came on because Darius really wanted to do it, and they wouldn't take him without me. But defiance might've played a small role. Maybe desperation, too. I felt the clock was ticking and yet…I couldn't find what I was looking for."

Grady picked up a seashell, rubbed the sand from it and presented it to her. "What're they going to say when they learn about me?"

She studied the grooves of the shell and the touch of pink on the underside. "They won't be happy."

"And your brother has done the same thing…"

"Yeah," she said with a wince.

"Oh, boy."

She gave him a sheepish look. "I hope you'll be patient with them. They—they mean well. They just…think we'll mess up our lives if they let us make our own choices."

She came out of the waves and put her flip-flops back on. "It's just one more challenge we'll have to deal with…" Then she offered him her hand, and he surprised her by smiling as he took it.

"We'll figure it out," he said.

"Will we?" She peered closely at him. "How badly do you want this to work?"

He studied her for several seconds. "More by the minute," he said, and she couldn't help grinning at his response. She thought he might kiss her. They hadn't really kissed yet and she was beginning to wonder what it might be like to feel his lips against hers in a kiss that contained more passion than restraint, more desire than politeness…and was surprised to find it left her slightly breathless.

"What is it?" he asked.

She lowered her gaze for fear he'd be able to read what she was thinking and feeling if she didn't. "Nothing. We'd better get back. Greg will be there looking for us."

Greg was obviously eager to see how they were getting along after spending the night together. When Grady let him in, he grinned meaningfully and looked from one to the other as if they might betray the fact that last night had involved more than just sleeping.

When they merely exchanged a glance, it must not have told him much, so he went to the deck, most likely looking for a pillow or blanket on the sofa. When he didn't find either of those things, he returned with a frown but began to film before actually asking.

"So…where'd you sleep last night?" He often prompted them by asking questions to start a conversation, but some or all of his part would be cut during editing, leaving the two of them talking about the subject he'd introduced.

"I slept in the only bed there is but nothing happened," Grady said.

"Then how'd it go?" he asked Aja.

Grady loved the innocent yet sexy smile she shot him. She had a way of being warm and friendly *and* just slightly out of reach, creating a challenge he was hoping to conquer. "It was fine, comfortable. I liked having him there."

"No civil unrest the first night?" Greg asked, as if he was teasing them, and he sort of was. It was his job to get some good footage, and the sooner he had what he needed, the sooner he'd leave. He wasn't supposed to stay all day, so Grady tried to open up a bit more, which wasn't easy because "open" didn't come naturally to him. "It's been peaceful, relaxing."

Fortunately, Aja chimed in almost immediately. "I thought maybe it would be too awkward getting into bed with a virtual stranger," she said. "I mean… I know this type of thing happens on a regular basis in the lives of some people. One-night stands are a thing. But they've never been part of *my* life, so I admit I was nervous. I want my mate to be sexually attracted to me, but I also want to know who he is before we… Before we take the physical aspect of our relationship that far."

"Bottom line, we're still just getting to know each other," Grady said. "This morning we got up and went for a walk on the beach, and it was nice to have the time to talk without anyone to overhear."

"What'd you talk about?" Greg asked.

"Our romantic histories, our families and some other stuff," Grady replied.

Greg came forward to get a close-up. "Aja's parents won't approve, right?"

"No," Grady said. "And it'll be a difficult thing when they find out—for them because of the shock and disappointment, and for me if they reject me."

"And since Darius is also on the show," Aja added. "It'll make things doubly difficult for them…and probably for us, too."

Greg shifted to change his shot again. "Do you have exes who might cause problems in the future?"

"I just broke up with my boyfriend before coming on the show," Aja said.

"Why'd you break up?"

"He asked me to marry him, but I found it necessary to say no, and I didn't feel it would be wise to stay together after that. He definitely won't understand why I would then go and do something like this. But…marrying him wasn't right. I knew that much."

Greg turned to Grady. "And have you heard anything from your brothers? What did they think of your new bride?"

"I think they loved her."

"Even the one who raised you and sat there glowering through the wedding? His name is Dylan, right?"

"Dyl's definitely not pleased with me marrying someone I don't really know, but I think Aja won him over."

Aja took the seashell they'd found on the beach from the pocket of her yoga pants and showed Greg and the camera. "Grady found this while we were out walking on the beach this morning and gave it to me. I consider it a symbol of hope—that we can find happiness together. Maybe we'll even return here in ten, twenty or thirty years to celebrate our anniversary."

"I would love to see that happen." Greg handed it back to her. "Have you given any thought to where you'll live?"

"I'm surprised the psychologists would pair two people who both have jobs that aren't friendly to relocation," Aja said. "But they must've seen something in our personality tests that made them feel we'd be perfect for each other despite that obstacle," she added quickly, which made Grady squirm.

"It'll definitely require one of you to make a sacrifice," Greg concurred.

"I guess I could sell my practice and start over in Whiskey Creek…" she mused.

"Or I'll have to open a franchise of Amos Auto Body in LA," Grady said. "But we don't want to get ahead of ourselves. Before we make any decisions, I think we should spend some time in Whiskey Creek to see how Aja likes it. Then we should spend some time here to see how I like it and decide from there."

"Sounds logical to me," Greg said. "What're your plans for the day?"

Aja talked about going to breakfast and playing tennis. Grady added he'd like to take Aja out on a sunset catamaran cruise. Then, seemingly satisfied, Greg lowered the camera. "Great job, guys."

"Do you know how my brother is doing?" Aja asked.

"Not yet," Greg told her. "JJ's over there filming them now."

"Are you worried about him?" Grady asked.

"A little," she admitted. "Not only is he younger than I am, he's more reckless by nature. But Barbie seems like a nice person. I really like her, so that provides me with a little peace of mind."

"Can you bring her some word when you come back this evening?" Grady asked Greg as he showed him to the door.

"Sure." Greg stepped onto the front stoop. "I'll text JJ now."

"Thanks." Grady was about to close the door when Greg caught his attention by pressing a finger to his lips to signal silence before handing him a small, sealed envelope.

Grady blinked in surprise. Why would the cameraman pass him something he wasn't also giving to Aja? He arched his eyebrows—silently asking that question—and Greg whispered, "Winnie told me to give it to you and not let Aja see me do it."

Perplexed, Grady slipped the envelope into the pocket of his shorts and nodded. But he felt apprehensive. He didn't want Aja to find out about his previous interest in Winnie, didn't want it to hurt her in some way, and couldn't help being a little nervous about what might be in the letter.

Chapter Twelve

Aja heard from Darius that afternoon while she and Grady were getting ready to go on their sailboat tour. They'd spent the day playing tennis and had so much fun they'd stayed at the court for hours, then stopped for ice cream on the way home. Then she'd showered and put on her swimsuit under a pair of cutoffs and a white tank, and now she was waiting for Grady to shower.

So? How's it going? her brother began.

Finally, you text me!

What do you mean? Did I miss a text from you?

No. She'd been hesitant to send anything after what'd happened with their last conversation. But there was far less chance of the same thing occurring again. Right now, they had more autonomy.

Grady asked a cameraman to check on you.

That's why I'm reaching out. I guess you've been worried about me.

Just wanted to be sure you're happy.

I'm fine. Everything's pretty new with Barbie, so I don't know what will happen in the future, but she seems like a nice person.

A nice person? That sounded rather apathetic. Aja was beginning to worry about things she hadn't really considered when she let her brother talk her into being on the show. What if he wasn't truly open to loving Barbie? What if he'd only married her because it was best for the career he coveted?

What'd you two do today?

She wanted to go to Disneyland.

Barbie had grown up in Nebraska and had come to Los Angeles to attend film school; she desperately wanted to work in the movie industry.

Did you have fun?

It wasn't what I would've picked. There's not much to do without kids, IMO. But you and I have been there almost every year since we were little, so it was probably a different experience for her.

Aja hesitated but was concerned enough about her new friend to say a bit more. Are you serious about Barbie? You're not just doing this for the show, are you?

Jury's still out. What about you?

She'd never been in it for the sake of the show. But she couldn't say that her future was any more certain.

You and I were wrong to do this, Darius. We could break someone's heart.

Or we could get our own hearts broken, right? We all knew the risks when we signed on. I'm not going to feel obligated to make a decision that isn't right for me.

She frowned as she read his response. He had a point. They'd all made the dangerous decision to get involved in this experiment.

So I risked my heart for *you* to get into showbiz?

I don't think you really believed you'd fall in love, did you? Even with as long as you dated Arman, you didn't want to marry him.

And he'd been perfect for her in every way. From the outside. There just hadn't been any…magic.

Don't tell me it's different with Grady.

She didn't know. There were so many reasons they shouldn't "work." And yet… She was enjoying him, certainly wasn't ready to call it quits. That said something, didn't it?

I don't know yet. One day at a time, right?

That's the way to approach it.

Grady came out of the bedroom. "All set?"

I've got to go, she texted her brother. Be sure to delete this conversation.

What conversation?

Rolling her eyes, she shook her head. *Very funny.*

"What is it?" Grady asked as she got up.

"I just heard from my brother."

"And?"

"He and Barbie seem to be getting along okay for now."

"I wonder how many couples will survive their first year."

"So do I," she said. And would she and Grady, or Darius and Barbie, be one of them?

It was getting late when they got back from the sailboat tour. Greg was with them, filming the second night of their honeymoon—and obviously trying to get something that would suggest they'd sleep together tonight—when Grady excused himself to go to the bathroom. He needed a break. Being on the show was wearing on him. He hated how awkward and difficult it was to get to know Aja while navigating the show's demands.

As he came back through the bedroom, he listened to Greg quizzing Aja about their day.

"Do you feel you two are getting to know each other?…Which part of the honeymoon have you enjoyed most so far?…Are you looking forward to tonight?"

As she did her best to answer those questions, Grady tried to psych himself up enough to go back out there. But that was when he remembered the note Greg had handed him earlier. Since Aja had been waiting for him at the time, he hadn't read it. He'd stuck it in his suitcase because he didn't want it falling out of his pocket while they were playing tennis. Then, in their hurry to make the sailboat tour, he'd forgotten about it.

He glanced at his watch. If he made it quick, he could read it without seeming to be gone too long. After retrieving the note, he went back into the bathroom, and closed and locked the door.

The card had a fancy *W* on the front. Inside would've been blank had she not written there.

Dear Grady,

I don't dare send anything to your phone in case Aja is with you when it comes in. But I wanted to let you know that I'm grateful for all you've done to help me with the show. I know this isn't something you'd typically get involved in, which makes me appreciate it all the more.

I loved meeting your brothers, by the way. They're tall, strong and handsome—just like you. All five of you seem to have overcome a challenging past, and I find that absolutely inspiring.

I mostly just wanted to encourage you. The show won't last forever. Then…who knows what will happen? I desperately want *Tying the Knot* to be a success. But I've never been attracted to one of my "grooms" before, and that leaves me torn when it comes to you.

We'll see what fate has in store for us, I guess…
XO Winnie

P.S. If you ever need to talk, and you can get away alone, here's where you can find my house.

He stared at the Hollywood address she'd given him. Did she think he might show up at her place one night while he was married to Aja?

He got the impression she wouldn't mind, that she was giving him the option for a reason. At the very least, this note was an attempt to let him know she was more interested than she might've made it sound before. Maybe she was having second thoughts about encouraging him to go ahead with the wedding...

He'd been so infatuated with her—infatuated enough to do something that was *completely* unlike him. And now? He wasn't sure why he'd wanted her quite so badly. Because when he closed his eyes and imagined the woman he couldn't wait to make love to, it was Aja—with her sweet, beguiling smile—that appeared in his mind. He could barely remember the details of Winnie's face.

He tore up her note and flushed the pieces down the toilet. Then he forced himself to join his wife and Greg in the living room. "You about ready to leave?" he asked jokingly to the cameraman, "because there's no room here for you to sleep, and I'm exhausted."

"I was just wrapping things up for the night. What do you two have planned for tomorrow?"

"More tennis," Grady said. "She beat me too many times today, and I'm too competitive to let that stand."

"And then we might body-surf and lie on the beach," Aja added. "Since we've both had very little time off in the past few years— well, since we can remember—we're planning to make the most of the downtime."

Except they'd still be working...for the show. Grady wished he could have just one day alone with Aja...

"Sounds fun. I'll get out of here." Greg stood but he was still filming, which became clear when he pointed the camera right at Grady's face. "How attracted are you to your wife?" he asked point-blank.

"I'm *very* attracted," he replied. "She's gorgeous."

"Which means…you might take things a step further tonight?"

He shook his head. "Not until she's ready."

He lowered the camera. "The crew has been placing bets," he informed them as he started to pack up. "They think you two will be last to consummate the marriage."

"Why's that?" Grady asked.

"Because Neal and Liz already have," he said with a laugh. "That just leaves you two and Darius and Barbie, and with them, it's Darius who's holding out."

Grady saw a worried expression pass over Aja's face. "You might be right," he said. "We're giving it time."

"Are there also bets on whose marriage will last the longest?" Aja asked.

Greg glanced over at her. "Of course."

"And?" she prompted.

He winced. "On that one…you're not last—you're first."

She stood, too. "Why?"

"Because no one can see what you have in common. How are you going to overcome having such different pasts? The anger you're going to get from her parents when they find out? And who's going to give in and move to a different place to be with the other? No one sees that happening, least of all Winnie."

"Winnie?" Grady repeated.

"Yeah. She told me she doesn't see where you two stand much of a chance, but she admires you both for trying to make it work."

Grady didn't say so, but he was beginning to believe if they stayed on the show, they *wouldn't* be able to make it work. They had enough challenges to overcome; they didn't need the unnatural intrusion of the public and the cameras—and all the stress that created—making things more difficult.

He walked Greg to the door and thanked him. The guy was only doing his job. But in the silence that followed the cameraman's departure, Grady turned to Aja and said, "How would you feel about quitting the show?"

* * *

"So…you really want to break our contracts?" Aja sat across the coffee table from her new husband. When she'd realized he was serious about leaving *Tying the Knot*, she'd asked for a few minutes to change into her nightgown and pour them each a glass of wine before they discussed it.

"I do," he said, as if he was growing more convinced of it by the moment.

She felt her eyes widen. "Since when?"

He spread his hands. "Since today, I guess."

"Then you obviously didn't come on the show for the opportunities it could provide…"

He raked his fingers through his hair. "No. Did you? Because if that's the case, I'll stay."

She could tell he meant it, which showed he wasn't only thinking of himself. She'd been looking for warning signs, traits and characteristics, not to like in Grady. If there was something wrong with him, she wanted to find out early so she could get out of the marriage before the show even aired. "I have no plans of—of going on TV for anything else. In case you haven't been able to tell, I'm an introvert."

"I've been able to tell," he said with a wry chuckle, "which is part of the reason I'm even suggesting this. If I thought it was what you really wanted, I wouldn't ask you to leave."

She tucked her legs underneath her and pulled a throw blanket over her lap. "I appreciate that, but the way our contracts read, quitting will cost us some money. And not a small amount."

"I'll pay the fine for both of us. It'd be worth it to me."

That such a loss wasn't a concern for him suggested he had plenty of money. His business had to be successful. "You want out that badly?" She took a sip of wine. "Can I ask why you've suddenly changed your mind?"

"Because I have this terrible feeling that…"

When he didn't finish, she leaned forward. "That…"

"That staying on the show will ruin anything we could have," he finally said.

She sat up straight. He was doing it for the sake of their marriage? Early on, she'd gotten the impression he didn't truly believe the show would result in a long-term relationship.

He was turning out to be so different than what she'd anticipated—better, which both excited her and left her feeling vulnerable at the same time. What if she truly fell in love with him? What if she wanted their marriage to continue, but *he* decided he wanted out? "Can you give me a little more?" she asked. "What makes you think so?"

"The constant intrusions," he responded with a gesture that suggested irritation. "The unnaturalness of all the stuff we have to do. The public scrutiny we'll endure once the show airs."

"Won't we still have to face that? They'll use the parts we've already filmed…"

"It won't be as bad if we quit early. The focus will be on the couples who stay, not the ones who wash out."

"Even if we're still together?"

"If we can make it as a couple—if we're happy enough to want to stick together—that'd be a good thing, right? I'd like to give us the chance to get to that point and feel our odds are better outside the show than in it."

"I see. But how will they get by without us? I don't want to ruin it for my brother and Barbie."

"We've gone far enough, what with the wedding and sharing part of our honeymoon. That footage should get them fairly deep into the season. We could even offer to send them more footage—selfie footage—from Whiskey Creek if they need it. At least then it'll be on *our* terms. We won't have a schedule to follow, or a cameraman showing up to say provocative things, hoping to film an argument or get us to discuss our sex lives, or the problems we have with various family members."

There was a lot to that statement, but one thing stood out above the rest. "You want to go to Whiskey Creek?"

"Why not?" he replied. "You've already arranged to have the next few weeks off work, right? I'd like you to see my hometown—to determine whether you could be happy there. Leaving LA also puts some distance between us and the production team. If we're seven hours away, they'd be much less likely to show up with a camera at our doorstep or talk us into doing more than we want to do at this point. And maybe…if they leave us alone for a few days, we might even be willing to come back for more filming later. I'm just…done with being a puppet. I want to feel like a normal human being again."

So did she. But once she decided to marry Grady, she'd assumed they'd finish the season.

"You want to stay in," he said, guessing when she hesitated.

"I don't," she admitted. "I've never been that excited about it. I just… I want to be sure we're not letting the others down."

"Our leaving won't hurt anyone. You came on the show for Darius, but they aren't going to kick him off now. They need him too badly."

"True, but we've come this far. Are you sure you don't want to see it through?"

"I would if I thought…" He huffed out a sigh. "I just want to take you home," he said.

His words made her happy, but if she went with him, she'd be giving him a certain amount of control over her life, and she didn't know him very well. Would she ultimately regret making such a decision?

Tough to say. But even if they stayed on the show, she'd have to figure out, at some point, whether she wanted their marriage to continue. Leaving would probably help her make that decision a lot sooner.

"Okay," she said.

He seemed surprised by her response…and eager to clarify. "Okay…what?"

"We'll quit the show and go to Whiskey Creek."

Chapter Thirteen

Winnie looked stricken. "What do you mean you're quitting? You told me… We agreed…"

Grady stood at the window of her office with his hands shoved into his pockets as she searched for the right words to convey her outrage. After his discussion with Aja last night, he'd gotten up early and texted Winnie to request a meeting before filming started, so the sun was barely peeking over the row of high-rises that made a canyon of the street far below. "I know what we agreed. But staying on the show will put too much stress on my marriage."

"You've got to be kidding me. Your marriage isn't real," she said. "I mean…technically it is, but it's more of an—an experiment for others to watch. You barely know Aja. You picked her instead of the women our psychologists felt were better suited to you. And now you want to protect that relationship by leaving the show?"

He turned to face her. "I knew this would be disappointing to you. But you were the one who encouraged me to proceed, who told me to give it my best. You said if it works out, great. If it doesn't, then…" He glanced away. "Well, we both know what we thought would happen then. But I've since realized that none of that is fair to Aja. I can't give our marriage my best effort if I'm thinking about you the whole time. That is inherently dishonest. And it gives me an escape hatch she doesn't have, a reason to bail out if she does the slightest thing wrong."

A muscle moved in her cheek. "Great time to grow a conscience," she growled.

"I didn't think coming on the show was a matter of conscience, didn't see where I was doing anything wrong. But it certainly feels like I'm doing something wrong now, which is why I'm trying to fix it."

"What about the cost of canceling?" she demanded. "It'll be expen—"

"Whatever it is, I'll cover it," he interrupted. It would be worth it to be able to ease his conscience.

"And you don't care about me or the show? How we'll get through the rest of the season?"

"Of course I care. Aja and I will provide you with the footage you need. It'll just happen a little differently, on our terms instead of yours. But who knows? That might go over even better with the audience. And it'll be free."

She shook her head. "I've never had a cast member do this."

"We both know I'm not your typical cast member. You understood what was motivating me going in. But the good news is that Aja and I don't want to let anyone down, so we're willing to help you in whatever ways we can."

"Staying would help me," she pointed out.

"Other than that," he clarified.

Tears filled her eyes, which made him squirm. He didn't know if she was crying because them leaving would hurt the show, and therefore its chances of success, or if she was truly interested in him. "I don't know what to say," she said.

He cleared his throat. "I feel terrible. I'm sorry."

Suddenly all business, she sniffed, blinked away her tears and stood. "It's fine. No problem. Since you're leaving early, we won't pay you for the time you've been on the show, but we won't charge you the penalty, either, as long as you give us enough access and video footage to finish the season."

He spread his hands. "I've already agreed to do that."

"You also agreed to other things and are now going back on your word," she pointed out curtly.

"And you know why!" he argued. "I screwed up in the beginning by—by doing what I did. I feel this is the only way to fix that—to give Aja the serious and honest attempt she deserves."

"But the marriage isn't going to work, anyway!" she said, obviously exasperated. "You're ruining my show—and any chance you and I might've had at a relationship when it's over—for nothing!"

"How do you know my marriage won't work?" he asked.

"What are the odds?" she demanded, coming right back at him. "You didn't even follow the show's protocols!"

"Exactly why I'm taking matters into my own hands. I'm trying to make up for that!"

Lifting her chin, she glared at him. "You've decided, then. I can't change your mind?"

He thought of Aja, how she'd cuddled up to him in bed last night. He'd wanted to slip his hand under that silky nightgown she was wearing, touch her, kiss her…

He'd held off, but it hadn't been easy. He'd lain awake long after she fell asleep, thinking about her and how crazy it was that they were actually married. There shouldn't be anything special between them—they barely knew each other and had nothing in common—and yet there was a small flame. If he didn't protect it and fan it, help it to grow, it would go out. In his mind, *that* would be the real tragedy.

"I'm afraid so," he said. "But I'll try to make it up to you."

"I'm not sure that's possible." She consulted her watch. "But I'll deal with it. Now, if that's all, I have to rush off or I'm going to be late. I'm meeting the crew to give them their instructions for the day."

He watched her cross the room as if she'd walk out and leave him there by himself. "So… Aja and I can pack up and leave?"

"If you're quitting, I guess that's up to you." She turned to face him as she reached the door. "But we've paid for the beach house through tomorrow. The least you could do is try to enjoy it and let us finish filming your 'honeymoon.'"

With a sigh, he scratched the back of his neck. "Fine. We'll do that much."

The next two days were some of the most enjoyable Aja could remember. In the past, she'd always had school or work on her mind—something she needed to get done. But she'd checked in with her office twice. All was surprisingly quiet. And she hadn't even heard from her parents. According to some pictures she'd seen posted on Arman's Instagram account, they'd gone to Palm Springs with Arman and his parents. They were all probably mad at her—and maybe even strategizing on how to get her back into a relationship with him—but she was trying not to think about that. At least for the moment they were giving her some space, so she didn't have to talk to them and insist she was having a great time on her trip to Europe with Darius. She felt guilty about lying in the first place, knew how angry they were going to be when they learned the truth.

"You got everything?"

She looked up from where she'd been packing the rest of her clothes in the suitcase on the bed when Grady came back into the cottage after taking their first load out to the car provided to them by the show for their honeymoon. "Just about," she replied and finished stuffing her makeup bag into one side of the suitcase before zipping it closed.

"I'll get that for you," he said as she started to grab the handle.

As she stood back so he could reach it, she couldn't help smiling at him. They hadn't even kissed since the wedding—had spent nothing but chaste nights together in their honeymoon bed—but she was beginning to wish he'd do something to change that. Or maybe *she* would. Grady smelled *so* good to her. And having his warm body in her bed at the end of each day was something she was beginning to look forward to. She'd slept with Arman on and off for years, of course, depending on what they each had going, and yet…it'd never felt quite so exciting.

Grady's gaze briefly lowered to her mouth, making her feel as though he was having similar thoughts. But then he grinned. "Should we go get something to eat? Celebrate the fact that we're about to reclaim our freedom?"

"Sure. I'd love to get a slice of quiche or something. What are you in the mood for?"

"I'm easy to please. If it's food, I'll eat it. Why don't you choose the restaurant?"

"There are so many I'd like to show you in LA…"

"That's one benefit of a big city, I guess." He gave her a worried look. "You won't have that many to choose from in Whiskey Creek…"

She laughed. "I don't live for eating out. I actually like to cook. I just haven't had the opportunity here."

"I didn't realize that," he said.

Resting a hand on her hip, she cocked one leg while she gave him a saucy look. "There's a lot you don't know about me."

His gaze moved down over her. "I'm looking forward to learning more."

"You're sure taking your sweet time," she said.

His eyebrows shot up. "I've been trying to wait until you're comfortable. But now you're asking for trouble."

She stepped back and put up her hands. "Okay. Maybe I went too far."

"That's what I thought," he said with an exaggerated wink and headed out with the suitcase.

She chuckled as she followed behind him. "Do your brothers know we're coming?"

"No," he said, looking back at her. "I thought it would be fun to surprise them."

Whiskey Creek looked as though it hailed from a different era. Wooden boardwalks lined the main drag that snaked through the small cluster of buildings constituting downtown. She liked seeing all the reminders of the town's past, including the small park with its gold-panning statue and the darling Victorian B&B they passed, not to mention the beautiful old mansion that was now used to host weddings.

"Where does this road go?" she asked as the buildings quickly gave way to raw land.

"There's another Gold Country town, not too different from this one, about fifteen miles away," Grady told her. They'd turned in the car the show had rented for them and were now in his truck.

"Are there a lot of such towns?"

"Quite a few, sprinkled throughout the foothills." He lowered the volume of the music they'd been listening to. The drive had been long—seven hours—and yet they'd talked the whole time about myriad subjects, including how Winnie had reacted to them quitting, what they'd try to do to make it up to her, his brothers and their wives and children…and his father, who was someone else she'd meet. "Does this place seem too…claustrophobic for you?" he asked, watching her closely. "Too rural?"

She studied the buildings as they passed them again going the opposite direction, until he stopped at one of the lights and turned right. A lot seemed to hang on her answer, but she wanted to be honest. "I'm not sure. It's definitely a cute town… Where's your business?"

"That's where I'm taking you now."

She knew he was hungry. They'd talked about where they'd grab dinner when they arrived. But he seemed so excited to show her around; that was taking precedent at the moment.

Two blocks off Sutter Street, where there weren't many businesses at all—just a few houses in among the dirt roads, trees and shrubs—he turned into Amos Auto Body.

"Here we are," he said. "Would you like to see the inside or wait until another time?"

She could tell he was eager to show her, so she said she'd love to see it all now, and he hopped out. "You don't lack for work," she said as she looked over at a large, fenced yard filled with vehicles that needed repair.

"Fortunately, that's true. We have a pretty good reputation in these parts. People come from all around," he said, then walked her inside and through numerous paint stalls and repair bays in the back part of the building .

"What're your hours?" she asked as they came out.

"Eight to five every day except Sunday."

She stopped walking. "You work six days a week?"

"Until now, I haven't had a reason not to. My brothers all have wives and children, so more demands on their time."

"Meaning you've been picking up the slack."

He shrugged. "Keeps the business running smoothly. But now that I have… Well, if we have kids…" He didn't seem to know how to finish either of those statements. "I'll be reasonable with my hours moving forward," he said instead. "What's your schedule like?"

"Typically, I work Tuesday through Saturday. I'd rather work Monday through Friday, but that can make it hard for some of my patients to get their teeth fixed. At some point I hope to go down to every other Saturday, at least."

"That'd be nice."

He showed her the store, with its counter area, vending machines and vinyl chairs in the small lobby. Then he locked up and they returned to the front yard. "Do you want to continue to work even after you have kids?" he asked.

"As a dentist?" she clarified. "If I need to."

"What if you *don't* need to?"

"If I have the luxury of going either way, I'd—"

"Have a ceramics studio," he said, finishing her thought.

"Exactly."

He opened the truck door for her. "What about your education? You'd let all that go if you could?"

She grimaced in uncertainty. "It probably wouldn't be wise. It required so much work and effort. But it wasn't what I wanted to do in the first place. And we're just dreaming here, anyway, so... yeah, I guess I would."

Cocking his head, he studied her as he raised a finger to trace her jawline. "Most of my brothers' wives don't work. As far as I'm concerned, you'd have your choice," he said and closed her door.

Aja wasn't looking for anyone else to take care of her. But Grady's self-assured manner—his confidence that he could carry the load—was almost as appealing as his generosity.

She smiled as he climbed into the driver's side and as soon as he started the car, she took his hand.

"What?" he said as she watched him.

"I really like you," she replied, and although it wasn't the most romantic place he could've picked for their first kiss, when he leaned over to press his lips to hers, it was so natural she sighed and kissed him back.

Chapter Fourteen

Grady hadn't planned on kissing Aja in that moment. He'd wanted to wait for the right time and the right place. But it'd happened spontaneously, probably because he'd been thinking so much about it.

She parted her lips, allowing his tongue access to hers, and a tidal wave of desire slammed into him. The memories of her lying next to him in bed the past few nights flooded his brain, making him want her even more. He craved the feel of her breasts in his palms, his mouth on her neck, or anywhere else on her body, and her legs wrapped around his hips as he moved inside her.

This was nothing like what he'd expected—he was falling for his wife.

Suddenly, a pair of headlights hit them. Surprised, since it was well after closing time, he pulled back and watched a man get out of a truck and approach them.

"Shit. It's my dad," he muttered and lowered his window.

JT scowled as he reached the driver's side and craned his neck to see around Grady. "That's her?"

Grady ignored the question. It wasn't a very polite way to greet Aja—his dad was a little rough around the edges. "What are you doing here?"

"Thought maybe I forgot to lock up. Came back to check."

"*You* closed for the day?"

"Dylan had kids' stuff. And don't act so shocked. I'm the one who started this business, damn it. I used to close all the time, back when I was still wiping your snotty nose."

That was before he'd lost all of Grady's trust. But JT was doing much better these days. Once he'd finally been pushed into rehab and had been convinced to make changes.

"Door was locked when we arrived."

"Just wanted to be sure."

"I appreciate that."

His father tried to look around him again. "Aren't you going to introduce me to my new daughter-in-law?"

Grady leaned back so that Aja and JT could see each other. "Dad, this is Aja Kermani. Aja, this is JT, my dad."

"Nice to meet you," she said.

He scowled. "What is she? Middle Eastern?"

"She's sitting right here, Dad. Don't talk about her in the third person," Grady said, but Aja spoke at the same time.

"I'm Persian," she told him. "My parents immigrated from Iran, but I was born here."

"No one mentioned anything about that," he said.

"Because it doesn't matter," Grady told him.

JT spread his hands. "I was just surprised, okay? And isn't her name Aja *Amos* now?"

He and Aja hadn't even talked about whether she'd take his name, eventually. That seemed like a discussion for later, after the experiment was over and they decided if they were going to stay together. "That remains to be seen."

"So why aren't you in LA? I thought you'd be filming the entire month," his father said.

"We decided we didn't really like being on camera."

"You quit?"

"Not entirely. We just…negotiated better terms."

"What does that mean?"

"It means we're going to be here for a few days, at least." Grady attempted to change the subject. "Where's Anya?" His father had always had an explosive relationship with his on-and-off-again romantic partner, so he was afraid they'd had yet another argument when he didn't see her with him.

"She works at the bookstore, remember?"

"I didn't think the bookstore was open this late."

"It's the owner's birthday. They're throwing a party for her after hours."

So she hadn't moved out while Grady was gone. That was a good thing, because his father was coming to depend on her.

"That's nice." Grady turned to explain whom he was talking about to Aja. He hadn't even mentioned that his father was with someone. As a general rule, he avoided talking about JT whenever possible. "Anya's my father's ex-wife, but they're back together." He didn't add "for now," even though, in the past, Anya and JT had split up too many times to count. But now that they were both clean and sober, Grady was beginning to believe they might actually make it. And for the first time in his life, he was starting to like Anya.

"Why don't you two follow me over to the house?" JT asked. "Anya should be home soon, and she'd love to meet Aja. She's crazy about *Tying the Knot*. She's watched both the other seasons and can't wait until it airs with you two on it."

"We'll come by sometime this week," Grady said. "We haven't had dinner yet, and Aja hasn't seen the house. Give us a chance to get settled in. Then we'll make the rounds."

JT wasn't happy with this response. Grady had known he wouldn't be. He needed a lot of time and attention. Grady was usually okay with trying to make sure he got what he needed, but he wanted to be alone with Aja tonight. "We're still on our honeymoon," he explained.

"Oh, right. Dylan told me you went through with the wedding. That, in itself, is unbelievable, especially for you."

Afraid that JT was going to wander into uncomfortable territory, Grady lifted a hand. "Dad, that's enough."

JT leaned in to make sure he had Aja's full attention...but, fortunately, changed the subject. "You married a good man," he said. "My boys make excellent husbands." He hesitated briefly, then added, "I used to be an excellent husband myself once."

"Which is where we got it from." JT hadn't been "excellent" for long, but Grady was saying what he could, hoping this conversation wasn't about to unravel.

Seemingly gratified, his father addressed Aja again. "Dylan said you're a dentist in LA."

She smiled. "I am."

"How are you two going to handle the fact that you own businesses in two different parts of the state?"

"We haven't decided," Grady responded quickly to save her the trouble of coming up with an answer.

A skeptical expression claimed JT's face. "I don't see how you're going to make that work."

Grady cleared his throat. "You don't need to worry about it. Aja and I will figure things out between us."

"I can't help but worry," he said. "We need you around here."

Grady and his brothers had needed a father, too, when they were kids. But JT had let them down. "Aja and I are going to go eat, Dad. I'll talk to you later."

JT nodded and backed away, but only because Grady put the truck in Reverse, signaling that he was about to drive off.

"Is he going to be okay?" Aja whispered as they pulled away.

Grady waved through the open window before putting it up, but he couldn't help glancing in the rearview mirror to make sure his father was getting back into his vehicle. "Yeah," he said. "He'll be fine."

Aja didn't seem convinced. She twisted around to look through the back window. "Maybe we should invite him to come to dinner with us, after all. He seems sort of at loose ends. Might be a vulnerable moment."

Grady stepped on the brake. "You wouldn't mind?"

"Not at all," she said.

This wasn't what he'd hoped for with regard to their first night in Whiskey Creek, but the offer she'd made was certainly kind. "It's our honeymoon, and your first night in town, and—"

"Grady..." She reached over to take his hand. "Your father is more important. And maybe once he gets to know me, he won't be so disappointed that I'm Persian," she added with a laugh.

He grimaced. "I'm sorry about that. Honest to God, I don't think he cares about your ethnicity. He just loves to rock the boat, and he might do more of that type of thing at dinner. That's what I'm afraid of."

"If he does, it's okay. He can be himself. I'm more resilient than that."

Finally convinced, Grady got out, walked to his father's vehicle and waited for JT to lower the window. "We're going to that new Italian place—Amalfi's—if you'd like to join us."

"Really?" he said. "You want *me* to come?"

"We do."

"Okay. Sounds good."

Grady jogged back to his own truck and climbed in.

"Is he coming?" Aja asked.

He shot her a grin. "Of course," he said and took her hand and kissed her knuckles. "Thank you for quitting the show with me, for being willing to leave LA with me—" he studied the soft, smooth skin of her face and her wide, dark eyes "—and for being the type of person who cares about others."

"Well… I certainly understand about difficult parents." She shot him a rueful expression. "Just wait until you meet mine."

Aja couldn't help wondering how she'd found herself in a small town she'd never even heard of, married to a man she'd barely met. Had she lost her mind?

Maybe. For the first time in her life, she was acting impulsively instead of carefully measuring what she wanted against what her parents wanted for her. She felt like she was living, *truly* living for a change, so it was hard to regret the decisions that'd brought her to this place.

At dinner with Grady and his father, she realized JT was every bit as unpredictable as Grady had told her he could be. Some of the things he said obviously embarrassed Grady. But she wished her new husband would relax. She understood that he couldn't control his father. Learning more about the man she'd married and his lifestyle did make her wonder if she'd be happy in Whiskey Creek, however. She'd never imagined leaving Los Angeles. But the challenges of starting an Amos Auto Body franchise in

LA could make Whiskey Creek their only option…if they stayed together.

Grady texted Dylan and Rod, the only brothers who were local, to ask them to come over to the restaurant to say hello and grab some dessert. That meant they weren't alone with JT for very long. The influx of people and laughter made it feel sort of like an impromptu party, because this time the brothers brought their wives and children. Even JT's significant other showed up eventually, when she was finished with the birthday party at the bookstore.

The restaurant was closing by the time they said their goodbyes. She and Grady were the only ones in the parking lot when he opened the passenger door to his truck for her. "That was quite the initiation," he said. "Are you ready to divorce me yet?"

Although he chuckled, she didn't laugh. His hopeful grin suggested he wanted to be reassured Aja was committed to their marriage, and she found that quite endearing. He'd been through so much in his life. As he'd said, he was probably afraid to love, which was why he'd married someone he *didn't* love. That way, in his mind, he could have a wife and children and not get hurt.

But he wasn't as impervious as he thought. He was lonely, or he wouldn't have come on the show. His defenses were wearing thin; she could feel his desire for love warring with his fear of actually loving. "Of course not, but I was a little overwhelmed," she admitted. "I can only imagine what it's like when Aaron and Mack and their families are here, too."

"The noise is deafening," he said with the same wry grin.

"You might have to remind me of some of the children's names. You have more family than I do—more immediate family, anyway."

"You don't have anything to worry about," he said. "I'll remind you as many times as you need."

Their eyes met and held, and his gaze lowered to her mouth. He was going to kiss her. Just the thought sent off a riot of butterflies in her stomach. When she'd first met Grady, she'd been worried about whether she'd be willing to sleep with him. She'd only ever had sex with Arman. But she wasn't concerned about that anymore. It felt as though they'd be *very* compatible in that way. And the fact that he hadn't even tried to make love to her yet—other than that brief interlude in the truck earlier, when he'd kissed her and it might've gone further had they not been interrupted—was driving her mad. If he was holding back on purpose, just to make her want that kind of contact, it was certainly working.

Catching her breath, she let her eyes close in anticipation. But when nothing happened, she opened them again and read fear and doubt in his expression. He was afraid to let down his guard, to allow her past the fortifications he'd built around his heart.

"You must be tired after such a long day," he said, stepping back. "I'd better get you home."

Chapter Fifteen

That Grady had backed away bothered Aja. She'd thought they'd been making progress. But instead of becoming more openhearted as he got to know her, he seemed to be building a wall between them.

They made chitchat as he drove a few blocks, then turned down a country lane that followed a creek. He lived in a two-story home that was too big for one person, but he explained that he'd grown up there.

While Grady showed her the house, Aja asked about his brothers and how they'd met their wives. They all had interesting stories and she liked hearing him talk about Dylan, Aaron, Rod and Mack.

"You definitely didn't have a conventional childhood," she said. "But at least you had plenty of love."

"And protection," he added with a ghost of a smile. "For a while there, it was us against the world."

They'd walked through the house and were in the kitchen when Aja said, "You sure keep the place clean."

He gave her a sheepish look. "That's not me. I have a housekeeper who comes every Friday."

"Must be nice," she said with a laugh.

"It's clean, but this place is getting old and outdated. I need to remodel. I just don't know where to start."

The house had everything most men would think it needed—a big-screen TV, plenty of recliners, a wet bar and a garage full of tools. But he was right about it needing to be updated. He could tear out the carpets and put in hardwood floors, maybe knock out a few walls to enlarge the kitchen and make a great room. The appliances looked fairly new, but she noticed that he needed to replace all the blinds and tear off a lot of wallpaper, too.

He headed toward a sliding glass door at the back of the family room. "I've already done the backyard, though," he said. "Come see."

They stepped onto an expansive deck with a huge barbecue area and a firepit a few stairs below the deck on the adjacent patio. He had expensive-looking lawn furniture, and a great view, since the back lawn sloped down to the creek.

"Did you pay to have all this done?" she asked.

"No, I did it myself," he replied. "Took me the better part of a year, but I was only able to do it in my off hours."

The smell of freshly cut grass rose to her nostrils. "Who takes care of the lawn?"

"I do, but my dad said he'd do it while I was gone. He must've mowed this morning."

"It's gorgeous out here, perfect for parties," she told him. "You didn't tell me you were *this* handy."

"Most people could do this," he said.

She knew *that* wasn't true. "My father can't even change the oil in his car let alone build a backyard like this," she said. "But he's an incredible ophthalmologist."

He rested his hands on his hips as he surveyed his own work. "I enjoyed the process, and I'll be happy to do whatever you want on the inside. I just haven't gotten that far, don't really have an eye for what's best in there, so I'd be happy to take some direction from you if…if you want to get involved."

If things worked out was what he was really saying. They always had the possibility of failure hanging over their heads, weren't quite as committed as a normal married couple would be. "That would be a fun project," she admitted.

"Oh, and there's this." He beckoned her to the side of the house.

She followed him to a freestanding shedlike building that had a padlock on the door. After he opened it, she could see that it contained a couple of motorcycles, some mountain bikes, several golf bags, a lawn mower and other yard tools. "We could clear this out and get a kiln, turn this place into a pottery studio for you."

She stepped back in surprise. "*Really?* But then…what will you do with all this stuff?"

"I can always build another shed," he said. "We got five acres here."

She turned in a circle, trying to assess how it might feel to have this place as a studio.

"I'd dress it up for you, of course—add air-conditioning, some windows, shelving and whatever else you need," he added.

"Thank you. That's so nice." Having a place to create the way she'd always dreamed certainly made Whiskey Creek more appealing. She couldn't have anything like this at her condo. If she wanted to do pottery in LA, she'd have to pay for studio time or rent her own space somewhere off-site, and that didn't make a lot of sense when she was at her dental practice most of the time.

"If you decide to stay, I want you to be happy here," he said.

She turned to face him. "Does that mean you're no longer considering Los Angeles?"

"Opening another franchise would take time, maybe three years, so it wouldn't be right away."

"You're saying you'd expect me to shut down my dental practice if we stay together?"

"I prefer to think of it as offering to let you live your dream instead," he said with a crooked grin.

"You realize, if I were to sell my practice, I probably wouldn't have an income for quite some time."

"I understand."

"And you wouldn't mind?" she asked.

He seemed taken aback by the question. "Why would I mind? If this marriage becomes a *real* marriage, what I have would be yours, too. I have some savings, and the business is doing well. We could make it."

But what if they tried to stay together and their marriage failed despite that? She'd have given up her practice, and he would've spent a fortune helping her get started in the art world.

That he'd be willing to take such a risk after marrying her the way that he had said so much about the type of person he was—how far he'd go for someone he loved.

Touched by his generosity, she wanted to kiss him again, feel his arms go around her and hold her close. But he didn't reach for her; he stepped out of the shed and held the door so she could follow him.

Aja had suggested they sleep in the same bed and Grady had agreed, but that had probably been a mistake. As she lay next to him that night, he wanted her so badly he couldn't sleep. But he was terrified to trust her enough to act on that desire. What if he fell in love with her and she let him down?

He continued to battle his growing desire. He needed to wait until he could be certain she wanted to be with him. What if there was a side of her he hadn't yet seen? Or what if she decided she'd made a mistake marrying him and wanted to back out?

There was a lot riding on their marriage. More than felt safe. She didn't seem excited to leave LA behind, and it would take a lot of time and effort for him to get into a position where he could safely move there. Would that be all it would take to make her leave him?

And what about her parents? They had to have considerable influence over her, or she wouldn't have found it so difficult to follow her own path before now.

That she'd allowed them so much control wasn't exactly a harbinger of hope that she'd defy them if they disapproved of him. But, possibly because of how she valued family, she seemed to be more tolerant of his father than he would've expected from just any woman. Although JT had said some things that'd made him squirm tonight, on the whole Grady had had a great time at dinner. For once, he wasn't the only one without a partner. At last, *he* had a wife and the chance to have a family.

Aja sighed in her sleep and cuddled closer. He could feel her soft breasts pressed against his arm and was so tempted to lift his hand to touch her. The scent of her shampoo rose to his nostrils and he closed his eyes to breathe it in, remembering the feel of her lips against his and the way she'd met his tongue with her own.

Nearly groaning in frustration, he rolled over to face the other direction. Surely, this unorthodox marriage wouldn't last; he needed to be prepared for when it ended.

Movement in the bed woke Aja. Grady seemed miserable, couldn't seem to get comfortable. She felt him shift one way, then the other and then onto his back, and when she squinted in the dark to see if she could make out whether his eyes were closed, she found him staring up at the ceiling.

She had no idea what time it was, but she knew it was late and got the impression he'd been tossing and turning for hours. He'd been so eager to come home, so excited to show her his business and his house and the shed he was willing to make into a pottery studio for her. And it'd all gone well—even dinner with his family. So why wasn't he able to sleep?

They'd shared a bed at the beach house, too, so she knew he hadn't been quite *this* restless since they married...

She almost asked him what was wrong. But she was afraid he'd misinterpret the question, feel he was disturbing her and needed to sleep somewhere else. That wasn't what she was hoping to achieve at all. She just wanted him to let down his guard. She couldn't really get to know him if he wouldn't, and she was so hopeful what she felt for him would continue to grow. That was why she'd quit the show and come to Whiskey Creek with him.

When he lifted his head to look at the alarm clock on the nightstand, she decided it was time to do something drastic. Without a word, she shimmied out of her nightgown, tossed it on the floor and slid over to pull Grady into her arms.

Grady was wearing pajama bottoms but no shirt. Summer nights in Whiskey Creek were too warm otherwise. So when Aja's bare chest came into contact with his, he nearly gasped. He'd been trying so hard not to even think of her sexually. But, of course, that had been impossible. He could no longer resist, was going to make love to her whether he regretted it or not.

Her hands delved into his hair as he began to kiss her, and she moaned as if that kind of contact was exactly what she'd been craving.

From that moment on, he could scarcely breathe. Pulling her more snugly against him, he slid his hands up her bare back, welcoming the incredible satisfaction of simply holding her naked body against him.

"God, you feel good," he muttered.

She didn't respond. She just kissed him again—this time holding his face in both hands while she did it—and the slow indulgent way she used her tongue, as if she was savoring every second, made the kiss more enjoyable than any he'd ever had.

Taking his time, he reveled in having such intimate access to her mouth and all the rest of her, but eventually rolled her onto her back and began kissing his way down her throat to her breasts. He liked curves—*loved* curves—and she had plenty of them, along with what seemed like miles of the softest skin he'd ever touched.

She moaned as his mouth reached her breasts, and he began to use one hand to explore the rest of her. When she arched her back, he knew he'd found something she liked.

Lifting his head, he grinned down at her. "Apparently, this is a good spot."

"It's a *great* spot," she admitted breathlessly, and he managed a chuckle, but all mirth fell away quickly because he was so intent on further discoveries.

He loved the smell of her, he realized, as he continued to kiss his way down her body. Not only the scent of the products she used, but also the scent of her skin and that musky, more intimate smell that was so individual to her. Everything about her appealed to him. He pictured her in her wedding dress as she came down the aisle toward him. That was the first moment he'd realized how truly beautiful she was.

She began to tremble as he kissed her thighs. He couldn't wait to peel off his pajama bottoms and bury himself inside her. But if he wanted to draw this out and make it last, he had to manage a little restraint, at least for now.

She tried to bring his head up...possibly to kiss him again. Or maybe being completely open to him made her feel too vulnerable.

"Let me taste you," he said, resisting, and when he reached the same spot he'd first located with his fingers, he felt her body jerk in reaction.

"That's...incredible," she said, her voice whisper-thin. Then, as her muscles grew taut and her breathing more ragged, he slid his hands under her so he could hold her lower body at just the right angle...until she shuddered and cried out.

Chapter Sixteen

She was making love to her *husband*. She thought it might be awkward being so intimate with a man she didn't know well. But it wasn't. All she could feel was Grady inside her, his fingers threaded through hers as he pinned her hands to the pillow above her head and stared down into her eyes. The way he was looking at her was probably the most erotic thing she'd ever experienced.

He moved slowly at first, as though he didn't want to miss one tiny nuance of having joined their bodies, but he couldn't seem to hold back for very long. Only a few moments later, his eyelids slid closed, and he began to move faster. Although he was using a condom, Aja had the somewhat curious thought that she wanted to get pregnant. Before tonight, she'd been so focused on her career that the idea of having a baby meant only calamity—at least when it came to reaching her goals. But a baby was becoming more and more appealing and important to her.

Closing her own eyes, she told herself to shut off her mind for once and simply feel. Even if her marriage didn't last, she had tonight, and she was going to make the most of it.

Grady went to the bathroom, then came back and dropped into bed. All the tension and anxiety that'd been building up inside him the past couple of weeks was suddenly gone, replaced with exhaustion.

When Aja scooted closer to him, he shifted so she could rest her head on his shoulder.

"That was the best," he told her.

"I think so, too." He could hear the smile in her voice as she curled more comfortably into him. "How soon would you want children if—if we decide to stay together?" she asked.

He felt it'd be irresponsible to have kids before they knew each other better. But he'd longed to start a family for a while now, so other than that, he was ready.

"Whenever you'd want to give them to me," he mumbled, and if she said something else, he didn't hear it because he sank into a deep, dreamless sleep almost instantaneously.

Grady was gone when Aja woke up. She stretched and yawned, then smiled as she remembered last night. Another gamble had paid off. She'd enjoyed every second of making love with Grady. And he'd seemed to enjoy it, too. But she had to wonder if her luck would hold…

Pulling the blankets higher, she listened for her husband.

When she didn't hear anything, she got up, dressed in yoga shorts and a tank top, and went to the bathroom to brush her teeth and put her hair up. Then she ambled downstairs and into the kitchen, where she found a pot of hot coffee with a sticky note.

Good morning, beautiful. Had to take care of a few things at the auto body shop but want to take you to breakfast. Call me when you're ready to go.

She checked the clock—8:08 a.m., which was an hour and a half later than she usually got up—and poured herself a cup of coffee. Could she get used to living in this town? she asked herself. Could she make this house her home?

She wandered onto the deck, where she saw two deer at the creek—they had to be used to seeing humans because they didn't run when she came out. She admired them as she sat at the patio table. It was beautiful in Whiskey Creek; she had to admit that.

She thought of how her parents would react to her moving away. They wouldn't like it. She'd be leaving the tight Persian community she'd been part of since she was born. But she wasn't sure that would be entirely bad. Whiskey Creek had a lot to recommend it, too.

Reminded of her family, she took her phone from her pocket and texted her brother.

How's it going? Aja began. Is it true love or what?

She didn't get an answer right away. She'd finished her coffee and gone back inside, was just rinsing her mug in the sink, when she heard the alert.

Barbie's a nice person. But probably won't last.

Aja bit her lip as she read that. Why not?

Just not right for me.

Does Barbie know that?

I can't imagine she doesn't.

Have you talked about it?

A little. We're happy to stay together so we can remain on the show. It could give us both the kinds of opportunities we're looking for. But other than that...

That makes me sad.

There's nothing to be sad about. She likes you a lot, too. We can all be friends. What about you? Are you falling for Grady?

That was a good question. She smiled as memories of last night floated through her mind. There's definitely something there.

Seriously? That's the last thing I expected my conservative, cautious older sister to say.

I know. It's scaring me, too. To be honest, I don't know whether to trust it.

So are you glad you quit the show?

It's been nice to be out from under those demands. But we'll take some video to send Winnie today.

How do you like Grady's hometown? Would you be willing to live there?

She frowned as she gazed out the window at the expansive front yard. The properties along the creek were large, which meant she didn't have any close neighbors. Jury's out, she wrote. But then she thought of the shed Grady had said he'd make into a pottery studio.

There was an entirely different life waiting for her here.

So which one would make her the happiest?

Grady was still at the shop when Winnie's text came in. Can you talk?

They didn't have anything more to discuss, not that Aja couldn't hear, but he got the impression Winnie was implying she wanted to talk to him without involving his wife. He wanted to write back "About what?" But he was afraid such a blunt response would come off as rude, so he called her instead.

"There you are," she said.

The sulky note in her voice confused him. "What's that supposed to mean?"

"I didn't hear from you all day yesterday."

He straightened. "We were driving, Winnie. Then I was introducing Aja to my father and showing her my house and business. Were we supposed to check in?"

"I just thought…" There was a pause, then she said, "I just thought you might have some video for me."

"Not yet. But I promise we'll get you something today."

"Like what?"

"Shots of us at breakfast after our first night in my house. That should be good, right?"

"That'll be great, but…how are things progressing?"

He wasn't sure what she meant. "If you're asking whether we're getting to know each other, we are."

"And you're enjoying each other?"

"I'd say so."

"What about sex?"

This was awkward because he knew she had a personal interest in the question. He wanted to tell her it was none of her business, but because of the show, it sort of was. Everyone would want to know if they'd consummated their marriage. "That part's good, too."

"Greg told me you hadn't slept together before you left here."

He swallowed a sigh as he looked out the window of his shop to see another customer pull in. "It happened last night, okay?"

"And?"

"And I don't know what else to say." He felt like he was somehow betraying Aja just by telling Winnie this much, and yet... surely Aja knew the show would be peppering them with such personal questions.

"You're falling in love."

It was a statement, not a question. "I don't know," he said.

"That's how it feels to me."

"I'm just trying to give Aja an honest effort. She's a beautiful woman, a great person. She deserves it."

"I wish I'd never paired you together," she said angrily and disconnected.

Grady stared down at his phone. Apparently, she'd been so confident his marriage wouldn't succeed, she hadn't worried about it. She'd thought she could use it for the show and he'd still be around after, and didn't like that things now seemed to be going in a different direction.

So...what might she do about it? He didn't want her to tell Aja the *real* reason he'd come on the show and gone through with the wedding. As if she knew he was thinking about her, his phone buzzed with a text from Aja. I'm ready.

I'll be there in five.

Then he sent a message to Winnie. I'm sorry. You know I didn't expect this.

You could stop it, she wrote back.

Actually, he didn't think he could. That was what made it so beautiful.

It was also what made it so scary.

Chapter Seventeen

Grady was excited to see Aja. He'd thought about their love-making the entire time he was helping his father and brothers get the shop open and going for the day. He could tell that with him gone they were beginning to fall behind. But he was only willing to do so much today, certainly wasn't going to spend more than a couple of hours at the shop when he was still on his honeymoon.

Aja must've been watching for him, because she came out as soon as he pulled into the drive. He admired her long black hair gleaming in the sunlight and the pretty white sundress that contrasted so nicely with her smooth skin.

When she reached the truck, he leaned over to open her door. "Morning."

She gave him a bright smile as she climbed in, and he realized that smile was what he loved most about her. It had to be the sweetest smile he'd ever seen. "Morning," she said. "How are things at the shop?"

"Busy. But that's better than not being busy." He reversed down the drive and swung out to return to town. "I hope you didn't mind that I ran over there for a bit while you were still sleeping. I didn't want to wake you."

"No problem. I know you have responsibilities."

"I appreciate it. What about you? Dental practice okay in your absence?"

"I just checked in with my assistant. Things there seem to be going surprisingly well. No real emergencies—nothing the on-call dentist hasn't been able to handle."

"Have you heard from Winnie?" He didn't want the producer to remain in contact with Aja. Knowing Winnie would rather see them break up, he didn't like the idea of the two of them talking.

"No. You?"

"She contacted me this morning, looking for more footage. I told her we'd take some at breakfast."

Aja wrinkled her nose. "Now that we've left the show, I'm so done with that. But we said we would, so, of course, we will."

"Yeah, we'll finish what we started, but I'm not excited about it, either."

Once they arrived at the restaurant, a kitschy place that'd been around forever called Just Like Mom's, he took Aja's hand as they walked in...and almost immediately spotted Heidi Fullmer, a woman he'd dated on and off over the past several years. She was sitting in a booth having breakfast with her sister.

He smiled and nodded because she looked up, but when the hostess tried to seat them on the same side of the room, he asked if they could sit over by the window.

She looked startled that he wouldn't just accept the table she'd offered him, and he could see why. He came here all the time and had never expressed a preference. "I just sat a party in that section," she complained. "It's Joanie's turn to get a table."

"Come on, Isabelle," he said. "I'm sure someone else will walk in soon. It's always busy in here."

She acquiesced with an irked "Fine," and led them farther from Heidi.

Once they were seated, had been given their menus and she'd walked away, Aja lifted her eyebrows. "What was wrong with the other table?"

"I just like sitting by the window."

Fortunately, she let it go at that, but while they ordered coffee, omelets and biscuits with gravy, Heidi and her sister finished their meal and got up.

Grady hoped they'd just go, but he didn't get that lucky. Her sister waited by the door as Heidi walked over.

"Hey." Although she spoke to him, she was eyeing Aja.

"Hey," he responded. "How are you?"

"Good. You told me you were going to California on vacation for a month. What are you doing back so soon?"

Why couldn't he have chosen a different restaurant? "Cut it short," he replied simply.

"Why? Didn't you like it there?"

"I liked it fine. I needed to take care of a couple things here."

"I hope everything's okay with your father and brothers…"

"I meant with the business." Feeling Aja's curiosity, he added, "We might go back in few days."

"We…" Heidi repeated and studied Aja that much more closely. "I don't believe I've ever had the pleasure of meeting your friend…"

"Aja, this is Heidi Fullmer. Heidi, this is Aja Kermani, a dentist from LA."

"My pleasure," Aja said.

"Did you two…meet online or something?"

Grady answered before Aja could. He wanted to retain control of this conversation. "We met in LA."

She finally held his gaze. "And you brought her home with you…"

He could tell Heidi was upset that he was with another woman, and he felt bad about that. But he'd never made her any promises.

"I see. That's great, just great," Heidi said sarcastically and turned to Aja. "I feel like I should warn you. You might think you've found a great guy and your relationship is really going somewhere, but I can promise it's not. He'll never marry you."

Aja blinked several times. Then she said, rather uncertainly, "But…he already has."

Heidi's jaw dropped and her eyes rounded as she turned to him. "You son of a bitch!" she cried before breaking into tears and rushing out of the restaurant with her sister trailing behind.

The silence after her departure felt deafening. "Sorry," he said. "I had no idea she'd be here."

"Does she have some claim on you?" Aja asked hesitantly.

"We've dated quite a bit over the years but have never been exclusive. It's always been difficult for me to make a commitment."

Lines appeared in her normally smooth forehead. "And yet you married me…"

"I didn't know you," he said. "Somehow, that made it feel like less of a commitment, I guess." It sort of was, he thought—on her part, too. Surely, she had to recognize that.

"And now?" she asked.

He spread out his hands. "I'm hoping this works. I'm planning on it, or I wouldn't have brought you here."

She looked out the window, where they could see Heidi being consoled by her sister at the car.

Afraid what'd just happened might make her have second thoughts about him or want to return to LA, Grady reached across the table for her hand. "Nothing's changed, Aja," he said.

She nibbled at her bottom lip as she met his gaze. "That's just it," she responded. "A lot has changed for me."

They spent the day kayaking at Lake Tabeaud, which was only twenty minutes from Whiskey Creek. Aja had never been kayaking before, but Grady seemed to have toys for every occasion...or he could borrow what he needed from one of his brothers.

Because breakfast at the restaurant hadn't gone as well as they'd hoped, they did some filming while kayaking and eating a picnic lunch on the big blanket Grady had brought. He wanted her to see the natural beauty of Northern California. But Southern California was equally beautiful, and the weather there wasn't quite as cold in the winter, or hot in the summer.

Still, Aja could see the appeal of this place—the unique history, the open spaces and opportunity to move around freely, without all the crammed freeways and lines at restaurants, and other places in LA—especially when she viewed it through his eyes. This was where he'd grown up. It was home to him.

After their encounter with that other woman this morning, she was just afraid she hadn't taken Grady's limitations seriously enough. She seemed to have broken down his walls a bit last night. It'd felt like they'd made a strong emotional as well as physical connection. But would he only put those walls back up?

"You've been quiet since breakfast," he said as they drank

wine from plastic champagne flutes after eating broccoli salad and pastrami sandwiches.

"It's peaceful here," she said.

He peered more closely at her. "So…you're just relaxed? You're not worried or upset?"

Finished with her wine, she put the plastic flute back in the basket. "I guess I'm…thinking."

"About…"

"Your brothers. Your town. Your business."

He plucked a blade of grass, then leaned back on his hands as he began to chew on it. "What kind of conclusions are you drawing?"

"I'm impressed that your brothers seem to be so in love with their wives."

"When we fall, we fall hard, I guess."

She could see why. Once they made up their minds, they made up their minds. But would he be able to get beyond the past the way his brothers had? He had so much to offer. Why was it taking him so much longer? "What are you most afraid of?" she asked.

He removed the grass from his mouth and tossed it away. "Psychology is complicated, right? But I think a psychologist would say I'm afraid of trusting the wrong person, that I don't want to lose someone I love."

"But what have you gained if you never love in the first place?"

"Nothing," he said. "Which is why I'm trying to overcome it."

"And I see the effort. But if you couldn't overcome it for someone you dated for so long, what makes you think you can overcome it for me?"

He dropped his head as he considered the question. "You and Heidi are completely different kinds of people, for one," he said. "What holds true for her won't necessarily hold true for you."

Her phone buzzed with a text. She was going to ignore it. This conversation was important. But a call came in immediately after, so she knew someone had to get through.

"I'm sorry, but there must be an emergency at work," she said. "I have to check."

She dug out her cell. But it wasn't her office that'd been trying to reach her; it was her brother. Her heart leaped into her throat as she read his text.

Grady could obviously tell something was wrong. He leaned forward. "What is it?"

She pressed a hand to her chest. "My brother's been trying to reach me."

"Because…"

"My parents have been in a terrible accident."

Grady had tried to insist he'd drive her home or fly to Los Angeles with her, but Aja knew, at this point, it would only make the situation more difficult to have him there. Her parents didn't even know she was married. She needed to get back to LA as soon as possible so she could be there for them. The accident had occurred while they were on their way home from Palm Springs and had been so bad that her mother was in intensive care. Aja had packed her bags as soon as they could get back to Whiskey Creek and purchased a ticket on the first flight out of Sacramento—which was the last flight of the day to LA.

The drive to the airport took a little over an hour, and other than "Let me get that for you" and "Do you want a snack to take on the plane?" Grady didn't say much. She didn't talk a lot, either. She felt guilty for being somewhere else when her parents needed her, especially because she was doing something they would never approve of.

"Are you going to be okay?" Once they reached the airport, Grady had pulled to the curb and gotten her luggage from the back of the truck. He was standing next to it, a worried expression on his face, his hands shoved into the pockets of his jeans as she rummaged through her purse for her ID.

"I'll call you when—when I can," she said in place of a more direct answer and took her suitcase without even hugging him goodbye. The news of her mother—the possibility that Esther might not make it—had jolted her out of the dream she'd been living in lately and brought her back to the world she'd always known.

After checking her bags with an outdoor gate agent, she grabbed her carry-on and hurried toward the sliding doors of the airport. She told herself not to look back at Grady. She'd have to decide what she'd do about him, and her future, later.

But she only made it as far as the ticket counters on her way to the escalator before she turned around and saw, through the glass doors, that he was still there, staring after her.

Regretting the fact that she hadn't even hugged him, she waved, but he didn't wave back. He just dropped his head before lifting it to respond to the security officer who approached him a second later. Then he walked around his truck, climbed in the driver's side and drove away.

Chapter Eighteen

Grady made it home by midnight. He told himself he shouldn't feel so bereft. Nothing earth-shattering had changed. Aja had been in Whiskey Creek for only twenty-four hours.

And yet the house felt strangely empty without her. He kept picturing her with that carry-on she'd wheeled away from him so fast. He felt terrible that she might lose her mother, knew how hurt and upset she'd been…and he couldn't blame her. But he was afraid she wouldn't come back.

He shouldn't have begun to think their relationship could last. He'd been beating himself up over it the entire way home. Even if her mother recovered—and he prayed she would—it would take time for her to get back on her feet, likely so long Aja would slip back into her old life and give up on what they could've had. She was already worried about whether she could rely on him from an emotional standpoint. Since he'd never had a close, long-term relationship, he was worried about that, too.

Even if she didn't want a divorce, after this she'd be more likely to decide to keep her dental practice in Los Angeles. She couldn't displease her parents after what'd just happened to them.

It wasn't easy to fall asleep that night. All he could do was smell Aja's perfume on the sheets and remember the feel of her naked body in his arms.

Aja stood beside her mother's bed. After Darius had picked her up at the airport and taken her to the hospital, they'd both spent the night in Esther's room in a pair of uncomfortable vinyl chairs. He told her a drunk driver had run their parents off the road, and because it'd been raining at the time, they'd hydroplaned and plowed into a tree going sixty miles an hour, essentially wrapping the car around the tree on the passenger side.

It was a miracle they were both still alive. Their father had whiplash, several cuts and bruises, a lost tooth, and a broken arm, but his doctor said he would be able to come home in a day or two. At this point, they were only keeping him for observation.

Their mother had suffered the worst of the impact. Esther's face and arms were burned from the hot gas in the airbags that'd deployed, but those airbags were probably what'd saved her life. Although she had no injuries from the neck down, she had a subdural hematoma and a subarachnoid bleed, and she'd fractured both eye sockets. Now, she was in a medically induced coma as they attempted to stop her brain from swelling.

"I'm going to get coffee. You want any?" Darius asked, covering a yawn as he got up and headed to the door.

"No, I can't drink coffee on an empty stomach," she replied.

"I can grab you a breakfast sandwich."

"That'd be great. Thanks."

Barbie wasn't with Darius. Like her, he knew better than to bring his spouse to the hospital. They couldn't even tell their parents about Barbie and Grady—not now. They needed to get through this emergency first. Since Darius was planning to split up with Barbie, he'd probably never have to tell them. They didn't watch much TV, certainly no reality TV, so unless one of their friends saw the show when it aired, or an advertisement for it came up somewhere, there was a possibility they'd never find out about Barbie. Even if they did, Darius could say he was merely acting, trying to get a start in showbiz. But…what would *she* say?

She had no idea. As she held her mother's limp hand, she felt guilty for doing something Esther would consider so "reckless," and yet she couldn't bring herself to regret it entirely. Neither could she forget the expression on Grady's face as he watched her leave. He obviously didn't believe she'd be coming back. And she couldn't promise otherwise. She had no idea what was going to happen, just that she was lucky she already had some time off work because her parents were going to need her a great deal in the coming weeks.

A male nurse poked his head in. "Still here, I see. You've got to be exhausted."

"I'm okay. Just hoping she can hear me when I talk to her or feel me holding her hand."

"I doubt it. She's completely out. So if you need to go home and get some rest, now would be a good time."

She considered it but shook her head. "I can't leave. Not right now."

"I understand," he said and gave her a kind smile before moving on.

Darius returned a few minutes later. "You haven't even changed positions since I left. At least come over and sit down while you eat."

Reluctantly, Aja let go of her mother's hand and circled the bed. "You went to Starbucks instead of the cafeteria?"

"It was just down the street." He handed her an English muffin with egg, Gouda and bacon.

"Good choice," she said as she took a bite.

He winked. "We've been to Starbucks together often enough for me to know what you like."

She chewed and swallowed but could barely taste the food. She was too tired and worried. "I feel so bad, Darius," she said, lowering her voice even though the nurse had assured her their mother couldn't hear anything.

He took a drink of his coffee, which looked to be the only thing he'd ordered for himself. "About the show?"

"About marrying someone without including Mom and Dad. Now how are we going to tell them?"

He put his cup on the side table and leaned forward. "Listen to me, Aja. If you and Grady work out, you have nothing to apologize for. That's the best thing that could happen. And if you don't? You won't even have to tell them you were really married. You can say you went on the show to support me, and it was all an act. They don't know any different when it comes to reality TV, and as long as everything goes back to the way it was, I doubt they'll care."

Somehow, he'd always been more immune to their parents' demands. He did a lot of what was expected of him—hence law school—but he cheated more than she did. He told them what they wanted to hear, then he did exactly what he wanted to do. He framed it as living his best life without "upsetting" them. She was too honest for that. She tried to be everything they wanted, even if what she wanted was something else.

"It's just bad timing to be doing something that will upset them so much," she said. "That's all."

"Not if you handle it right," he reiterated. "What did Grady say when you left? Does he expect you to come back?"

"I didn't promise anything."

He grimaced, as if it shouldn't be that hard to decide. "I can't see you selling your practice and moving to some small town in NorCal, can you?"

"Probably not," she allowed…and yet there was something charming about Whiskey Creek, something innocent and untainted. She liked that warm, fuzzy Hallmark movie feeling…

"So will he move out here?"

"It would be harder for him."

"Hard for an auto mechanic? There's got to be a thousand places he could work in LA."

"He's not just an auto mechanic, Darius. He's a business owner, and he's done quite well for himself."

"How do you know? Did he go over his finances with you?"

She thought of the moment when they were standing at the door to the shed, and he'd said he'd turn it into a pottery studio for her. "No, but I've seen his property and his business. He grew up the hard way, and it made him strong, resilient and confident. He doesn't owe his success to anyone else."

"Neither do we," her brother said. "I mean… Mom and Dad have given us a lot, but we got the education."

"He didn't even have a mom and dad. He was raised by his older brother."

A grin split his face. "Sounds as though you really admire him."

Grady was so different from her, but that was part of the appeal. He was more independent, more rugged and more self-sufficient than any man she'd dated so far. Even when they didn't have anything to say, she found it comforting just to be in his presence.

It was his quiet strength that set him apart. But if she stayed with him—and moved to Whiskey Creek—she'd be changing *everything* about her life.

Again, she wondered why the psychologists on the show had paired them together. What was it about their personalities that made them compatible? If she knew the answer to that question, maybe she'd have more reason to believe and hang on.

So this time, instead of just wondering, she decided she'd ask.

Grady couldn't believe he was back at the shop as if nothing had changed in his life. It was so anticlimactic, so…deflating. He loved his business—loved working with his brothers, too—but seeing Rod or Dylan walk in with a kid on their shoulders or with a cell phone pressed to one ear while they talked to their wives made him feel even more isolated and alone than when Mack had married and moved away, and he'd become the only single Amos brother.

He figured he'd continue to work the longest hours and do more to take care of their derelict father. No one else had the time. But he'd been excited to think he might have more to look forward to—like the birth of his own child.

"What is it?" Dylan asked during a momentary lull when it was just the two of them behind the counter. For the first time since they'd opened a few hours ago, they didn't have people coming and going, dropping off or picking up cars, and the phone wasn't ringing off the hook.

Grady hadn't told him what'd happened to Aja's mother or that she'd left. He didn't trust himself to talk about it without betraying too much emotion. He focused on straightening up the front counter so he wouldn't have to meet his older brother's gaze. "What's…what?"

"Something's wrong."

"Nothing's wrong," he insisted.

Dylan stepped closer. "Then why are you here? Did you have a fight with Aja?"

"No. Aja's not really the type to fight. She's strong because she has a good self-image and she's accomplished a lot. But she's sweet and calm at the same time. If I said something harsh, I think she'd just start crying, which would make me immediately back off."

"That's real strength," he said. "Being strong enough to show vulnerability without feeling it makes you weak. So what's happening?"

"Her parents were in a terrible car accident last night," he said. "I had to take her to the airport."

"And you didn't say anything until now? You made me pull it out of you?"

Because he was too upset. He didn't want Dylan or anyone else to know how deeply it would hurt him if his marriage imploded right when he was beginning to believe in it. "I… It's been busy around here."

He had a feeling Dylan could see right through him but made a calculated decision to let it go at that. "Are they going to be okay?" he asked instead of calling Grady on that bullshit answer.

"I don't know. It's too soon to tell."

He rested his hands on his hips. "Why didn't you go with her? She could probably use the support."

"Because it would be easier for her without me," he said and explained why.

Dylan leaned against the counter as he listened. Then he said, "I knew they wouldn't exactly welcome you into the family."

Someone pulled into the parking lot; they had only a few seconds before another customer came into the store. "And that hasn't changed."

"Once they see how you treat their daughter, how happy you make her, they'll come around," he insisted.

Bill Thorne pushed the door open, effectively ending the conversation. Dylan gave Grady a nod, as if to add an exclamation point to what he'd said, and Grady tossed his brother a smile for the encouragement.

But he wasn't optimistic Aja would give him the chance. He'd already tried to text her—twice—this morning. He'd called, too. He wanted to make sure she'd made it back safely and ask about her mother.

Unfortunately, he hadn't gotten a response.

Chapter Nineteen

Even with her mother in a coma, Grady filtered through Aja's mind constantly, especially because she knew he'd been trying to reach her. She planned to call him back, but she was waiting to get her legs underneath her again—didn't want to say anything that might cause more instability. Her parents' accident had leveled her. She was still trying to come to terms with it, was waiting to see how things would go so she could decide what she should do in her personal life.

It was almost noon when Darius insisted she go home, shower and get some rest. He said he'd sit with their mother and call her if anything changed, and only her trust in those assurances had released her from the responsibility she felt to stay at the hospital. She was exhausted, mentally and physically, and needed to do exactly as he said—take a long, hot shower and fall into the comfort of her own bed for a couple of hours. Then she'd go visit her father and update him on Esther, if there was an update, before relieving Darius, so he could get home in time for his next filming segment with Barbie for *Tying the Knot*.

While she was in an Uber to her condo, she called Winnie to let her know what'd happened. Darius had been planning to break the news of their parents' accident once he had more of an idea of how it would impact his schedule in the coming weeks, but she'd asked him to let her handle it.

Fortunately, Winnie picked up immediately. "Winnie, it's Aja… from the show," she said as soon as she heard the other woman say hello.

The subsequent pause gave Aja the impression Winnie was surprised to hear from her, and that sort of made sense since they'd been communicating through Grady since the wedding. "What can I do for you?" she asked. "Were you and Grady able to get some footage for me yesterday? Because I haven't received anything yet."

"After what happened last night, Grady probably forgot to send it. I'll remind him."

"What happened last night?" she asked.

"I'm afraid my folks were in a car accident and are both in the hospital. Although my father will be okay, the situation is less certain with my mother. I had to fly home at a moment's notice, so I'm back in LA."

"That's terrible!" she said. "I'm so sorry. But… Grady didn't come with you?"

"No. Considering the circumstances—the fact that my parents don't even know I'm married—I thought it would be better to take care of this on my own."

"I see."

Surprisingly, Winnie didn't sound too disappointed.

"I apologize for having to change everything once again, because this will definitely impact our ability to do what we said we'd do when we left, but—"

"That's not a problem," she interrupted. "You just take care of what you need to. Your parents' well-being comes first, of course."

Grateful that the producer was being so accommodating and understanding, Aja felt some of the tension leave her body. "Thank you. I was worried that this might trigger the penalty and—"

Winnie cut in again. "No, of course not. Don't even think about that."

"But…what will happen with the show? How will you get by without us?"

"We'll use the footage we've already taken to maximum advantage. And we'll fill in with the couples from previous shows who are still together." Her tone suddenly changed. "Unless… I mean… Is your brother quitting the show, too?"

The idea of *that* definitely alarmed her. Aja could hear it in her voice. "No. I talked to him only an hour or so ago and told him I'd stand in for Mom and Dad as much as possible so that he and Barbie can continue filming."

"That's a relief. We can adjust their schedule here and there, if necessary."

"Great. I'll let him know. He's at the hospital right now, but he'll be able to film this evening."

"Great. So…you don't think Grady will join you even on weekends?"

Aja hadn't let herself consider that option, or any options. She'd just felt she needed to be free to focus and do what she needed to do. But now that such an easy solution had been suggested, she knew it would sound odd that she couldn't make something like that work. "He could, I guess. We'll probably try to arrange that at some point. And if he does come, maybe we *could* get some more filming done."

"No, that'll make things too difficult. You're going through enough. Don't worry about it. There will be no penalties if you'd rather just focus on your family."

She sounded so sincere, and that came as a relief. "I appreciate it, Winnie."

"No problem. Be sure to check in now and then to let me know how your folks are doing. Darius can keep me in the loop, too, of course, since I'll be seeing more of him. And if you decide you'd like to be on the show again in the future, we'd love to have you back. We've never had a contestant return for another try. And you're such a great catch. Any guy should be excited to have you as a partner, and I know the audience would love to see the return of a former contestant."

She'd said that as if she expected Aja to be single. But in Aja's mind, that had yet to be decided. She was just taking a break to find herself again…and figure out how to navigate the next few days and weeks. "I haven't given up on the marriage," she clarified. "We're still…going to try."

"Oh! I didn't realize that. I assumed if things were going well he'd be staying at your place or something, trying to support you through this."

"I had to drop everything and catch a plane, and…" Her words fell off. She supposed he *could* join her, and her parents wouldn't have to know about it, at least not until they were well again. But having him around while she was at the hospital all the time and couldn't be forthcoming with her parents would be so difficult—make her feel torn in two.

"And deal with a tragic event," Winnie said, finishing for her. "You don't have to explain yourself to me. I'll make do with the material we've got already, okay? You don't have to bring Grady out here."

Aja almost said "okay" and hung up. But she couldn't figure out why Winnie didn't care more about whether they stayed together. When they were starting out, she'd seemed so invested in the success of each couple.

Maybe it was just that she'd already given up on her and Grady since they left LA and started to dictate the parameters of their own participation.

Still, Aja had one more question for Winnie, who was saying she had to run.

"I hate to keep you," she began. "But before you go, can you tell me why I was paired with Grady? What was it the show's professionals saw in us that suggested we might be well-suited for each other? I mean… I can't help but wonder. We don't even live in the same area."

There was such a long silence that Aja thought Winnie had hung up.

"Winnie?"

The producer cleared her throat. "Yes, I'm right here."

"I was wondering if the psychologists indicated why they thought Grady and I would be good for each other," she reiterated in case Winnie had missed her question the first time.

"I'm afraid they didn't leave any notes, Aja."

"So…how does it work? They just match brides with grooms and don't give you any supporting documentation?"

Aja heard Winnie sigh, then the other woman said, "If you're beating yourself up because you think you should be able to make this marriage work, and yet you can't, you should stop that right away. Because the psychologists didn't pair you with Grady, I did."

Aja gripped her phone that much tighter. "What do you mean? We took those personality tests for a reason, right?"

"Yes, but you weren't even interested in coming on the show. You did it for Darius. So I didn't think you really cared who I paired you with."

"But you offered the psych evals as reassurance, never told me—"

"The psych evals are just so we don't let anyone dangerous on the show. We have to do our homework. The personality tests are used for pairing. But check your contract. It's all perfectly legal. The psychologists merely make suggestions based on the personality tests. As the producer, I have the ultimate say."

"So you ignored their advice and overrode their opinion, sabotaged my chances of success on the show? *Why?* Why would you ever do that?"

"I wasn't sabotaging your chances on the show. The way everything played out, I just…didn't have a better option. But I wanted to tell you now so that you didn't continue to try to make something work that—that isn't, especially while you're dealing with your parents' car crash. Otherwise, I wouldn't have mentioned it."

"You would've continued to keep that secret to yourself, in other words."

"It wasn't a secret. It was just…one of the decisions I had to make for the good of the show."

"And Darius? Did you do the same with him and Barbie?"

"No, I went with everyone's recommendation there."

"And the other couples?"

"I used their recommendations for the other couples, too."

"So it was just Grady and me."

The Uber driver had come to a stop in front of Aja's condominium complex. "Hello? Can you hear me?" he said. "We've arrived."

If he'd said it before, she'd missed it. She'd been too focused on her conversation to even realize where she was.

Numbly, she forced herself to get out of his car. But then she stood on the street looking up at the place she called home until another vehicle came and honked for her to get out of the way.

"Aja? Are you still there? What's going on?" Winnie asked, and Aja finally tuned in to the conversation again.

"Nothing, but I won't be doing anything more for the show," she said and disconnected. She felt duped, betrayed, and she had no doubt Grady would feel the same. Maybe this would make him decide to give up on their marriage, but she felt it was only fair that he know the truth, too.

After dragging her luggage into the elevator and up to her second-story condo, she turned on the air-conditioning as soon as she walked through the door to help dispel the summer heat and rid the place of the musty odor that often came with living so close to the beach.

But she didn't get in the shower and then drop into bed as she'd planned. Although her eyes felt like sandpaper, she knew she wouldn't be able to sleep.

Grady's morning had been a busy one, and when his newest tech ruined an expensive paint job, it grew frustrating, as well. But the moment he saw Aja's call come in, he told Dylan, who was working the front counter, to put out the bell and take over for him in back. Still, by the time he'd stepped outside he'd missed her call, so he called right back.

"Hello?"

Grateful to finally have the opportunity to talk to her, he breathed a sigh of relief when she answered. "Hey. How are you?"

"Not so good," she replied.

"What's going on? Don't tell me your mother is even worse than we thought."

"I don't know about that yet. The doctors won't say much. They managed to stop the bleeding and the swelling of her brain, but…there could be some long-term damage. We just have to wait and see."

"I'm sorry this happened, Aja. What about your father?"

"He's banged up, but it's nothing that won't heal."

"That's good, at least. Have you had anything to eat today? Been able to get any rest?"

"I've had a little food, no rest. But I saw your missed calls and wanted to get back to you. And I have something to tell you that's probably going to upset you."

Afraid of what she was about to say, he lifted his ball cap, then put it on again. Was this where she asked for an annulment? Told him it was over between them?

Because that wasn't what he wanted at all. The more he thought about her and the past week—their wedding, their honeymoon at the beach, talking for hours in the car on the drive to Whiskey Creek, dinner with his father, making love in his bed—the more he was coming to believe that, against all odds, she might actually be the perfect woman for him. And even if she wasn't "perfect" for him, he wanted to be with her, overcome whatever problems came up. "What is it?"

"We weren't paired together by psychologists, Grady. That was all bullshit."

He'd never heard her swear before, which showed him how upset she was. "What do you mean?"

"Winnie paired us together. That's why we have nothing in common and don't even live in the same part of the state."

His heart began to pound. "Who told you that?"

"She did. Can you believe it? And it's right there in the contract we signed—that she has ultimate say. We just never paid attention to it because we didn't see any reason for her not follow the psychologists' advice—not after giving us all those tests—and we didn't truly believe we'd meet someone we'd want to spend the rest of our lives with."

Grady felt sick. "How'd that even come up?"

"I called to tell her about my parents. I wanted to make sure she wasn't going to charge the penalty—especially for you—when we have no control over the fact that we can't finish what we agreed to do for the show."

"What'd she say?" he asked, scrambling to come up to speed with what was going on.

"She said we don't need to worry, that she won't charge us. But then I asked her why the psychologists paired us together even though we didn't seem to have anything in common, and she said they didn't pair us, that she did."

Shit. He squeezed his forehead. "Why would she tell you that?" he asked, but he was talking to himself more than her.

"She said she didn't want me to feel I'm failing at something I believe I should be able to succeed at while I'm going through this with my parents."

"So she was looking out for you?" he said dryly. "She wanted to let you know that our marriage didn't have much of a chance to begin with so you wouldn't worry about sticking with it?"

"Something like that, I guess." She sounded slightly confused, and he couldn't blame her. "But she could've told us from the start that she'd decided to override the psychologists' advice. Instead, she led us to believe we had that going for us."

He didn't know what to do. He couldn't react with outrage, couldn't pretend he didn't know. That would be a lie. And he cared too much about Aja to destroy her trust in him.

But this was such a terrible time to have to confront this issue. He'd hoped they'd be able to get further into their relationship before he had to address the truth of how they'd come to be together.

Unfortunately, Winnie had forced his hand. She hadn't told Aja the full story, but she'd told her enough to put him in a terrible position. And he knew why she'd done it. She didn't want their marriage to last. He could tell how much it was bothering her during their last phone conversation. Having him unavailable and no longer interested made her want him that much more. Or she'd really believed his marriage wouldn't be successful, that it was just a matter of time before he'd be able to date her and was willing to wait…until she realized it might not go the way she'd expected.

Bottom line, she wanted to see their marriage fail.

"Grady? Don't you have anything to say about that?" Aja prompted when he didn't respond.

He rubbed his forehead for a second, bemoaning the fact that he seemed to have only one choice. Then he drew a deep breath and said, "I feel terrible because this is hitting at the worst possible moment, but there's more to it than you know."

Her voice went deadly serious. "What are you talking about?"

"I *promise* I was going to tell you at some point. But thanks to Winnie, I guess that moment is now."

Chapter Twenty

Too tired to fight the tears that welled up, Aja pulled her pillow in close to her body. The conversation she'd had with Grady had been a difficult one. She could tell he felt bad about how everything had played out, and she believed him when he said he would've told her the truth eventually…because he could've lied and *not* told her earlier.

But by the time they'd hung up, she was pretty disillusioned.

The real reason he'd come on the show was for Winnie? He'd just been putting in his time with her? He'd admitted he'd chosen her because he thought she was the *least* likely woman to be compatible with him…

With a sniff to stop her nose from running, she turned onto her other side and punched her pillow to get it right. That he hadn't been completely honest until today bothered her, of course, but it was the idea that he and Winnie had had this secret thing going on all along that upset her the most. She felt *so* stupid for joining the cast of the show and allowing them to use her as a pawn in their little game.

But as angry as she was tempted to be—with both of them—she had no one to blame but herself. When she signed on as a contestant, she'd known she was opening herself up to only God knew what. Otherwise, she would've been honest with her parents about what she was planning to do, and they would've told her that she was a fool for taking a leave of absence at her office to meet a man who would most certainly be "unsuitable" for her. They would've strongly advised her *not* to marry a complete stranger, especially one who had nothing in common with her.

Even Darius would say she'd taken it all too seriously. Look at him and Barbie! They were getting along just fine—were friends, he'd told her while they were at her mother's bedside—and working together to navigate the show so they could use it as the launchpad they'd intended it to be for their acting careers.

But somewhere along the line, Aja had screwed up and begun to let her emotions get involved. Now she was married to a man who lived seven hours away, in a town of only two thousand people, and she didn't know whether to have the marriage annulled and go on with her life as it was, forgive Grady and try to manage a long-distance relationship until they knew each other better, or throw caution to the wind and move to Whiskey Creek. If she did that, and the marriage ultimately ended in divorce, she would've ruined her dental practice for nothing. She might even have kids by then and be facing custody issues.

She sighed as she pictured her poor mother connected to all the tubes and machines in the intensive care unit. Esther and Cyrus would probably never forgive her for deviating from the careful plan they felt would bring their family the most happiness. She couldn't even tell them what she'd done; not while they were in such a fragile state.

"What a mess," she muttered to herself.

Her phone signaled a text. She'd left her notifications on in case Darius or someone else from the hospital needed to reach her, so as soon as she heard the sound, she shoved into a sitting position and reached over to the nightstand.

But it wasn't Darius; it was Arman. She hadn't heard from him since she refused to marry him, but she'd told him she wanted to remain friends. He probably just wanted to check on her parents, anyway, so she didn't feel it would be kind to ignore his call.

Drawing a deep breath in an effort to keep the tears out of her voice, she answered. "Hello?"

"Aja, my parents and I just heard from your father. We had no idea he and Esther had an accident after they left us in Palm Springs and feel absolutely terrible."

"I appreciate that," she said. "It's very nice of you to call."

"I'm worried about you. Is there—is there anything I can do?"

"Nothing. It's all up to the doctors now. They're working hard, trying to minimize the damage to my mother's brain. My father probably already told you that he'll recover."

"He did. But he's *so* worried about your mother."

"We all are."

"Would you mind if we came by the hospital?"

How could she say no? The two families were very close. "Of course not."

"What time would be best?"

She was *so* exhausted she couldn't face dealing with him or his parents tonight when she returned to the hospital to relieve Darius. "How about tomorrow morning?" she asked and held her breath, hoping he'd accept the slight delay and not press for something more immediate.

"Sure."

She exhaled. "Thanks."

He lowered his voice. "I want you to know I'm here for you, if you need me."

His kindness caused tears to well up again. Should she have accepted his marriage proposal? It seemed as though she'd veered widely off course the night she refused. "I appreciate that."

"But...you don't want me around?"

She was married to someone else now! She gripped her forehead. *What* had she done? "It's not that. It's—it's just a very difficult time, but I'll manage."

"Don't you miss me? Let me help you through this."

"Arman, I can't deal with anything emotional right now. I'm in a difficult enough situation as it is."

"I thought it might make things easier. But...okay. I'll see you in the morning," he said and let her hang up.

She sat there for several minutes after that conversation, thinking about him. He knew her so well, knew her family. Her parents loved him; his parents loved her. Esther and Cyrus were probably right—he would've made a good husband. So...was she being spoiled by refusing to go that way? Selfish? Asking for too much?

She closed her eyes as she slouched back down in the bed. Maybe what she'd done would turn out to be an even bigger regret than she'd imagined.

* * *

Although Grady had tried to call three times, Winnie didn't pick up until that evening. He had a feeling she knew—or had guessed—the reason for his call. She had no business revealing what she'd revealed to Aja. She should've left that to him, which made him wonder if it wasn't a subtle form of revenge.

"You told her?" he demanded as soon as she finally answered.

There was a long pause. Then she said, "Calm down, Grady."

"I haven't even raised my voice."

"But there's a steely note in it. I can tell you're not happy."

"I'm *not* happy," he admitted, "and for good reason. Why'd you take it upon yourself to tell Aja that *you* paired us together?"

"Because I didn't want her beating herself up, thinking she had to make the marriage work because it was…supposed to, especially while her mother's fighting for her life in the ICU."

"Did Aja tell you she was struggling with our marriage? Or was she just letting you know she couldn't finish filming for the show?"

After another long pause, she said, "Either way, I felt I had to be more honest with her."

He got up and began to pace on the deck. "And what about me? You couldn't have talked to me about it first?"

"Grady, if she gives up on the marriage that easily, she wouldn't have stuck it out for the long haul, anyway, especially now, with her parents in the hospital. They are *heavily* involved in her life, which is completely foreign to you and me. They don't even know about you. What do you think is going to happen when she tells them?"

"Her mother might still survive and be fine, and if she does, we could've dealt with everything else after. I didn't need you getting involved, trying to sabotage the marriage you helped facilitate."

"That's just it! It was *because* I helped facilitate it—because I put her in the position she's in—that I felt guilty about not being more up front."

"That can't be true," he said with a scoffing laugh. "If it was guilt that motivated you, you would've told her the real truth. *You* didn't pair us. *I* did. You allowed me to do that, remember?"

"I couldn't go that far, and you know why," she said. "It would be terrible for the show if that ever got out, so I came as close to the truth as I dared."

"In other words, you told her what served your purposes," he clarified.

"So what? Do you want me to admit that I'd rather you be free? Of course I would!" she said, finally moving past the bogus excuses. "You know I'm attracted to you, and I thought you were attracted to me. But you're so caught up in trying to force this marriage to work that you're going to make us both miss out on what we could've had!"

He stood at the railing of his back porch and stared out at the creek. Was she right? Was he missing the main attraction? Winnie was gorgeous and smart and engaging. He couldn't argue with any of that. But so was Aja. And she had a wholesomeness to her that appealed to him more than anything else he'd ever encountered...

"Grady?"

"I'm still here," he grumbled.

"Aren't you eager to see what *we* could have?" she asked.

He tested that question on himself, but the answer was...no. Not anymore. Since Aja had come into his life, she'd changed everything. "I'm sorry, Winnie. I'm not trying to force my marriage to work because I don't want to fail. And it isn't just because I want to be fair to Aja. It's because..." He struggled for the words to finish that sentence and couldn't seem to grasp the right ones, but only because he couldn't believe what kept coming to the tip of his tongue.

"Because..." she prompted.

"I think it's because I've fallen in love with her," he said incredulously.

This met with dead silence. "You've only known her a couple of weeks, Grady."

"I realize that," he said. "But... I think she's got me. I never saw it coming, so I must not have put up my normal defenses and—"

"Oh, my God!" she moaned. "You actually mean it."

He did. As shocking as that was. The man who'd been unable to open his heart had finally lost it to a sweet, sincere, beautiful Persian woman he'd met only because he'd done something most people would call completely idiotic.

He thought Winnie might insist he didn't know Aja well enough, that he had to be wrong, but she didn't. She didn't say another word. There was no click or anything, either, but the phone went dead.

The night had been long and hard. Morning seemed to take forever. Aja had tried to get out of the hospital before Arman and his parents arrived. But Darius had called to put her off an hour, said he had to do a quick segment for the show before he could come relieve her, and the Kahns arrived first thing, right at eight.

Aja felt self-conscious when Behar and Behram walked in and saw her curled up in the vinyl chair where she'd been sleeping. Dropping the thin hospital-issue blanket she'd been using, she got up to greet them, still stiff and sore and with eyes swollen from all the crying she'd done last night. They'd never seen her so unkempt, but it was difficult to care too much about her appearance when she had so many other, more pressing concerns.

She wasn't sure what to expect from them. They'd known her since she was just a baby and had always been warm. But she'd recently refused to marry their beloved son. Maybe it was her imagination, but she thought they were decidedly cool toward her, despite their concern for her mother.

"Good morning," Behram said, sounding much more formal than usual. Behar merely dipped her head. But then, Arman walked in, and his big brown eyes showed much more sympathy.

"Have you been here all night?" he asked.

She nodded and tried to fix the hair that was falling from the messy knot on top of her head. "Darius has been…busy. Stuff he has to do for school," she quickly added so they wouldn't ask what he was doing or be tempted to judge him.

He came over to hug her, and the familiarity of his embrace, and the scent of his cologne, proved so enticing she couldn't help melting into his chest. "You must be exhausted," he murmured above her head.

Once again, tears pricked the backs of her eyes, but she blinked them away. "I'm tired," she admitted.

Behar moved to her mother's side and took her hand. "Have you heard anything?" she asked, her face pinched with concern. "What are the doctors saying?"

"They don't know what to say," Aja replied. "Not yet. They plan to bring her out of the coma sometime today. I guess we'll know more when she wakes."

Behar frowned. "This must be so frightening for you."

Extricating herself from Arman's embrace, she continued to try to fix her hair. "It's been terrible, upsetting."

"Of course," Behar said. "Why don't you let us sit with her now while you go home and get some rest?"

Aja longed for her bed. The hour nap she'd ended up getting last night just wasn't enough. But she couldn't leave. "I don't dare. I don't know when the doctors will be bringing my mother out of her coma, and I definitely want to be here for that."

"Of course you do," Behram said.

"Check with them," Behar directed. "If they aren't planning to do it until this afternoon, you'll have plenty of time."

She was too out of sorts to even think straight, felt overwhelmed by the simple task of tracking down that information. "I don't know where any of the medical personnel I need are at the moment. They come in periodically and then they disappear."

"There's a nurse's station outside," Behram said. "Ask there."

"I'll do it," Arman volunteered. Then his gaze met Aja's. "Go ahead and sit down. Can I get you something to eat while I'm gone?"

It would be so easy to lean on him, she realized. He could step back into her life, and they could pick up right where they left off. Then she'd have the love and support she needed to get through the coming weeks, and there'd be no upset to her parents, no upset to her parents' best friends, no need to sell her practice and move, no question as to what she was ultimately getting in a mate.

Should she just let go of Grady and choose the safe and ordinary path? Right her wrong before it was too late?

She happened to glance down and catch a glimpse of her wedding band. She'd been so caught up in everything that was going on she hadn't even remembered she was wearing it, let alone considered removing it.

Terrified that Arman or his parents would notice it, she slipped her hand behind her and stretched her back to make it look like a natural movement. "That'd be great—anything would taste good. I'll pay you via Venmo, so get something for yourself, too. And while you're gone, I'll talk to the nurses myself and try to tie down when the doctor will be back."

"Okay, but you don't have to pay me," he said and left.

Aja edged around the bed and gestured toward the seat she'd just vacated. "Behram, feel free to sit down. I'll let you know what I find out before I leave—if I'm able to leave."

Behar was still at her mother's side and didn't seem to hear her. "Can you believe this happened?" she said to her husband. "If we'd left when they did…who knows? We might've been following closely behind and…"

Then they could've been involved in the accident, too.

"She's going to be fine, Behar," Behram insisted. "Have faith."

Aja escaped the room, moving far more quickly than she'd been capable of moving just a few minutes ago, and found the nurse's station, where—after they'd made several calls over nearly twenty minutes—she learned that her mother's doctor was planning to bring Esther out of the coma around four.

Before returning to the room, Aja moved her wedding ring to a different finger, even though it barely fit, because she couldn't take it off entirely without the threat of losing it. She was wearing yoga pants and a stretchy top with no pockets.

"Sounds like I can head home for a few hours," she told the Kahns. "The doctor won't be here until later this afternoon."

Behar hadn't moved; Behram had taken the chair she'd been using before they arrived. "We'll stay until you get back."

"You don't have to. Darius is coming." Aja checked the time on her phone. "Allowing for the drive, he'll be here in another forty-five minutes or so."

"We'll stay," Behar repeated as if it was more of a decree, and it was then Aja understood she probably wouldn't get rid of them today.

She approached her mother's bed from the other side and peered down into Esther's empty, slack face. Surely, this nightmare wouldn't last. Surely, her mother would recover. She was the strongest woman Aja had ever known.

Silence settled upon them. Only the wheeze and rattle of the ventilator and other machines filled the void as Aja waited for Arman to get back. She felt awkward and wanted to leave, didn't care enough about eating to wait, but she couldn't ask him to get her food and then be gone when he returned.

At last, he walked into the room and handed her a sack. "Sorry it took so long. There was quite a bit of traffic. But I got you the *halim* you love, with some flatbread, of course."

Halim was a stewlike dish made of meat, barley and dal with a delicious blend of spices—something Grady had probably never even tried, let alone something he'd ever bring her. "Thank you," she said. "That's...very nice."

"Do you want to stay here to eat it?" he asked. "I can request a rolling table—"

"No," she interrupted. "It'll be easier at home. But...thanks again."

"Arman's a good man," Behar said sullenly. "Any woman would be lucky to have him."

"Mom!" Arman snapped, and she shot him a look that suggested it was only right she say something before going back to her vigil.

"I know he's a good man," Aja said. The question was...was he the right man for her—or was Grady?

Chapter Twenty-One

"You've been moping around all day," Dylan said. "What's going on?"

JT answered before Grady could, even though the question hadn't been directed at him. "He's butt-hurt. Fallen in love with that beautiful Persian woman he married, and now he thinks he's lost her."

Dylan leaned the bumper he'd been carrying out to the paint bays against the wall and walked over to the counter, where Grady had been working since he came in this morning. "Things haven't gotten any better? I've been hoping she was just supporting her parents and the situation would improve."

Grady didn't want to admit that wasn't the case, that he'd screwed up what was probably his best chance at happiness. He felt he shouldn't have gotten carried away thinking he might've *finally* found the right woman. That was stupid. He'd never been lucky in love. "She *is* supporting her parents, but—"

Dylan cocked his head when Grady didn't finish. "Are we still talking about the fact that her parents won't accept you? Is she backing away from the marriage because she knows they won't approve?"

"That's part of it. Aja doesn't even want to tell them about me—not now. And that's understandable, given her mother's in a freaking coma."

"A *medically induced* coma," Dylan clarified. "There's a difference. They're trying to save her, and they might pull it off. So don't give up hope too soon."

Grady shoved the invoice he'd just marked *paid* into the appropriate basket. "It's not only the family thing. It's… Never mind. It's a long story—that's what it is."

Dylan didn't budge. Neither did JT. They both stood there looking at him expectantly, and since they had a strange lull in business, no one else was there to interrupt.

"We'll take the time," Dylan said when Grady didn't succumb to his meaningful stare.

"I made a mistake, okay?" Grady said in exasperation. "And I feel terrible, so the last thing I want to do is talk about it."

"What'd you do?" JT demanded.

But Dylan didn't bother with that. He caught Grady's eye and said simply, "Then ask her to forgive you."

Grady blew out a long sigh. "I can't imagine she will, not at this stage of our relationship. I'm sure I've scared her off."

"She went on a TV show looking for love," Dylan pointed out. "I can't imagine she'll give up *too* easily."

Grady gave him a look that said, "Nice try."

"She went on the show for her brother. *He* wanted to be a cast member, and the producer wouldn't take him without her."

"Oh! That sucks," JT said as if he now understood why all was lost.

JT's response irritated Grady. But that was often the case with his father. Fortunately, Dylan was the man who'd raised him and didn't have the same effect. Grady respected and loved Dylan more than anyone in the world.

"All I know is that if you want her, you need to fight for her, so you won't kick yourself later," Dylan said.

"And how do I do that?" Grady asked. "She's not even returning my messages."

Dylan walked back to the fender and lifted it over one shoulder. "You know where LA is, don't you?"

"You want me to drive to Los Angeles and interrupt everything that's going on? I don't want to bug her—"

"She came to Whiskey Creek because she wanted your marriage to work, right?" he interrupted. "She had to break her contract with the show in order to do it, give up whatever they were paying her. She cares about you, was hoping for a future with you, or she wouldn't have done that."

"But with the accident, I feel like my hands are tied."

"You can be supportive without going too far," Dylan said. "Just don't be demanding. All you have to do is show her you care."

That was the hardest thing in the world for him. When it came to love, he'd never been capable of taking much risk.

Dylan stepped toward the back door as he added, "But the window you have to save your marriage might be closing, so I'd leave right away. If you go now, you can be there by…what? Ten or eleven? And if she won't see you that late, maybe you can take her to breakfast—or bring her breakfast at the hospital—first thing in the morning."

Grady considered what showing up unannounced might be like. "That's…bold," he said.

"Sometimes you need to be bold," Dylan responded. "At least then you'll know that you did everything you could."

Aja slept deeply for six hours, until her alarm went off, bringing her to a foggy awareness. She had little doubt she could use even more sleep, but she felt somewhat refreshed after she showered, threw on a pair of jeans and a long-sleeved T-shirt, since it was always cold at the hospital, and rushed to reach her mother's room before the doctor showed up.

Darius had sent her a message while she was getting ready, saying the Kahns were still there and didn't seem to be planning to leave any time soon, so she knew she was about to have another awkward encounter with her ex and his family. Unfortunately, it would happen at a vulnerable moment. But she was so worried about her mother, nothing else mattered. The doctor had no idea if Esther would even be able to speak, let alone function in other regards, and the thought of her waking up and not even recognizing them was terrifying.

When she arrived, the room was as crowded as she'd expected. Her father was sitting in a wheelchair, and Darius was there along with a nurse, her mother's main doctor and the anesthesiologist. Thankfully, the Kahns were gone, after all.

"There you are!" Darius said with obvious relief.

She hurried to her father's side and dropped a kiss on his cheek. "What's wrong? Is everything okay?"

"I hope so." Her father looked pale and sounded uncertain, which was so unlike him. He'd always been large and in charge.

"Everything's fine," the doctor assured her. "My schedule changed a bit, so I juggled things around and arrived earlier than planned, that's all. But this process takes time. Dr. Nguyen will slowly lower the propofol keeping your mother's brain quiet so that she can wake up gradually, at which point we'll change the mode on the ventilator to allow her to breathe on her own."

"You've already started that process?"

He nodded, but he was clearly focused on monitoring her mother's heart and brain activity. "Just a few minutes ago."

Aja sidled closer to her brother. "Where are the Kahns?" she whispered.

"The doctor asked them to leave, said there were too many people in here," he replied.

"Thank goodness."

He brought her forward, next to their father, who'd been wheeled to the edge of the bed, and left his arm around her shoulders. She knew then that as cavalier as he sometimes acted, he was as frightened as she was.

"How long will it take?" she asked the doctor.

"Depends," he said. "Some people take longer than others. Maybe thirty minutes or so?"

She felt as though they were in the way. "Should we step back?"

"No, we'll manage," he said. "We want her family to be the first thing she sees. This process can create a lot of confusion and anxiety. Having her loved ones close will reassure her."

Aja felt her brother's grip tighten on her shoulder. "Okay," she said.

"She'll be fine," their father said, but tears were gathering in his eyes. He was part of the medical community. He understood the risks and the odds.

Scarcely able to breathe, Aja gripped the hand he lifted for her, and they waited—grouped together and hanging on to each other—for what seemed like an eternity. Each minute, each second that ticked away created more fear. Would Esther wake up at all?

"Come on, *eshghe man*," her father muttered, his words a chanted prayer he'd probably been saying under his breath that'd finally become audible.

That was when her mother's eyelids fluttered open.

Aja gasped and her father dropped her hand to grab Esther's. "We're here with you, and you're going to be all right," he told her. "*Dooset daram*. Just relax. Don't fight those who are helping you and all will be well."

The distress in her eyes eased, and although she groaned when the doctor adjusted the ventilator to allow her to breathe on her own, she didn't try to grab at anything or resist.

She was awake! She'd come back to them! And she seemed to recognize Cyrus, at least. Otherwise, why would his words have calmed her so quickly?

That was all *very* hopeful. Now they just had to wait and see if things got better—or worse—from here.

Grady had no idea what to expect. He hated to drop into the middle of a family emergency, especially one this serious. But it also felt weird to be in Whiskey Creek while his wife was in LA.

He'd decided he wouldn't be intrusive. He'd get a motel and stay out of the way—simply let Aja know he was close and available to support her if she needed him. Then *she* could decide whether she wanted to see him.

Just in case it was a mistake and Aja absolutely *didn't* want to see him, he'd sent a message to Darius to let him know he was coming. He'd hesitated to bother her brother, so he hadn't requested any type of response. He'd just felt as though someone should know he was coming.

He arrived at midnight and stopped at a moderately priced motel along the freeway not too far from the mansion where they'd filmed the show. His phone lit up while he was dragging his suitcase into the room. He assumed it was Dylan, making sure he'd arrived safely. His oldest brother had called him twice to make sure he wasn't getting sleepy behind the wheel.

But once he dropped onto the bed and checked his phone, he saw that the text had come from Darius.

They took mom out of her coma today. No one can say If there's been any lasting damage to her brain. The doctors are trying to ease her back into functionality, so we haven't tried to communicate with her too much. We'll know more tomorrow. Barbie and I are staying at my place for now. It's not as nice as hers, but it's closer to the hospital. You're welcome to sleep on the couch. Just know that my apartment is on campus, so very small.

There was so much Grady wanted to say that it would be difficult to put it all in a text, so he decided to take the chance of calling Darius and was relieved when he picked up. "Sorry to disturb you, especially this late," he said. "But I wanted to let you know that I'm set for the night. I've already got a room."

"No problem. I just got home from the hospital. Barbie says she'd love to see you. But I wasn't joking when I said my place was small."

"I'm fine," Grady insisted. "But it's nice of you to offer."

"Why wouldn't I? You're my brother-in-law," he said with a laugh.

That was the thing. Was he *really*? Would his relationship with Aja—and Darius—last? Because of the way he'd come to be married, Grady didn't know if he could count on it being real. He felt like he was trying to turn a dream into something tangible he could rely on, and that wasn't an easy task. "How's your sister?" he asked.

"This is hitting her hard, as you probably know."

"She hasn't said much to me recently. I think she's withdrawn completely."

"Because of the guilt. She feels bad having such a tragedy happen right when she was doing something that would upset Mom and Dad. She also feels bad for lying to them. She's always been too honest for her own good," he added as an obvious joke.

Grady chuckled. But it wasn't just the family dynamic that stood between them, and Grady knew it. Aja had good reason to be disappointed in him. He didn't see where he could've told her about Winnie and the psychologists before he did, however. Thanks to Winnie, he'd told her too soon as it was…and Aja's reaction proved it.

"I keep telling her that Mom and Dad are *both* going to be okay," Darius said. "Today couldn't have gone any better. Mom came out of her coma right away and began to breathe on her own, so they've removed the respirator. She even ate a little soup tonight. Now they're just trying to keep her comfortable and stable until she feels strong enough to interact. That's when we'll know if—if she's truly herself."

"Not knowing must be hard."

"It is. But I'm feeling better now than I have since the accident— I can tell you that much."

"Do you think it was a mistake for me to come to Los Angeles, Darius?" Grady asked. "Does Aja consider our marriage over? I don't want to make this any harder on her."

As the silence stretched, Grady imagined he was thinking it over. But if it required that much thought…

He braced for the worst.

"Depends," Darius finally said.

"On what?"

"Are you doing it for the show—so that you look attentive and don't come off like an asshole? Or do you really care about her?"

"I can promise you it's not for the show."

"Which means…"

As difficult as it was for him to talk about his feelings, if he wanted Aja, he had to dig deeper, allow himself to be vulnerable. "She's *all* I care about."

There was another pause, this one much shorter, and Grady knew his sincerity had come through when Darius said, "I'm happy to hear that. I'm going to send you the address to her condo—along with the code for the gate so you can get to her door. My dad felt well enough to stay with my mom tonight. He wanted to have some time alone with her. So Aja is on her way home right now. It might be the perfect time to talk to her."

Grady breathed a huge sigh of relief. Maybe, just maybe, he had another chance. "I appreciate it."

Aja had just pulled on the tank top she planned to sleep in when she heard a knock at the front door. It was likely her neighbor, DeeAnn, checking on her; she'd told her about the accident earlier. With a yawn, she pulled on her robe, belted it at the waist and padded out through the living room in her slippers to peer through the peephole.

Then she froze. It wasn't her eighty-year-old neighbor. It was Grady, and he was holding a huge bouquet of purple and white hydrangeas.

She stepped back while trying to decide what to do. He didn't fit into her life. They lived in two different parts of the state, and she couldn't leave LA—not now that her parents needed her. She wasn't going to do anything more for the show, either. She felt like she'd gotten burned by it, was done with Winnie. She just hadn't told him that she'd come to these conclusions yet. It wasn't a conversation she was looking forward to having. She cried whenever she started rehearsing it in her mind, which was odd. She hadn't shed nearly as many tears over Arman.

But Grady had come all the way from Whiskey Creek. She couldn't leave him standing at her door. She wasn't even sure how he'd gotten through the security gate.

Steeling herself, she withdrew the bolt. "Hi," she said.

He studied her for a moment. "I'm sorry to surprise you. But… you haven't been responding to my texts."

"I apologize for that. It's been—"

He lifted a hand. "I know. I'm not criticizing or—or trying to put pressure on you. I just… I bought these flowers for you before I left Whiskey Creek and needed to get them into some water."

She couldn't help chuckling. "So you drove them seven hours?"

He grinned. "I did. And if you were in San Diego or anywhere else, I would've driven them farther. I've been dying to see you, Aja. I'm sorry. Truly sorry. I didn't intend for what happened to happen. Everything just got away from me. Because I was skeptical that the show could truly find me a wife I'd love. I was still trying to manage that on my own."

Politeness dictated she step back and let him in. It was rude to keep him standing on her stoop. But she wasn't ready. If she invited him in, it would be almost impossible for her to ask him to leave, because she was far too excited to see him. Then all the decisions she'd made recently would be upended, and she'd be faced with the same difficult questions she'd been asking herself all along—what she would do with her practice, her condo and her parents if they stayed together. "And now?"

"I'm glad I took matters into my own hands, because *they* never would've paired me with you."

She took the flowers and stared down at them. "That's very nice of you to say, Grady, but I don't see how we could ever make it."

"We can make it if we want to," he insisted. "I'm nearly forty, Aja. It's taken me a long time to fall in love. So I know how special this is. I don't want to lose you."

"You're saying you *love* me?"

"I must! You're all I can think about, all I want."

"But your business and my business—"

"I'll move here, help you take care of your parents and work for another auto body shop until I can get my own again."

Aja felt her jaw drop. "You'd do that?"

"If that's what it takes."

She gave him a wry smile. "Winnie's going to hate that she missed getting this on the show."

"Forget Winnie," he said. "Just tell me you feel the same way about me—that you'll fight for what we could have, in spite of the obstacles between us."

All the turmoil inside her suddenly eased, and her path forward seemed clear. Maybe Grady wasn't anyone her parents would've picked for her. Maybe they didn't have a lot in common. They'd have to figure out where to live and who would do what for work. But those were practical problems. As he'd said, they *could* overcome them if they wanted to badly enough.

"Aja?" he prompted, tilting his head to catch her eye.

She stood on her tiptoes as she threw her arms around him. She nearly dropped half the flowers she was holding in the process, but she didn't care. *This* was what felt right. It was the *only* thing that felt right. So they'd just have to deal with everything else. "I'm willing to fight for our marriage, too," she said.

Epilogue

Esther was getting stronger all the time, and there didn't seem to be any lasting brain damage. Although she was still fragile and would remain in the hospital for probably another week, she had no trouble with her speech or memory or motor skills. The doctors marveled at her recovery. And except for the cast on his arm, her father was back to his old self.

Aja nibbled at her bottom lip as she waited for her mother to finish eating lunch. Her father was in the room, too, reading the news on his phone. Darius was off somewhere, filming for the show. Since he and Barbie weren't going to stay together, he didn't plan on ever telling their parents about the marriage, and Aja certainly wasn't going to out him.

She did, however, need to tell them about Grady. He'd been staying with her in the condo for eight days so far, but had just recently started commuting to Silver Springs to help at the Amos Auto Body shop his youngest brother was running.

That seemed to be working out in the short term, but after her mother healed and they could make all the arrangements, they planned to move to Whiskey Creek, after all. Although Grady insisted he'd be the one to relocate if she wanted him to, she'd decided, since her parents were going to be fine, she'd go ahead and sell her dental practice and open a new one in Grady's hometown. She wanted to be able to contribute to their living—although he'd told her on numerous occasions that she didn't have to work if she didn't want to.

Maybe if she got pregnant, she'd focus on raising their children and building a pottery business instead.

It was nice to have options.

"What is it with you?" her father asked, jerking her out of her reverie.

She glanced up to see him studying her quizzically. "What do you mean?"

"You've always got a dreamy smile on your face these days."

Her mother put down her fork and peered at her. "Don't tell me you and Arman are back together…"

"I'm afraid not." The Kahns had been to the hospital several times, and she and Arman had been friendly to each other, but there'd been nothing to indicate they'd ever get back together. This was just another of her mother's many attempts to get her to yield to their wishes.

But that wasn't going to happen. And her father had unwittingly given her the perfect opening to bring up what she'd been waiting to talk to them about. "I've met someone else," she announced.

They both blinked in surprise. *"Who?"* they said in unison.

"His name's Grady Amos."

"Where'd you meet him?" her father asked.

She figured the less said, the better. "Here in LA."

Her mother shoved the rolling cart containing the remains of her lunch to one side. "At your practice? Is he a patient?"

"No, at an acting gig I participated in for Darius's sake."

Her mother stiffened. "Darius is acting now?"

"He's been doing a little of it lately." She had to admit certain things, just in case they learned about the show later. But she could keep it relatively vague—felt that was the smarter way to go.

"Why hasn't he mentioned it?" her father asked.

"Because of everything the two of you have been going through. He didn't want to worry you by making you feel as though he's been taking too much time away from studying for the bar."

Her father set his phone on the counter. "Who is this man you're seeing? And what kind of a name is *Grady*?"

"It's an American one," she replied and got up to show them a picture of him. She still wasn't wearing her wedding ring; she didn't plan to tell them she was married. She'd break that news later, maybe months later, once they'd adjusted to having Grady in her life.

Her mother frowned at his picture. "You're dating this man?"

"I am. And he's the most wonderful person on the planet. You're going to love him."

Her parents didn't look as though they believed it; she wasn't sure she did, either, because she wasn't convinced they'd ever be able to admit they were wrong about Arman. But their approval no longer mattered so much to her. She was finally happy. Better than happy—content in a deep-down, fulfilled sort of way. She'd managed to find what she was missing.

"What does he do for a living?" her mother asked skeptically.

"He owns his own business—an auto body shop." She didn't mention where. That they'd be moving was also something she was saving until they got to know Grady.

The whine of the bed motor sounded as her mother pushed the button that would raise the back up even higher. "You were with Arman until just recently. Is this why you broke up? How long have you been seeing him?"

"Grady isn't the reason I broke things off with Arman," she admitted. "I didn't meet him until right after. But we're already starting to get serious. I think he's the one."

Her parents gaped at her. "When were you going to tell us?" her mother asked.

She smiled as she walked to the bed and rested her hands on the railing. "When I was ready," she said.

Her mother's gaze grew stern. No doubt she thought Aja was being impertinent. "What's that supposed to mean?"

"It means who I date—and marry—should be *my* choice, right?" Aja spoke gently but firmly—firmly enough that her parents looked at each other as if to say "What's going on with our daughter?"

"I hope you know what you're doing," her mother grumbled. She often resorted to instilling fear as another form of manipulation.

Aja kept her smile firmly in place. "It feels like I do, but there are no guarantees. Even if I married Arman, there'd be no guarantees. And as much as I love and respect you both, I need the freedom to make my own decisions."

"We've never stopped you from doing that!" her mother snapped.

Aja could've argued that point, but she didn't bother. They weren't going to see things from her perspective, not today. That would take time, if it *ever* happened. She now understood that if the way they interacted with her was ever going to change, she had to be the one to make it happen.

A nurse came into the room, drawing her parents' attention, so she slipped out to text Grady.

I told them.

She got a text right back.

What'd they say?

It wasn't what they said, it was what I said. And I feel good about it.

* * * * *

WHEN WE TOUCH

Prologue

Present Day

It was Kyle Houseman.

Olivia Lucero hesitated when she saw her ex-boyfriend through the peephole, even though she'd already yelled, "Coming," at the sound of his knock. It had been three years since he'd broken her heart by marrying her sister, Noelle. He and Noelle were now divorced, but it was still awkward to confront him, especially on her own.

"What's wrong?" Lorianna Beck, a friend who'd come to town for Victorian Days, a celebration Whiskey Creek hosted every Christmas, held her coffee cup in one hand and rubbed her eyes with the other.

Olivia forced a smile and shrugged. "Nothing," she said, and finished turning the knob so she could open the door.

A hint of relief eased the anxiety on Kyle's forehead. His hands were shoved deep in the pockets of his jeans and, when she'd spotted him through the peephole, he'd been wearing a scowl. "Thank God you're home," he said.

That wasn't the greeting she'd expected. She'd assumed he'd come to see Brandon. Whenever Kyle showed up these days, he asked for her husband. They were finally establishing a relationship, but it was still tentative.

"Brandon's at the shop," she said, maintaining a polite smile. After her husband had retired from professional skiing, he'd opened a ski-and-snowboard shop in the center of town. He was usually out of the house early, particularly during the cold season— not that there'd been much snow this year.

"I'm not looking for Brandon." Kyle's breath misted in the morning air. "I was hoping I could have a few minutes to speak with you alone."

Olivia glanced over her shoulder at Lorianna, who was sitting at the kitchen table. Although she and Lorianna, the wife of one of Brandon's old ski buddies, had bonded quickly, Lorianna was a relatively new friend. She had her own problems, and that—rather than Victorian Days—was the real reason for her visit. But Olivia wasn't sure she wanted to share anything too personal with her. Besides, with the issues Lorianna was facing, the poor woman was going through enough.

When Olivia turned back, she could tell that Kyle hadn't realized that she had company. Lorianna had arrived late last night, so she hadn't been seen around town. And she didn't have a car with her, parked out front or otherwise. She'd flown in from Denver, and Olivia and Brandon had picked her up at the Oakland Airport. "It looks like this might be a bad time," he said. "So maybe…maybe you can call me later?"

"Wait! Don't go on my account." Lorianna dried what was left of her tears and jumped to her feet. "I'm no reason to postpone anything. I was just about to get in the shower, anyway." She scurried out of the kitchen before Olivia could argue, so Olivia stepped back and waved Kyle inside. She wasn't dressed for company, but she was curious enough to hear what Kyle had to say that she wasn't concerned about her appearance.

"Who was that?" he asked, once Lorianna's footsteps could be heard on the landing overhead.

She and Kyle had grown up in the same small Gold Country town and knew almost all the same people. Olivia could understand why he'd be slightly surprised to find a stranger in her house. "Have you ever heard Brandon talk about Jeff Felix?"

"The skier?"

"That's his wife, Lorianna."

"She seemed upset. Is she okay?"

"She'll be fine."

"Where's he?"

"Home in Denver. He was too busy with the restaurant they recently opened to join her, and she wanted to see Victorian Days."

"She doesn't seem too impressed so far."

"She hasn't been yet. That'll be tonight. And she's working through a few…issues."

"So she's staying with you?"

"For a short time." Until she could make a few decisions about her life—or Christmas arrived next week. Whichever came first. Olivia had agreed to provide a temporary safe haven where Lori-anna could rest, relax and do some soul-searching under the guise of hanging out with a new friend.

Kyle scratched his head. "I didn't mean to chase her off."

"It's okay. I'm sure she doesn't mind." She motioned at a chair. "Have a seat while I get you a cup of coffee."

He didn't say anything, but he seemed ill at ease as he waited, looking around at the Christmas tree in the other room, the garland running up her staircase railing, and the other decorations and furniture. She guessed that he was wondering if this was how their house would have looked if they'd ended up together.

"Thanks," he said when she brought him his cup. Then his gaze lowered to her belly and she guessed he was thinking about the baby. She and Brandon had made the announcement last week, so word was getting around. Obviously, he'd heard.

She slid the cream and sugar closer. She knew him so well—or used to—that she could've fixed his coffee for him, exactly the way he liked it. "So…what's going on?"

His chest lifted as he took a deep breath. "Your mother came to see me last night."

A jolt of concern went through her as she perched on the edge of her own seat. "She did? *Why?*"

He grimaced. "She asked me to help heal her family."

Olivia clenched her jaw. "Let me guess—she's worried about Noelle."

"Yes."

"That's why you're here? To patch things up between my sister and me?"

"If I can."

"That's all in the past," she said in a tone indicating they should leave it there.

"I realize that, but it hasn't been forgotten, not if you and Noelle can't be in the same room—not even at Christmas."

Olivia stood and went to the counter to get her herbal tea. Why hadn't her mother come to *her* about this? Nancy never faced what was bothering her head-on. Instead, she tried to ignore it or slip around it somehow, which irritated Olivia. "What happened wasn't all your fault, Kyle," she said.

"Still, I'm sorry for my part in it."

"I know. You've apologized and…and I've forgiven you."

"Have you?"

She shifted beneath his intense regard. "Yes."

"Then maybe that's the problem. She doesn't understand how you can forgive me but not your own sister."

Olivia couldn't stifle a bitter laugh. "Because I know my sister! Does my mother think I don't understand what Noelle did? How badly she wanted to steal you from me? How calculated she was in her approach? I mean…was there even a baby, Kyle?"

He sighed and rubbed his chin without answering.

"You can't say for sure, can you? You don't even know whether she was lying about that."

"I saw the pregnancy test results. There was a baby. I'm just not sure if she miscarried, like she claims, or…"

"It says a lot that you're still not sure, don't you think?"

"Look, I understand your anger. Trust me, I can get angry over Noelle, too. But we can't escape the past and hang on to it at the same time. What upsets me is that your relationship with her—with your whole family—is compromised, even three years later, because of me. It makes me wonder if I'll ever be able to atone for what I did."

"It's not you who needs to atone! That's the thing."

"What we did takes two. I'm fully aware of that—and if I wasn't, there've been plenty of people telling me," he added dryly.

She'd been one of them. "So what do you want me to do?"

"Give Noelle another chance. Let this Christmas be a fresh start."

"I'd be a fool to trust her again! I can't believe you came to help my mother."

"She wants to put her family back together. And I want the same thing, for you more than her. What good does it do to hold a grudge?"

"Who wouldn't hold a grudge after what Noelle did?"

"That may be true, but it ended well." He lowered his voice. "Look at what you've got. Look how happy you and Brandon are."

He had a point. Without Noelle, she probably would've married Kyle herself, and then she would never have known what she was missing. Kyle was wonderful, but Brandon was more than she could have dreamed.

"It would be easier to forgive her if she was even the slightest bit contrite," she said. "Or if I had some hope that she wouldn't stab me in the back again at the first opportunity."

"She's jealous of you. She wants what you have. Somehow, no matter what happens, no matter how hard she tries, you always end up better off."

"And I've felt bad for her before. But I don't anymore. She's her own worst enemy."

"I know it's not easy to forgive someone who doesn't deserve it."

Olivia wasn't sure she was capable of such a magnanimous gesture, but Kyle seemed to be suggesting that he thought she was.

What if she could let go of her resentment? What if she could put her family back together again, allow them to look forward to holiday gatherings as they used to? For her parents' sakes if not Noelle's?

As enraging as it had been that her mother had supported Noelle through the whole painful debacle of her marriage to Kyle, in her heart Olivia understood why she'd behaved as she did. Nancy had known that her "good" daughter would be okay in the end. It was Noelle who worried her. Noelle screwed up so much she needed someone to be on her side when the rest of the world walked out.

"Damn it," she grumbled.

"What?"

"You know what. But I'll think about it."

He nodded. "Thanks. I hate the fact that...that there are any residual negative effects of what I did, especially when it comes to you."

He still loved her. Olivia could feel it. If she could wave some magic wand that would heal his heart and free him from regret, she would. So why couldn't she feel the same way about her sister?

There were a lot of reasons. But she needed to overcome them.

"You'll find someone else someday," she whispered as she gave him a brief hug and walked him to the door.

"What was that all about?"

Olivia had just said goodbye to Kyle when Lorianna appeared, dressed in a robe and wearing a towel wrapped around her head.

"Nothing important. Aren't you going to get dressed? There's a Christmas shop down the street that might cheer you up."

"I was going to ask if I could borrow a blow dryer. I forgot mine."

"Of course. There's one under the sink in my bathroom."

"I'll get it, but you really won't tell me who that man was? Here I've been blubbering on and on about my problems, and you're going to keep yours all to yourself?"

Olivia considered her new friend. Maybe it would help Lorianna to know that she wasn't the only one trying to forgive someone for something painful. Maybe that was even the reason fate had brought them together. "You've been wondering if you can get over the fact that your husband's been with someone else."

"I don't think I can," she said, sounding adamant. "My heart is broken. My trust is destroyed."

"Well, I'm trying to move beyond a hurtful situation, too. I've just got a little more perspective on it—thanks to the passage of time."

Lorianna studied her more closely. "What kind of situation?"

Olivia smiled. "Are you sure you don't want to finish getting ready first? Because it's a long story."

Lorianna pulled off the towel and fluffed her hair with her hands. "I'll let it air-dry," she said. "I'd rather hear this."

Chapter One

Three Years Ago

Returning for her sister's wedding would've been difficult had it merely meant pretending to be a happy and supportive bridesmaid. But being in charge of the whole event? That added insult to the most heart-wrenching emotional injury Olivia Arnold had ever sustained.

As she drove back to Whiskey Creek for the first time since learning that Noelle would be marrying Kyle Houseman—the man she'd been dating herself until three months ago—she wished she'd had the nerve to refuse her parents. Noelle tried to beat Olivia at anything and everything she did. It had been that way since they were children.

But Olivia planned weddings for a living. She was also the family peacemaker, so it came naturally to try to forgive, to move on. And, as her mother had pointed out, she was the one who'd asked Kyle if they could take a "break" while she moved to Sacramento to build her business. She'd wanted one year to see if she could develop it into something spectacular in a bigger city before marrying Kyle and settling down in Whiskey Creek.

Given all that, how *could* she refuse to help? Especially when she could save her father so much money?

Despite her determination to soldier on through everything that was happening, an odd sense of panic welled up as she reached the edge of town. Pulling over just beyond the sign that said Welcome to Whiskey Creek, The Heart of Gold Country, she tried to get hold of herself but almost turned her Acura around. Within an hour, she could be home in Sacramento. She could hide away until this wedding was a distant memory and, if she was lucky, avoid her sister and new brother-in-law for a decade or two. Maybe by then she'd be able to face them without wanting to cry.

And why shouldn't she turn back? If she stayed, the humiliation of the next few days would be as painful as the heartbreak. Whiskey Creek was a town of only two thousand people. Thanks to the fact that she and Kyle had been a couple for three years, and had separated so recently, she couldn't possibly escape the whispers, the pitying looks or the condolences of the friends and neighbors who'd known her most of her life.

"Shit. Shit, shit, shit!" Bumping her forehead against the steering wheel, she pictured Kyle kissing "the bride" and groaned at the disappointment and betrayal. Noelle had waited for just the right moment. When Olivia was in Sacramento, trying to experience something new before starting her life with Kyle. When he was alone and not coping well with the separation. Then she'd made her move. Olivia wasn't sure she'd ever be able to forgive her sister, especially since it was Olivia's own tears and confidences that had armed Noelle. They'd never been particularly close, but they came from the same family and had lived under the same roof until Olivia relocated to Sacramento last February. That gave Noelle certain insights she wouldn't otherwise have had.

But if she left, if she ran, her sister would know she was just as hurt today as she had been that terrible evening the horrible truth—that Kyle and Noelle had been seeing each other—came out. Why give Noelle the pleasure? Why confirm that her sister, younger by two years—which only made it worse—had finally landed the coup de grâce of their sibling rivalry?

"Ahhhhh!" She pounded the steering wheel with her fists this time, before hitting everything else in sight. Somehow, seeing her hometown looming ahead had destroyed her restraint. Rage seemed to be a monster growing in strength and power until it was bursting out of her chest—

A knock on the window interrupted her midsob. She'd been so focused on her distress, on screaming and beating her dashboard, she hadn't heard anyone approach.

Mortified to realize she had a witness to her behavior, she turned to see a tall, blond man dressed in a white T-shirt, khaki shorts and flip-flops. His mouth, tense with some emotion, made a slash in his face beneath a pair of mirrorlike sunglasses.

Oh, God... Despite those glasses, it wasn't a cop, as she'd expected. Worse—it was Kyle's stepbrother, Brandon Lucero. He was younger than Kyle by a year, which made him almost a year older than her, and he appeared to be...concerned. No doubt he thought she'd lost her mind.

Her only consolation was that Brandon wasn't likely to tell Kyle what he'd seen, even if he connected it to the upcoming wedding. There was no love lost between the two men. They'd lived together while in high school, after Kyle's older sister had married and moved away and his father married Brandon's mother. But that hadn't made them friends.

Brandon waited to speak until she rolled down the window. "You okay?" he asked, his teeth a stark contrast to his golden tan.

After getting abusive with the interior of her innocent car, her right hand hurt so badly she was afraid she'd fractured it. She cradled it in her lap, hoping he wouldn't notice the swelling, and wiped her other hand over her wet cheeks. This kind of behavior wasn't like her.

"Don't I look okay?" she countered as if she hadn't just lost control.

He shook his head. "Tell me this has nothing to do with Kyle."

She dabbed at her eyes, inadvertently smearing her mascara, which she wiped onto her white shorts. Cut low at the hips and high on the leg, they'd been purchased with one goal in mind—turning male heads. In her current situation, she needed the ego boost. But what did it matter if she looked better than she ever had? Noelle was marrying the man Olivia thought would be *her* husband. "Would you believe I broke a nail?"

His biceps bulged, stretching the sleeves of his T-shirt as he folded his arms. "Not a chance. Want to try something else?"

"No. Who cares if you think I'm an idiot?" she grumbled as she pushed her long hair out of her face. "You've never liked me much to begin with."

This seemed to surprise him. "What gave you that impression?"

"I don't know." She managed a facetious smirk. "Maybe the way you scowl every time you see me? Or, if you can't avoid me, which is always your first choice, you just grunt so you don't have to say hello?"

He scowled when she'd expected him to laugh. "Would you believe I was saving you from myself?"

"No."

"I can be chivalrous when I want to be."

"That's definitely not an adjective I'd use to describe *you*. I'm sure all the women with broken hearts you've left behind would agree with me."

His scowl darkened. "What women with broken hearts?"

She could've named a few. But he didn't give her the chance to be more specific. He was still talking.

"I'm going to assume you're angry or you wouldn't have said that. You're obviously having a bad day."

Ah, the understatement of the year. And since she had to face Kyle and Noelle as well as her parents in the next few minutes, her day was going to get worse.

"We had a class together, remember?" he added. "I took you to my junior prom. I've always liked you just fine."

She couldn't see his eyes, but she sensed that they were moving over her, taking inventory of what her clothes revealed. Instinctively she wanted to cover up. The only thing stopping her was the sure knowledge that doing so would draw more attention to her atypical attire. "And—" he grinned "—from what I can see so far, I'm going to like the new you even more."

What had she been *thinking* when she'd put on this outfit? If Kyle didn't regret what he'd done by now, a pair of short shorts and a low-cut blouse wouldn't do the trick. It was too late to save what they'd had, anyway. It wasn't as if she could take him back.

"I dressed in a weak moment," she explained, her face burning. "I needed to feel attractive."

"Mission accomplished." He whistled. "You could stop traffic. You stopped me, didn't you?"

She considered the amusement on his face. "I'm pretty sure you thought I was having engine trouble."

"To be honest, I thought a bee had gotten into your car and you were under attack."

"Thanks for the visual. But it wasn't that bad."

His eyebrows rose above his sunglasses. "It was alarming. But back to your changed wardrobe. I don't think showing that much skin is the best way to recover." He scratched his smooth-shaven chin. "I mean… I'd hate to see you wind up with the wrong kind of guy. *Again*."

"Kyle was the wrong kind of guy?" She was anxious to hear his justification for that statement. The general belief was that *Brandon* was the less reliable of the two. Kyle had attended UC Berkeley on an academic scholarship while getting a degree in electrical engineering. He'd started his own company manufacturing solar panels after that, which was currently making him rich. He was strong, kind, talented.

Maybe he wasn't *quite* as handsome as his stepbrother, but his attention wasn't nearly as fleeting, either.

"For you he was *completely wrong*," Brandon maintained as if he'd been able to see it all along.

The uncertainty she'd always felt in his presence returned. She'd caught him watching her since that prom. Most of the time he turned away the second she noticed, but occasionally their eyes met and held, and she remembered how badly she'd once wished he'd call.

Mouth quirking up on one side, he said, "Why don't you follow me to my place and put yourself back together before you walk into the lion's den?"

It was a kind suggestion. One she never would've expected— not from him. But she could guess why he was suddenly so helpful. He'd love nothing more than to shove a connection with her in Kyle's face.

And therein lay the appeal of his offer…

"Do you think your stepbrother will hear about it if I do?" she asked.

He chuckled softly. "We can make sure of it."

That kind of petty revenge was beneath her. But the idea of turning the tables was tempting. "He'd hate it," she mused. "Whether he's marrying my sister or not." She knew because of that last call, the apology, the crack in his voice when he'd said he'd always love her. The memory of it brought fresh tears to her eyes…

A truck was coming up from behind. To get out of its way, Brandon stepped close enough that she could pick up his scent in the air that blasted into her car as the truck whooshed by. He smelled as good as he looked. But that was no surprise. She recalled dancing with him as a sophomore, pressing her nose into his warm neck in an effort to remember his scent. She'd instinctively known that was the only part of Brandon a girl could safely capture.

"He wouldn't want you to be with anyone else, but me least of all," he agreed.

Obviously he liked the idea of upsetting Kyle as much as she did. Problem was…what if she fell into her own trap? Brandon was like a meteor. He burned hot and bright as he crashed through a woman's orbit, but he left a lot of damage in his wake and nothing, no one, slowed him down. Although some girls welcomed the thrill of trying, Olivia was already nursing a broken heart. She had no business being alone with this man, especially while she was on the rebound.

On the other hand, she was tired of trying to turn the other cheek. She was also tired of being so darn careful with her love life. Kyle was supposed to have been a wise choice, a man who wanted to settle down and have a family. And look how well that had turned out. He was having a family, all right. *With her sister.* Noelle was pregnant, hence the rush on the wedding. Her mother wanted Noelle married off before she started to show.

"Are you coming?" Brandon asked when she didn't answer.

Were they going to be allies? She found that a bit ironic, considering that, after prom, they'd never even been friends. "If I go to your house, it doesn't mean I'll be sleeping with you," she said, taking a stab at his motivation for inviting her.

He jammed his fists into the pockets of his baggy shorts. "Kyle won't know that."

Her injured hand was beginning to throb. She should head to her parents' house, change into something more sensible and make an ice pack. But if she showed up there in the next few minutes, they'd question her about her red eyes even if she concocted a good excuse for her hand. She couldn't stand the thought of that, especially if they cornered her in front of Noelle, who would know exactly what was wrong and take great satisfaction in being the cause of it.

"Do you have an ice pack?" she asked, finally letting him see her injury.

He slid his sunglasses down to take a look, and she felt the full effect of those eyes, which were several shades lighter than hazel. "Do *I* have an ice pack?"

"You have a lot of them." Of course he did. As a professional skier, he probably needed one often.

"Come with me and you'll feel better in a few minutes. I guarantee it."

She squinted up at him. *I think that's what I'm afraid of*, she thought but all she said was, "Thanks."

Chapter Two

Olivia had never been inside Brandon's house. Kyle had driven her past it once, when they'd been coming back from a picnic near the old mine. Brandon had been abroad at the time, or they never would've taken the chance of running into him. Kyle preferred to have as little contact as possible. Since then, she'd noticed the turn-off that led to his solitary cabin whenever she drove up this way to hike or bike. Brandon had always been a bit of a mystery to her.

She could understand why he'd like living here, with the peace and quiet and the spectacular view afforded by one wall made entirely of glass. His home reminded her of the *Swiss Family Robinson* tree house, probably because it was two stories high and dug out of the mountain—very much a part of nature. As if that wasn't unusual enough, a telescope held pride of place in the middle of the living room, beneath a giant skylight.

Most people wouldn't put a telescope in the living room because it would obstruct their view of the television. But Brandon's TV was in the loft area above. Down here, various geodes and old weapons, artifacts and sculptures lined bookshelves that also contained a surprising array of books, mostly nonfiction. She spotted one on astronomy, another on Buddhism and a third on the history of China.

She'd never taken him for a scholar. Since he made his living as an extreme skier, he was often videotaped plunging down the steepest slopes in the world. She thought he was foolish to risk his life doing a thing like that *once*, let alone again and again, but there appeared to be some fringe benefits to his job besides the high pay and adrenaline rush. Obviously it had taken him to many different countries.

"Are you an art collector?" she called, studying several paintings.

He came into the room carrying the most technically advanced ice pack she'd ever seen. "Not really. I pick up what appeals to me. Most of it's from unusual places. I love to travel."

"I can tell."

"What about you?" he asked.

She pulled her gaze from a photograph of an African woman holding the hand of a child in some faraway jungle she'd probably never see. "I don't get the opportunity very often."

Although she'd been planning weddings and other events since she'd graduated from Sac State with a degree in business administration, moving to Sacramento had required she take on some expenses that she'd never had before. Not only was she living on her own for the first time since college, she'd leased an office and was paying for advertising in the hope of attracting new clients. The money she'd saved needed to be held in reserve, just in case.

"Would you like to see more of the world if you could?" he asked.

She fingered an elephant carved out of wood. "Absolutely," she replied, but she wasn't really considering the possibility. She was too preoccupied wondering how the Brandon suggested by this house could be so different from what she'd taken him to be, which was much more the typical jock.

"I'm planning a backpacking trip across Nicaragua in a few weeks." He bent to look into her face. "You could come with me."

The idea of escaping held massive appeal. But she wasn't sure it was a legitimate offer. Most people didn't extend invitations like that off the cuff. "You're going across the entire country?"

"Nicaragua's not that big."

"I have a feeling it might seem big if you're *walking*."

He smiled. "That's the best way to see it."

"I wish I could," she said in a throwaway statement that took for granted he hadn't been serious.

He didn't press the issue. He motioned to a soft leather couch. "Have a seat. Let's get this on your hand."

Once she was settled in, he examined her hand before putting the ice pack on it. "You should get this x-rayed."

"I couldn't have broken any bones throwing a tantrum," she said, but she knew that was denial talking.

"I'm not so sure," he responded. "If the pain doesn't go away in the next day or so, definitely have it checked."

He should know about broken bones. Not long ago, he'd tumbled off a cliff in Switzerland and broken his right leg in three places. They'd replayed the footage of it on the local news over and over. As a result of that spill, he'd been on crutches, convalescing for much of the last year she and Kyle were dating. In the past twelve months, she'd seen him around town more often than she had in the ten or so years since prom.

He arranged the ice pack on her hand and headed back to the kitchen.

"Do you ever get lonely out here?" she asked, looking toward the giant window directly across from her. From where she sat, she couldn't see the water, but she knew the river cut through the ravine below.

"Not really."

That was a stupid question, she told herself. Why would he get lonely? He could have a woman visit anytime he wanted.

"Do you ever get lonely in Sacramento?" he called back.

After living at home with her family since college, and dating Kyle for three of those years—seeing him every day—Sacramento had been a big change. She'd been *more* than lonely; she'd been positively bereft. But other than that lapse of sanity in her car, she thought she'd managed to absorb the pain without showing how bad she really felt. "I try to keep myself so busy I don't even have time to think about stuff like that."

"No wonder you lost your cool."

His response surprised her. "Excuse me?"

"You haven't dealt with the blow."

"I refuse to feel bad about a man who could do what Kyle did. That's all."

He reappeared with some painkillers and a glass of water. "Here, take these."

She swallowed the pills, then eyed him dubiously when he said, "To be honest, I don't understand why you're here."

"You invited me," she pointed out, purposely misunderstanding.

"You know what I mean."

With a wince, she adjusted the ice pack. "I felt it was best to come back with my head held high. Not coming would only have confirmed to Kyle and Noelle that I'm still hurt."

"I admire your courage, but…"

He thought she'd bitten off more than she could chew. That episode in the car proved it. "I won't break down again."

"There's no shame in loving someone, Olivia."

As if he knew anything about it. She almost said that, but stopped herself. Why be unkind? *He* wasn't the person who'd wronged her. "There is if that someone is marrying your sister," she grumbled. "Everyone's watching me, waiting for the tears to flow." And he'd actually witnessed them…

His expression softened. "Kyle screwed up."

"I appreciate the sentiment, even if you are sort of obligated to say that."

"Just because you're in town doesn't mean you have to stay," he said. "I'm the only one who's seen you."

"You're suggesting I leave? Miss the wedding? She's my sister."

"That goes both ways. Most people would say she had no business hooking up with your boyfriend."

The fact that Kyle had been her boyfriend made him that much more desirable for Noelle. It was a strange but undeniable dynamic. Noelle had always coveted what she had. "What good would it do to nurse my resentment? To tear my family apart?" she asked. "Besides, I *have* to attend the wedding. I'm planning it."

His thick eyebrows jerked together. Because he'd removed his sunglasses the moment they walked into the house, she could see his eyes. She wasn't sure that was a *good* thing. They were so beautiful they could render a woman helpless with a single, smoldering glance—especially a woman who needed to feel desired again.

"You're *planning* it?" he said. "Why the hell would you do that?"

The anger in his voice made her stiffen. "That's what I do for a living. That's what I've been doing since college."

"Doesn't mean you had to do *this* wedding. Why didn't you say no?"

"To my *parents*?"

"They had no right asking *you*."

"They couldn't afford anyone else. I could do it much more easily than they could themselves. Besides, they *want* me to forgive her. They want to maintain peace and harmony in the family."

"That's bullshit. They should've protected you, told her to elope."

Olivia had never dreamed she'd be commiserating with Brandon Lucero. Apparently their mutual dislike of Kyle had pulled them onto the same team. "Why haven't you ever gotten along with your stepbrother?" she asked.

"Kyle's not bad," he replied. "Not anymore." He returned to the kitchen a third time and came back with two glasses of wine, one of which he handed to her.

"That didn't really answer my question."

"I was fifteen when he came into my life."

"And?"

He seemed reluctant to continue, acting as if it didn't matter anymore. But she could tell it did.

"Oh, come on," she said. "He was sleeping with my sister within a week of our break. We weren't even supposed to be seeing other people. I'm not going to stick up for him."

"There's no need for anyone to stick up for *him*. Everyone knows *I'm* the black sheep."

"You're saying he's had it easier than you?"

He took a sip of his wine. "By the time he came into my life, it'd been ten years since my dad died. I was only five when it happened." He sat across from her. "But by the time my mother remarried, I was comfortable, no longer craving a father or a brother. My mother and I were doing just fine."

"Until she met Bob Houseman and everything changed."

He nodded. "Suddenly I lost the company of my friends and found myself in a new town, a new school. Not only that but I had this father figure who was bossing me around and laying down strict rules. I had a brother, too, who meant the absolute world to him, which meant I could never compete. That made having a dad more of an illusion than a reality." He studied the wine in his glass. "The worst part was how it affected my mother. She was so eager to please them both that I was quickly relegated to the back seat, expected to understand and adapt." He fell silent before finishing with, "There were just a lot of changes."

So he felt that Kyle and Kyle's father had stolen his previous life and his mother from him. When she looked at it from his point of view, she could see why. It sounded as if Kyle had been in a better position to enjoy the new family dynamic. It would be hard to start over in high school, hard to have your position usurped.

Was that why he'd used his good looks and charisma like a weapon?

"How do you feel about Kyle now?" she asked.

"None of what bothered me then seems to matter anymore. I've come to terms with it."

She got the feeling that wasn't completely true. Maybe the animosity had died down, but… "Do you think you'll ever be close?"

"Probably not. Imagine taking two boys with strong personalities, both only sons, and trying to force one to become 'the little brother' after years of living a different life. Although I was younger, I refused to let Kyle best me at anything, and he resented the constant challenge."

"I'm sure it didn't help that you went your own ways so soon after your parents were married."

"I don't follow you…"

"You never really got a chance to adjust." Kyle had headed off to college just two years after the wedding, right after she and Brandon went to Brandon's junior prom, which was something that had always bugged Kyle—even though he and Olivia weren't dating back then. By the time he returned, Brandon was gone. Then they started their careers and, with Brandon out of town so much, it'd been easy for Kyle to forget he even had a stepbrother.

"Actually I think we were both relieved by the separation," he said with a wry grin.

"If he finds out I'm here, you could be looking at another challenge to your relationship."

He winked at her. "I'm willing to take that risk."

She glanced around the room. "You're willing to take *any* risk."

His eyes never left her face. She could feel his close regard, even though she avoided eye contact. "Only if I want something badly enough."

Olivia's phone rang, saving her from a response. She was glad. Whether or not he'd meant what he'd said as a pickup line, she'd felt a tingle down to her toes.

She checked caller ID. It was her mother. Nancy had been expecting her and must be getting worried. They were supposed to make the favors for the reception after dinner tonight.

Sending Brandon a look asking his forbearance, she overcame her reluctance to take this call and answered, infusing as much lift into her voice as possible. "Hello?"

"Where are you? I was sure you'd be here by now."

Olivia allowed herself a grimace. "I, uh, had a little accident." *"With your car?"*

"No. I tripped while loading up and hurt my hand. So I'm running late."

Brandon was watching her, but she continued to avoid his gaze.

"How bad is it? You didn't break any bones…"

"I doubt it," she said, removing the ice pack to take a look. "I'll be there shortly."

"Dinner's at six."

She heard the subtle threat in that statement. They'd eat without her if she wasn't there. "I'll make it."

"Good. Kyle and Noelle are here waiting."

"I bet they are."

Her mother had to have heard the sour note in her voice, but, wisely, she didn't react to it. Since the news of Noelle's pregnancy, Nancy had done her best to minimize Olivia's previous relationship with Kyle. The way she told the story, Noelle was marrying an "old friend" of her other daughter's. Never mind that she and Kyle had talked about marriage themselves.

"Hurry. We have a lot to do."

"See you soon." After she hung up, she returned her attention to Brandon. "It was very gallant of you to rescue me from my imaginary bee attack, but I've got to go."

"You sure you're ready for what lies ahead?"

"No, but I never will be." She rolled her eyes. "Noelle and Kyle are anxiously awaiting my arrival."

"Lucky you," he said dryly.

"Exactly."

"Where are you staying?"

"My parents'."

He made a face. "Isn't your sister living there?"

She drank the rest of her wine, put her glass on the coffee table and got up. "Until Saturday night, when her new husband whisks her off to wedded bliss."

"You're more forgiving than I am."

"I could pay for a hotel, but I'd be a hundred bucks poorer. How would that bother them?"

"Good point." He stood, too. "Just don't let loose on any inanimate objects again. You might break your other hand."

"I've learned my lesson," she responded, but just hearing her mother's voice had put a lump in her throat. She couldn't help feeling betrayed by her parents, too, because they were so eager to throw their support behind this wedding. She knew they had a grandchild at stake, but still…

After using his bathroom to fix her makeup, she found Brandon standing at the window, looking outside. "What do you think? Can you tell I've been crying?"

"I never would've guessed. If it gets too bad, you could always come back here."

She raised her eyebrows. "So we could…"

His grin turned her knees to water. "Sleep. Of course. And I won't charge you for the room."

"Maybe you'd let me check out your big telescope," she said, widening her eyes in feigned innocence.

"If you want to see the stars, I could give you a night to remember," he said, playing along.

She laughed. "The ultimate revenge?"

"No," he said, growing serious. "What I've wanted since prom."

"That's why you dropped me off at the end of the night and have avoided me ever since?"

"I knew I wasn't what you needed. You're too sensitive."

That had been true then, and it was true now. If someone as trustworthy and admired as Kyle could hurt her so terribly, how would she ever survive the kind of emotional damage someone like Brandon could wreak?

"But I'll go easy on you," he added with a grin. "My number's in your phone, in case you need it."

"Thanks." She was surprised he'd taken the liberty. She was a little flattered, too. But she had no intention of returning. She *couldn't* come back. She'd only get herself into trouble if she did, because it wasn't Brandon's telescope she wanted him to share.

Chapter Three

Kyle's work truck sat in her parents' driveway. Olivia had expected to see it, but her heart sank all the same.

Taking a breath, trying to bolster herself, she got out of her Acura and started toward the front door, rolling her suitcase behind her with a sense of determination and purpose that belied the pain.

You can do this. Just keep your chin up and try to forget that this is Kyle and Noelle. Pretend they're no different from any of the other couples you've worked with.

It was a wedding, a job, she told herself. But she hadn't been home since she'd moved away. Her only contact had been through her mother, who shared various details over the phone.

Olivia felt strange marching up to her parents' front door knowing that nothing was as it used to be, that Kyle wasn't waiting for her in quite the same way as he'd waited for her in the past.

She spotted a flurry of movement at the window. Then the door flew open and her mother descended on her. "There you are! I've been worried. Let me see what you've done to your poor hand."

Grateful for the distraction, she displayed her injury.

"Oh, dear." Her mother's eyebrows knit. "Look at that. Of all times for something like this to happen. Well, come on in. We'll get some ice. Maybe we'll be able to put you on the left side when we take the wedding pictures so the swelling doesn't show."

"I don't need to be in the pictures at all," she said before she could stop the words.

Nancy's smile faded. The expression on her face suggested she was about to respond, but whether she was going to warn her not to ruin the wedding, or say she was sorry about what Olivia must be feeling, Olivia never heard because Kyle strode out to greet her.

Olivia thanked God that Noelle wasn't with him. Seeing him was bad enough. He seemed reluctant yet eager to approach, which added more confusion to the emotions currently assaulting her.

"I'm glad you're safe," he said.

Their eyes met briefly before she jerked hers away, but he kept his smile stubbornly in place as he hurried to assist with her suitcase.

"I've got it." She made an effort to keep the resentment from her voice, but it was impossible. No doubt he picked up on her tone. They were too familiar with each other for him to miss the slightest nuance.

Why had this person she'd trusted so deeply betrayed her? There were moments, moments like now, when she couldn't believe that their lives had taken such a dramatic turn.

He attempted to grab her case in spite of her refusal, but she hung on and kept walking, leaving him no choice but to fall back and follow.

"Where's Dad?" she asked her mother as they reached the front patio.

"Out back, grilling some steaks."

Olivia didn't ask where Noelle was. She didn't want to see her sister.

The smell of a home-cooked meal enveloped her as soon as she entered the house—evoking the only pleasant sensation Olivia had experienced since she'd left Brandon's. Everything else cut like broken glass.

A buzzer went off in the kitchen, and her mother hurried to remove whatever she had on the stove. Sensing Kyle's presence at her elbow, she left her suitcase and pivoted to go back outside, already eager for a reprieve from the tension twisting her stomach. "I've got the stuff for the wedding favors in my trunk. I'll grab it."

"Not with your hand hurt," Kyle said. "Let me."

"No, thanks. I can manage." She had no intention of allowing him to do anything. But, to her chagrin, he joined her, anyway. So she tried to ignore him. She didn't want to see him any more than she wanted to see her sister.

Once they were out of earshot of her mother, he caught her elbow to get her to face him and lowered his voice. "I'm so sorry, Olivia. I know… I know how hard this must be. It's killing me that I'm causing you pain."

He seemed sincere, but maybe he was just being arrogant. She'd begun to doubt everything she'd ever known about him, except the physical sensations that had been such a major part of their relationship. Looking at him made her crave the familiarity they'd enjoyed. Losing his friendship hurt as much as all the rest.

Battling the threat of tears, she manufactured another smile. "You're not causing me pain," she said. "As a matter of fact, I'm already seeing someone else."

Dropping his hand, he blinked in surprise. "Your mother said… I mean, she didn't mention that."

"I haven't told her about him. There's enough going on around here. This is *your* week, *your* wedding. I'll save my announcements for later."

Did he go pale? Or was that her imagination?

"Is it someone in Sac?" he asked.

She could've said yes and left it at that. She wasn't entirely sure why she didn't. Maybe it was because a mere name wouldn't have the same effect. "No, actually. He's from Whiskey Creek. Someone you know quite well."

A muscle flexed in his cheek. "Who?"

She'd already gone too far. But the same desperate compulsion that had overtaken her in the car when she injured her hand seemed to goad her now, until the name that would hurt him most passed her lips. "Brandon."

The color returned to his face, staining his cheeks a bright red. "My *stepbrother*?"

"You're not really related," she reminded him. "That happens to be important to me, even though it wasn't to you."

He seemed to struggle with words. "His mother is married to my father."

"You lived together for two years. Sadly I've had to put up with Noelle my whole life."

He shook his head as if she'd just coldcocked him. "Brandon?" he said again. "You've got to be joking."

She lifted her chin. "Why?"

"Because he'd be terrible for you!"

"In what way?" she challenged.

"He…he doesn't know what it means to really love anyone. The second he gets bored, or a skiing opportunity presents itself, he'll be gone and you may never hear from him again."

She sneered. "Funny *you* should say that."

"I know I let you down." He lowered his voice. "But…that doesn't mean I don't care about you."

"Did you think I'd mope around indefinitely?"

"No, of course not. That isn't what I want. I want you to be happy."

She smiled broadly. "Brandon makes me happy."

A scowl replaced his stunned expression. "Don't cut off your nose to spite your face, Olivia. He hasn't been able to maintain one serious relationship. He'll only hurt you in the end."

She popped the trunk. "I doubt it. Thanks to you, I'm older and wiser than I was."

"You're no match for him. He'll take advantage of how innocent and trusting you are and how deeply you love—"

"I'm not planning to marry him." She rolled her eyes. "I'll leave making the big commitment to you and my dear sister. Brandon's good in bed. Right now, that's all I need."

When he sagged a little, her heart twisted so painfully she almost admitted the truth. But Noelle's voice, filled with suspicion, rang out from the patio. "What's taking so long?"

Olivia raised the trunk lid, revealing the many boxes of wedding paraphernalia she'd borrowed from River City Resort Club & Spa. She'd been planning to tote it all in herself, regardless of her throbbing hand. But if Kyle was going to dog her footsteps, she figured he could handle the job.

"Looks like there's more here than I remembered. If you could bring it into the living room, we'll get started on the wedding favors right after we eat. I have to leave soon. Brandon's expecting me," she said, and walked past her sister without saying hello.

Chapter Four

Noelle was angry during dinner. Olivia could feel her sister's animosity. She wasn't sure why Noelle felt *she* had the right to be upset. But every few seconds she'd glance over at Kyle, who was keeping his eyes on his plate, before sending Olivia an accusing glare.

What did she think happened before she came upon them outside?

Olivia didn't care. Not really. Most of the slights Noelle perceived were imagined. Olivia just wanted to get the wedding favors assembled so she could leave. She couldn't stay here, as planned. The unspoken hurt and anger were too agonizing.

But she wouldn't go to Brandon's. Sacramento wasn't that far. Although it would waste time and gas, she'd drive home and come back in the morning. She did, however, have to tell Brandon what she'd said to Kyle. She wasn't looking forward to that conversation. She'd already embarrassed herself once where he was concerned.

After dinner, Kyle went in to watch a true crime show with her father, Noelle disappeared into her bedroom and Olivia helped her mother wash dishes. Olivia had just started to relax, thanks to the comfort of routine, when Noelle called to her.

"Can you come and tell me how to wear my hair?" she asked, but Olivia wasn't fooled. Noelle had played nice long enough.

"I'll be right back," she told her mother.

Nancy's forehead creased in worry, as if she, too, suspected that Noelle wasn't interested in opinions on her hair, but she nodded, and Olivia silently promised to do all she could to keep her temper in check. Noelle and Kyle were going to have a baby. She needed to keep that in mind, especially if she wanted to be part of her niece or nephew's life. Olivia just hoped that someday she'd be able to look at her sister's offspring, at *Kyle's* offspring, without cringing.

"Are you thinking of an updo?" she asked as she walked down the hall.

Noelle was waiting by the door. She closed it as soon as Olivia walked in. "What are you doing?" she whispered harshly.

Olivia studied her flushed face. She was pretty; there was no denying that. They both had wide blue eyes, long blond hair and even features, but Noelle, shorter by two inches, had a curvier figure. Despite that, Olivia had never been jealous. Due to Noelle's demanding nature, self-absorption and terrible mood swings, she'd never been particularly popular with the opposite sex. Olivia figured men could sense that her looks wouldn't be worth the cost of involvement. She'd always thought Kyle understood that, too. "I don't know what you mean," she said.

"You know *exactly* what I'm talking about!"

Did Noelle believe Olivia had said something inappropriate to Kyle? That she was trying to stir up trouble?

Olivia started to explain that she was at a complete loss when Noelle made the reason for her anger clear. "You're seeing *Brandon*? *Really?* Kyle's *stepbrother*?"

And then Olivia remembered. For most of one summer, Noelle had had the worst crush imaginable on Brandon. She'd done everything possible to gain his attention, including driving past his house numerous times a day, calling him incessantly, showing up wherever she guessed he might be. Olivia had forgotten that, largely because it'd been so long ago—eight years or more. And he hadn't given her so much as a second look. When August rolled around, he told her flat-out that he wasn't remotely interested and she'd better quit stalking him or he was going to the police.

The police threat came—understandable enough—after she'd spied on him with another woman, but his unequivocal rejection had done significant damage to Noelle's ego.

"Why are you smiling?" Noelle snapped.

Olivia sobered. "I guess I still don't understand why you're upset."

Noelle grabbed her arm. "I'm upset because you're doing this on purpose! You're trying to ruin my wedding!"

"What?" Olivia jerked loose. "I've been planning your wedding— *for free*! Not only have I donated hours and hours of my time, I've called in favors from all the vendors I've ever worked with."

"For Mom and Dad. Not for me."

Olivia couldn't argue with that.

"This is your revenge," she continued. "This is how you think you'll get the last laugh."

"What are you talking about?" Noelle had liked a lot of boys over the years. She couldn't claim proprietary interest in *all* of them. Besides, after that summer she'd never had a nice thing to say about Kyle's stepbrother.

"I'm talking about you sleeping with Brandon!"

So Kyle had shared that information. "I don't see why my being with Brandon would bother you. You're in love with Kyle, right? You're having his baby. And because of that baby, he's marrying you."

"Not because of the baby!" she cried, stamping her foot. "Because he loves me! I knew you'd try to cheapen it, try to convince yourself that he's still in love with you. But he's not. He hates that the two of you were ever together!"

When they talked on the phone for the last time, Kyle had said the years they'd spent together were the best of his life, but Olivia didn't give him away. His feelings had probably already changed.

"Fine. I don't care. He's all yours now. You got exactly what you wanted. So enjoy him and leave me alone."

"I didn't get pregnant on purpose. I know you think I did."

"At this point, it doesn't matter what I think." She turned to go but Noelle wasn't finished yet.

"Your relationship with Brandon won't last," she said suddenly, changing tactics. "He isn't the marrying kind."

"Fortunately, after what I've been through in the past few months, I'm only looking for some fun." Unable to resist, she lowered her voice. "And, God, can he provide it!"

* * *

Kyle had the hardest time keeping his eyes from gravitating to Olivia. She looked better than ever—tall, tan, hair streaked from the sun. But she'd always been beautiful to him, the only woman he'd ever loved. Just seeing her made his determination falter.

How had he gotten into such a terrible mess? These days, he constantly asked himself that. But he had no answer—except the obvious. He'd been an idiot, foolish enough to make the kind of mistake that would change his life forever.

"*Honey*, you have to put *three hugs* and *three kisses* in each box," Noelle said.

He blinked at the foil-wrapped chocolate candies. Wasn't that what he'd been doing? He opened the last wedding favor he'd assembled. She was right. He'd put in five kisses and only one hug. He'd thought as long as they each included six pieces, it wouldn't matter. But every little detail mattered to Noelle.

"Got it." He smiled as congenially as possible to keep Olivia and her parents from knowing how badly Noelle's voice grated on him.

Three kisses, he silently mimicked. *And three hugs*.

"Kyle, is something wrong?"

He glanced up to see his future mother-in-law watching him. He hadn't realized he'd slipped into inactivity.

"No." His cheek muscles ached with the effort of yet another smile. "I was just wondering if I'd remembered to invite my aunt Georgia."

"You invited her," Noelle said without looking up. "You had so many on your list I had to cut twenty from mine, remember?"

He didn't know if he was supposed to apologize. He'd tried to keep his list small. His was certainly smaller than hers, by a significant margin. He hadn't wanted a big wedding.

But thanks to Noelle's insistence on creating the fanfare she'd always craved for her wedding, they were looking at a long, painful weekend. One that included Olivia, making it impossible to avoid the fact that, if not for one foolish night, this could've been *their* wedding.

Actually, he'd been with Noelle more than one night. It had been a whirlwind couple of weeks, during which she'd flirted and teased and cajoled and pleased. Caught in the aftermath of Olivia's proposing a break and moving to Sacramento because she didn't want to settle down without experiencing a little more of life, he'd been feeling rejected, unsure she'd ever really come back and angry enough to tell himself he didn't have to suffer while she was gone. Their break hadn't been *his* idea. The fact that they weren't together but weren't really apart left him feeling irritable and foolish.

And this was where it had gotten him...

Suppressing a groan, he started filling boxes again.

"Did you find the right tie and cummerbund for your tux?" Olivia asked. It was the first time she'd initiated any conversation between them. He would've been grateful for her attention, except he knew she was only asking as the wedding planner.

"I have."

"And your groomsmen have the right ones, as well?"

"Probably. I've told them where to go."

"You need to check."

"I will."

"Do they know the rehearsal dinner tomorrow has been moved to seven instead of six thirty?"

He kept forming little boxes and filling them with the appropriate chocolate candy before adding them to the stack in the middle of the table. The women took over from there, tying on a delicate pink ribbon imprinted with Kyle's and Noelle's names and the date of their wedding.

Two days. The worst will be over in two days... "I've notified them of that, too."

"Even Brandon?"

He'd invited Brandon to be in the wedding party for the sake of his parents. He felt it would be too obvious a slight to leave him

out. But other than receiving a brief email confirming his participation, Kyle hadn't heard from his stepbrother. "Even Brandon."

"I'll double-check with him tonight."

The idea of Olivia spending time with Brandon for any reason
made Kyle flinch. She hadn't meant much to him when the two
of them went to a prom together years ago. But she meant a lot to
him now. "I can email him again."

"Why don't you just call him?"

He met her gaze. "Maybe I will."

Ham, as Olivia's father was called, paused in his work to raise
his eyebrows at this exchange. But, as usual, he didn't say anything. Sometimes Kyle wished he would. He wished *someone*
would admit that this wedding was a huge mistake. Because he
couldn't.

Chapter Five

Relieved to be away from her parents' house, Olivia dialed Brandon's number as she sat in her car, in the empty parking lot of Just Like Mom's. The diner was closed, along with almost everything else in town, including the touristy shops dedicated to Whiskey Creek's gold rush heritage. It was late enough that she was hesitant to start the long drive home.

"I'm not sure how to break this to you," she said as soon as Brandon answered.

"Break what to me?" he responded, his voice husky, which made her wonder if she'd awakened him. "You *couldn't* have found someone with a bigger telescope."

She knew he was teasing but, feeling herself flush, decided to ignore the innuendo. "I, uh, told a little white lie about you."

"Did it make me look good or bad?" He didn't sound too excited by the prospect either way.

"Maybe a little opportunistic?"

"Okay. Let me have it."

She drew a deep breath. "Kyle and Noelle think we're seeing each other."

"That's it?"

"Not quite."

"I'm waiting…"

"They also think we're sleeping together."

"Really."

"I don't know what got into me," she said. "Kyle pulled me aside and said it was killing him to know he was causing me pain, and I… I couldn't stand being so transparent and vulnerable. So I told him I'm not hurting at all, that I'm already seeing someone else."

"Me."

"Right. I could've named someone from Sacramento. That's what I *should've* done, obviously. He couldn't have proven that one way or the other. But…"

"It wouldn't have been half as much fun."

"No, it wouldn't have had the same impact." She'd found No-elle's reaction even more satisfying than Kyle's, but she didn't mention that. "I hope you're not too sorry you stopped to help me."

"Not at all. I just wish I could've seen Kyle's face."

She smiled as she remembered. "He went white as a sheet."

"Good. Maybe it gave him the jolt he needs."

"In what way?"

"I haven't given up hope that he'll come to his senses and call the whole thing off."

Olivia pictured Kyle and Noelle as they'd been at dinner. They hadn't seemed particularly close, but they were dealing with a lot of stress, even more than normally accompanied a wedding. She wasn't convinced she could get an accurate reading from what she'd seen. "Maybe he loves her."

"You and I both know who he loves."

She hadn't expected Brandon to be so candid. "There *is* the baby—"

"Jumping into a marriage destined to end in divorce won't help the baby." He lowered his voice in a way that demanded an honest answer. "Would you take him back?"

"No!"

"You're done with him no matter what he does, no matter how much he begs?"

"He won't beg. You know Kyle. Once he's made up his mind, that's it. Whatever else he might be, he's a man of his word. But I'm done with him."

"And now you're all mine."

The zap she'd experienced earlier, the one that left her feeling slightly giddy, struck again. Which made no sense. She was still in love with Kyle—although their relationship was completely and totally *over*.

Assuming it was basic chemistry, the kind that could come out of nowhere even with a complete stranger, she shrugged off her reaction. He was merely referring to what she'd said earlier. "Or so they think. I'm sorry I went that far. I had no right to drag you into something that could have long-term repercussions inside your own family. But I let both him and Noelle know it's not serious."

"You're saying you implied we're not making love, just having sex."

"Exactly. But I made sure they knew it was mind-blowing." She tried to joke a little herself but the images that flashed through her head—images of Brandon's mouth on hers—made her words anything but funny.

"There's only one problem," he said.

"What's that?"

"If you told them it was casual, they already know you were lying."

For some reason, she was having difficulty catching her breath. "What makes you say that?"

"Honey, you're not capable of casual."

She'd certainly been more circumspect than he had. But that didn't mean she couldn't play the same game of Catch Me If You Can. "How do you know? I'm just as capable of being free and easy as anyone else."

"You're speaking from experience? You've had other 'free and easy' relationships?"

She thought of the two men she'd slept with. Both had been long-term, steady boyfriends. "Not yet," she admitted. "But after what I've been through, I'm not looking for a commitment. Emotional entanglements are too…sticky and…and confining." The memory of Kyle coming forward to tell her he'd been with Noelle made her want to bang her head on the steering wheel again. "Not to mention painful," she added. "And when they don't work out, you have to deal with regret for getting involved in the first place."

"I couldn't have said it better myself."

"Why shouldn't I have my fun just like everyone else?" she asked, warming to her defiance. "I'm an adult. I can do whatever I want."

"Now you're getting me excited."

She heard the humor in his voice but chose to ignore it. "Maybe

I've been playing it too safe. Maybe I wouldn't be the one nursing a broken heart if I was willing to take a walk on the wild side once in a while."

"I'll buy that."

Again, she ignored the subtle smile in his voice because she loved feeling empowered. Just the idea of breaking the rules and getting away with it seemed to revive her flagging spirits.

But her enthusiasm dimmed as fast as it had dawned when he said, "Great. Come on over. Venus is out tonight. I'll show you."

Shit. She'd gone too far. She'd merely wanted him to respect her as someone equally competent to make that choice. Instead he'd called her bluff.

Suddenly feeling the need to backpedal, she searched for a good excuse. "I would, but…you're not the right kind of guy for my first hookup."

"Are you kidding?" he said. "I'm the *perfect* guy. And I'm volunteering."

"That's kind of you, but…it wouldn't be…*smart*."

"Define smart."

"We wouldn't gel. We're not…compatible."

"Because…"

She swallowed hard. He knew he appealed to women, knew she was no exception. What would he accept that would allow her to save face? "I'd be a boring partner for a thrill-seeker like you."

"That's like saying you have to wash your hair," he said flatly. "If you're stepping up your game, you're really going to have to do better. You're all talk."

"No, I'm not," she said. "Think of the women you've been with. The variety. The experience. I'd be…meat and potatoes when you're used to caviar."

"Olivia?"

It wasn't hot outside. As a matter of fact, it was a bit chilly. Yet she was sweating. "Yes?"

"Why don't you let me decide what turns me on?"

Because she'd long ago eliminated Brandon as a romantic

possibility. She knew she couldn't remain as aloof as he did. He seemed to sense the same thing, seemed to understand that she wasn't good at dealing with someone like him. "You've never even acted interested."

"Do you remember prom?" he asked.

Of course she did. That night was tucked away in a special file in her brain, one she accessed every now and then so she could relive his good-night kiss. No one else had ever kissed her in quite the same way.

But she didn't want to think about that now. She was too scared. "That was years ago."

"I know. But I've wanted you ever since. I'll be here if you change your mind," he said, and hung up.

Olivia pressed her good hand over her face. She wasn't sure what had just happened, how she and Brandon had rounded the corner from "acquaintances who'd once had a class together and went to a school dance" to "I've wanted you ever since" in such a short time. She figured it was her fault. She'd sent the wrong signals, especially when she'd had to let Brandon know she'd been telling others they were having sex. But she couldn't accept what he'd offered, no matter how reckless and angry and fatalistic she might be feeling. One night with him would be enough to set her recovery back by months.

Somehow, her life just kept getting more complicated…

She told herself to head back to her parents' house and turn in. She had so much to do in the morning.

This wedding had to go without a hitch, had to run more smoothly than any event she'd ever planned, or she'd get the blame for anything that went wrong. After all her efforts, she certainly didn't want to be accused of sabotage.

Too bad she didn't have internet, or she could work on her computer right here, she thought with a frown. Her parents had service, but she was still dragging her feet about returning there.

Briefly she considered renting a room at one of the two bed-

and-breakfasts in town. They'd have internet. But she didn't dare spend the money. Her savings were off-limits. Besides, one of Kyle's best friends owned The Gold Nugget. That crossed it off her list right there.

Sexy Sadie's, a local bar fashioned after an old-time saloon, caught her eye. She watched several people come and go, was contemplating stopping there for a drink, when her cell phone rang.

It was Kyle. She almost didn't answer. But if he was at her house, her mother, father or sister had likely asked him to pass on a message. She had to stop thinking of him as her ex and start thinking of him as her brother-in-law.

"Ick," she muttered but, with a sigh, hit the talk button. "What can I do for you?"

"You can answer one question," he replied.

This didn't sound as though he was planning to pass on a message. "Does Noelle know you're calling me?"

He didn't answer. "Are you already with Brandon?"

"No."

"Are you really seeing him?"

She curled her fingernails into her palms. Making up a relationship that didn't exist was pathetic. She should never have done it. Look what had happened with Brandon as a result! Just the thought of him lying in his bed, waiting for her, made her yearn for more than the memory of that one kiss all those years ago.

"No!" she said, as much to herself as him.

"Thank God."

"Not that it should matter to you," she added, feeling more sane.

"I know, it's just… I believed you."

After the doubt Brandon had shown that anyone would be convinced they were seeing each other, she knew she should feel vindicated. But he obviously understood who she was better than Kyle did. Which was odd. "Even though I've been living in Sacramento for the past few months?" she said.

"He'd be willing to make the drive. He has a thing for you. I could sense his interest the whole time you and I were together."

Strange though it seemed, given their limited contact over the years, she'd always had a thing for him, too. She'd just never allowed herself to entertain the possibility of letting it go anywhere.

"I'm telling you we almost got into a fight at Thanksgiving because of the way he kept looking at you."

Olivia hadn't noticed anything amiss, nothing beyond the usual push-pull she felt whenever Brandon was around. He'd shown up for dinner, but he'd stayed only long enough to eat. As far as she was concerned, he'd done nothing wrong.

"He didn't even speak to me," she said.

"He might try now."

"So you're...what? Giving me fair warning?"

"I'm letting you know that getting involved with him wouldn't be a smart move. You remember how he treated your sister—"

"I like that better than how *you've* treated my sister!"

"Ouch," he said, but she ignored him.

"Besides, that was years ago, when he was home from college for the summer. And she was *stalking* him, Kyle. She spied on him with another woman. That would make anyone angry."

"That's not the way she tells the story. She says he was pursuing her, leading several women on at the same time."

Because she didn't want to admit the truth. He'd discover that was a common occurrence. "I believe Brandon."

"Over your own sister?"

"Yes. Absolutely. Look, I appreciate all the brotherly love, but—"

"*Brotherly* love?" he interrupted. "Would you just...stop? Please? Do you think this is any easier for me?"

The desperation in his voice surprised her.

"I screwed up," he went on. "And now I'm paying the price. But I don't want you to suffer any more than you already have because of my stupidity."

Somehow his words made her even angrier than if he'd said he adored her sister and always had. "If you're having second thoughts, I'm not the one to talk to."

There was a long silence. Then he said, "I realize that."

"What is it you hold against Brandon, anyway?" she asked.

"You know how he is. He's stubborn and egotistical and…and difficult to get along with."

She wrapped her arms around herself and stared out at the town she loved so much. Kyle had cost her even this. She'd planned to come back but now…she felt as if she'd been cast adrift, as if Whiskey Creek was no longer her anchor. "How does that affect me?"

"He can't commit, and as much as you're trying to pretend you're not looking for love, I know you too well. He's not the kind of man you need."

As if Kyle was any better! He'd set himself up with that statement. But this time she let it go. "Have you talked to him recently?"

"I don't need to."

"Maybe you're going by dated information. Maybe he's matured and you're missing out on having a great brother."

"I'm not missing out on anything."

"You could cut him a little slack, you know. He's in your wedding party."

"For the sake of my parents."

She understood how familial obligation played a role this weekend. She doubted she'd even be attending the wedding were it not for Nancy and Ham. "Now you know why I'm here."

"I knew that before."

Again, the door opening and closing at Sexy Sadie's caught her eye. "I have to go."

"Wait—"

"For what, Kyle? Get some sleep. You'll need to be in top form this weekend."

He'd dared to call her, so she knew he wasn't with Noelle. Her sister was probably in bed, getting her beauty rest. That meant she could return to her parents'.

But Olivia couldn't go back there quite yet. Telling herself she'd have just one drink, she drove down the street and parked in front of the bar.

Chapter Six

Brandon's phone woke him. "Hello?" he muttered, squinting to see the time displayed on his digital alarm.

He was pretty sure it read 1:10 a.m.

"Brandon?"

Olivia. He recognized her voice immediately—although he could tell there was something wrong. "Yes?"

"I'm sorry, Brandon."

She sounded genuinely distraught. "For what, honey? It's okay that you didn't come over. I wasn't really expecting you."

"I meant for b-bothering you in the middle of the night."

When she sniffed, he gripped the phone harder. She was crying. "That's okay, too. What's wrong?"

"Um…do you think… Would it be too much trouble… I hate to ask this, but…"

"Where are you?" He was awake enough to hear that she was slurring her words. That, together with the loud music in the background, indicated she was at a bar.

"S-s-sexy S-S-Sadie's!" she announced, laughing. "I think I'm drunk. I was only going to have one drink, but… I don't know what happened."

"You had more."

"Yep."

He'd assumed she left town. He'd known she'd never show up at his place. "Do you need me to come get you?"

"Would you?" She seemed infinitely relieved.

"Of course." He rolled out of bed and began to dress.

"I shouldn't have called *you*. Today's the first time we ever really talked since prom so…it's rude, right? To do that to a new friend?"

"Is that what we are?"

"Aren't we?"

He smiled at her distress. "Of course we are."

"Okay, good. Anyway, I'd call someone else but...all my other friends belong to Kyle."

"They what?"

"They're *his* friends. Callie and Eve and Riley and Ted and Cheyenne..."

She seemed to lose her train of thought before she could name all the members of the tight clique Kyle had belonged to since grade school. Rattling them off by memory wouldn't be that easy to do sober, since there were at least ten.

"Losing them, along with everything else, must've been hard." He doubted they liked her any less, but he could see why she could no longer hang out with them.

"Cheyenne's *so* nice," she was saying.

He found his shoes and headed to the kitchen for his keys. "Cheyenne's nice," he agreed.

"And here I am wallowing in self-pity because my boyfriend got my sister pregnant."

"You'll get through this. I'm coming, okay? I've got my keys in my hand. I'll talk to you when I get there."

"I'm sorry, Brandon. You shouldn't have to come out so late."

"I don't mind," he said. "Just stay put. I'm on my way."

Chapter Seven

Brandon felt as if he deserved a medal. He'd managed to stop Olivia when she'd started peeling off her clothes. There'd been one moment when he'd almost succumbed when she looked her arms around his neck and tried to pull him into bed with her. She kept insisting she could do casual sex, and, Lord, did he want to believe her. With her body up against his, the silk of her panties coming out the back of her loosened shorts, he'd nearly thrown honor and decency to the wind. Sternly reminding himself that she wasn't in any condition to give consent, he helped her remove the shorts she was so intent on getting off but refused every advance.

And now he was paying the price. Tense and completely unsatisfied, he tossed and turned while the girl he'd dreamed about for over a decade lay in the next room wearing nothing but her T-shirt and a pair of pretty panties. He felt her soft skin in his mind every time he closed his eyes.

The memory alone made him hard.

He could only hope she'd want him as badly in the morning, but he knew her better judgment would take over by then. As much as she *thought* she wanted a wild affair, something to fill the sudden loneliness, it was all too typical of being on the rebound.

Frustrated with his inability to shut down, he rolled over to search for his phone on the nightstand.

He scrolled through his pictures, looking for one his mother had sent him, months ago, from Thanksgiving. It was a group shot with Kyle and Olivia and the whole family.

As he stared at her image, at her and Kyle smiling for the camera, he remembered how difficult it had been to see them together. He didn't want to sacrifice the life he had, but she'd always been a temptation. He'd hated the idea that his stepbrother, of all people, would end up with her, knew it would make every family event a challenge.

The ding signaling a text drew Brandon from his thoughts.

Have you been calling her since we took our break? Did you wait even that long before making your move?

What does it matter to you? he replied. Aren't you getting married this weekend?

Have you been chasing her?

Brandon didn't bother to deny the attraction. Was waiting to see if you were going to wake up and realize you're ruining your life.

This time when there was no response, Brandon figured it was just as well. He leaned over to return his phone to the nightstand—but another message appeared.

I have no choice.

Propping his pillows behind his back, he typed, Yes, you do. Don't let your sense of duty drag you into making a bad situation worse.

What about the baby?

What about it? Did you ever think she might've gotten pregnant on purpose? That she's manipulating you? Brandon wouldn't put it past her.

She's still pregnant.

You can support the baby, be a good father regardless. Maybe it's not optimal to do it single, but you can make it work. That sort of thing happens all the time.

There was a long wait before the next text came in. Brandon had just decided Kyle must've gone to sleep when he heard the reply arrive.

Not to me it doesn't. I want my kid to have my name, my presence. I don't want to be a part-time dad with a stepparent joining the action.

Brandon could sense the resolve in those words. He could easily understand the sentiment behind them, too. But he was afraid that Kyle's background and misguided nobility were pulling him into a nightmare of catastrophic proportions.

So how should he answer? He'd spent the past decade telling himself he didn't really care about his stepbrother. But...he couldn't help admiring Kyle's determination to fall on his sword. He was a much better person than Brandon had ever given him credit for. Maybe Bob had a right to be so damn proud. Brandon couldn't have made himself marry Noelle.

But no one—even Olivia—knew her the way he did. Although he was trying to believe she'd grown up and changed, he'd seen her at her worst, when she was obsessed and unrelenting and so narcissistic he couldn't even *like* her. He'd done everything he could to let her know he wasn't interested. But it made no impact whatsoever. If anything, she became *more* determined. He'd come home to find her waiting in his driveway, turn to see her staring in his window, "bump" into her so many times a day she could only be following him. He couldn't imagine a woman so out of touch with reality being successful in a marriage, even to a white knight like Kyle, who was willing to do 90 percent of the work.

I wish you'd listen to me, he wrote. There's something missing in Noelle.

I already know she had a crush on you. She was just being young and stupid and too forward.

Too forward? Her behavior went far beyond that. You're saying the Noelle she is now would never cross the lines she crossed back then?

Of course not, Kyle responded. Anyway, I could never undo the damage I've done. I can't go back to Olivia while Noelle has my baby. I might as well have some integrity and stand up and take responsibility for my actions.

Brandon wanted to reiterate that he'd be sorry if he married Noelle. But what good would it do? Kyle had made up his mind and nothing was going to change it. Then you need to let go of Olivia.

Again, Kyle's answer took a while to arrive. But Brandon waited because he knew it would come.

Won't be easy.

Olivia woke up to a splitting headache. It took effort just to open her eyes. She could see sunlight peeking around the cracks in the blinds, enough that she could make out an overburdened desk, a computer, a ship in a bottle and some tribal masks on the wall—but she didn't recognize any of it. Where was she?

Then it came to her. She'd gotten drunk last night, and Brandon had brought her home. She could remember him fighting to keep her clothes on. She could also remember trying to kiss him. She'd wanted him so badly…

Surprisingly enough, he was the one who'd resisted. "You're not interested?" she'd breathed.

"Not like this, sweetheart," he'd told her, and helped her remove only her shorts before tucking her in. She'd gotten the impression he'd been tempted despite those words, was fairly certain he'd almost turned back at the door. But she was embarrassed all the same. Now both of the Arnold girls had thrown themselves at him.

Brandon interrupted her moment of regret with a brisk knock. "Olivia? You awake?"

She cringed at the fact that she was going to have to face him, and so soon. She'd made a complete fool of herself last night, first by getting drunk, then by trying to get him into bed.

"I'm awake, but I'm not very happy about it," she replied.

He poked his head inside. Freshly showered and wearing a black V-neck T-shirt with a pair of well-worn jeans and flip-flops, he looked better than ever—which was saying a lot. She wasn't sure what accounted for that, unless just getting to know him made him more and more attractive. Maybe it was that she finally had some respect for him, since he'd rejected her advances.

"How are you feeling?" he asked.

She shoved a hand through her messy hair. "Like roadkill."

He chuckled. "I was afraid of that. Would you like something to eat?"

Could her stomach tolerate food? She didn't dare take the risk. "No, but a pain pill would be nice. What time is it?"

"Nearly nine."

"Oh, no!" She shot out of bed, then staggered and nearly fell.

Somehow, he managed to get inside the room quickly enough to catch her and guide her back to the bed.

"I've missed my first appointment," she explained, raising her good hand to her pounding head. "I was supposed to meet Abby, the event planner, at the Pullman Mansion, at eight. I've got to go!"

He frowned at her. "I don't think you're up to it."

She'd been stupid to drink last night. She wasn't used to that much alcohol. "I don't have any choice." Her tongue felt thick and unwieldy. "Have you seen my phone?" She glanced around but couldn't locate it.

"Your purse is out on the counter."

When she started to get up, he pressed her back. "I'll get it."

He returned with a glass of water, two ibuprofen tablets and her purse, which contained her phone.

"She's tried to reach me five times," she said as she checked her call record. "My mother and Noelle have both called twice." She lifted her eyes to his. "What am I going to tell them?"

"I say you tell them that you're not feeling well and to get by the best they can without you."

"I can't do that! The wedding's tomorrow night." She rubbed her temples, hoping to mitigate some of the pain. The hand she'd injured was no longer swollen, but it was still sore, which didn't help with her hangover.

He urged her to swallow the painkillers and watched as she obeyed. "Fine. Get in the shower. I'll call and tell them you're on your way." He took the glass. "Then I'll drive you to your car."

It wouldn't go over very well to have Brandon act as her secretary when she'd blown such an important appointment. They'd assume she was purposely causing problems. But it would postpone the confrontation until she felt more equipped to handle it. And letting them believe she was having an affair was better than the pathetic truth that she wasn't handling Kyle and Noelle's union quite as nonchalantly as she'd planned.

Regardless of anything else, she deserved one small rebellion, didn't she?

"Thanks." She handed him her phone. "They're right there on my list of favorites."

"Towels are on the rack to the left of the sink," he said.

Despite the pressure she was feeling to hurry, she could only move gingerly. She made her way to the door before turning back.

They stared at each other for a few seconds. Olivia didn't understand why, but she couldn't look away.

"You could steal him back if you want," he said at length. "You know that, right?"

He was serious. He was telling her that if Kyle was the man she really wanted to be with, she could fight for him and would probably win.

But it wasn't so simple. There were other people involved. Not to mention the baby.

"I wouldn't want to hurt the people that would hurt," she said.

"Despite what Noelle has done to you?"

She sighed. "Yes."

"Then you must not want him enough."

"I don't," she said. "Not anymore." That didn't mean what she was going through didn't hurt. But she couldn't get back with Kyle knowing he had a child with her sister.

At least, for the first time since falling in love with Kyle, she was feeling desire for another man. The excitement that brought told her life after Kyle was possible; she just had to be careful or she'd land herself in an even worse situation.

"I'm glad to hear it," he said.

Suddenly she became very conscious of the fact that she was wearing nothing but her panties and T-shirt. She was better covered than if she were wearing a bathing suit. But what had almost happened last night, what she'd *wanted* to have happen, made her feel very exposed.

The way his gaze traveled over her body, as intimate as a caress, made her breasts tingle. She struggled to find her voice. "Did I really try to rip off my clothes when you put me to bed?"

He grinned, which was answer enough.

"Thought so." She'd actually brought it up so she could apologize. "I'm sorry. From what you said on the phone, I assumed that…that you might welcome a bed partner."

"You think I was rejecting you?"

She felt her eyebrows slide up. "Weren't you?"

"Next time ask me when I have the option of saying yes."

Chapter Eight

Olivia had left her luggage at Brandon's house. Since her family already knew she was with him, there was no reason to leave his cabin on their account. He'd invited her to use his guest room for as long as she wanted, and she figured she might as well take him up on it.

That meant she'd be going back…

"Olivia, what do you think?"

She blinked before focusing on her mother, who was wearing a flowery dress and had her hair sectioned off in rollers with a scarf tied over the lot, making her look very 1960s housewife. "About what?"

"The bows that go on the chairs!" The impatience in Nancy's voice suggested she'd already asked once. "Noelle doesn't think they match the table runners. Are you sure these are the shade we ordered?"

Olivia had expected these meetings to be difficult. But she was so preoccupied with Brandon, she was finding them more of a nuisance than a challenge.

"They're a shade off," she admitted. "I borrowed these from River City to save money, remember? That's what you wanted me to do."

"But will they look bad?" Nancy refastened a roller that was threatening to fall out. Olivia had tried to convince her that a round brush and a blow dryer would give her the curl she wanted, but she insisted her hair looked best when she "put it up" for a day— and she was going all out for the wedding.

"I think they'll be fine," Olivia assured her. "They won't be right up against each other. See?" She held the two fabrics a few inches apart. "You won't notice they're not exact, especially with all the shades of pink and peach in the flower arrangements."

Noelle shot her an accusing glower. "I thought they'd match better than *that*."

She said this as if it was Olivia's fault they didn't, although it had been Noelle's choice. She'd wanted to save money on the chair covers so she could get a pair of very expensive heels, which wouldn't even show beneath her dress.

But it wasn't only the color of the chair bows that was bothering her. She'd been hostile all morning. Olivia could *feel* the animosity; she just wasn't sure of the cause. Was it the difficulty of pulling off an event like this? Or was it that Noelle knew Kyle had called her last night?

Maybe she'd been the cause of a fight…

Or was Noelle upset that she was hanging out with Brandon?

"Regardless, it's too late to change now," Olivia said. Normally she would've gone to greater pains to reassure the bride, but she meant that statement in more ways than one. Noelle had made her decision. And in the process, she'd hurt and embarrassed Olivia, cost their parents a great deal of money by demanding such an expensive wedding, made a public fool of Kyle and humiliated herself.

Now she was carrying Kyle's baby.

It was time for her to quit being so selfish.

"We could do without the bows," her mother suggested, obviously trying to placate Noelle.

"Is that what you want?" Olivia turned to her sister, making it clear by her tone that she didn't care either way.

Noelle pressed her fingers to her eyes. "Ugh! This is turning into a nightmare! Some wedding planner *you* are. I thought having a wedding was supposed to be fun."

"I think it helps to be in love," Olivia murmured. Fortunately Nancy didn't hear. Abby was showing her where they'd set up the table for all the candy.

"I *am* in love!" Noelle insisted.

"With Kyle or Brandon?" Olivia asked.

Noelle's lips thinned, and her eyes grew so cold they gave Olivia chills. "You're trying to ruin my wedding!"

Seriously? Was that all she was concerned about? There was so much more at stake!

"I'm afraid you're going to ruin Kyle's *life*," she responded, realizing, for the first time, that what she'd suffered might turn out to be paltry by comparison.

"How'd it go today?" Brandon asked as he let her in.

Olivia was so tired she could scarcely move. This week had been emotionally draining, and she was ready to crawl into bed. She hadn't even taken the time to have lunch. She'd been running too late, so she'd gone all day without a meal. But they had to be at the rehearsal dinner in an hour. She'd eat then.

"It was weird," she told him.

He went into the kitchen as she dropped onto his couch.

"It's always weird when your sister is marrying the man you love," he said.

Love? Or loved? She couldn't decide anymore.

She thought back on the past seven hours. Her sister had grown more and more hateful throughout the day. "It got even weirder than that," she said.

"In what way?" He brought her a sliced orange, which she accepted gratefully.

"I'm beginning to feel sorry for Kyle, if that makes any sense."

"Makes all the sense in the world to me. I feel sorry for him, too."

She offered him a tired grin. "That's harsh. Just because she stalked you for a few months?"

A chuckle let her know he understood she was teasing. "It was the creepiest thing I've ever been through, seeing her face staring in at me through the window."

"I suspect she still has a thing for you."

He tried to shrug it off. "Don't say that."

"It's true. Our…relationship is driving her crazy. I'd tell her we haven't slept together, but I don't think she'd believe me."

"She's getting married. It shouldn't matter to her either way."

She savored the sweetness of the orange he'd given her. "Unless she's only in it for the shoes."

"The shoes?"

"The celebration, the attention. This wedding shines a bright light on her and announces to everyone in Whiskey Creek that Kyle, a guy highly admired, prefers her to every other woman, including me."

"The sad truth is…he doesn't."

"I don't even care anymore." Pushing her plate away, she leaned back and closed her eyes. "All I want is for this wedding to be over."

"You're exhausted."

She didn't answer. She told herself she could rest for fifteen minutes. Then she had to get through the rehearsal dinner. But Brandon nudged her before she could drift off. "Come on. Nap on the bed. It'll be more comfortable."

"I can't move," she objected, but that didn't deter him. He simply scooped her up and carried her down the hall.

When he took her to his room instead of hers, she didn't have the energy to protest. At the moment, she was worthless as a sex partner. The next thing she knew, she was face down on his pillow, as his fingers massaged the tight muscles in her neck and shoulders.

She groaned. "Why are you being so nice to me?"

He laughed softly. "Don't trust it. Considering what you do to me, I have only evil intentions."

"Would it make you any less of a villain to lie down with me?"

"I suppose that wouldn't hurt my reputation too much," he said wryly, and scooted in beside her.

With his shoulder as her pillow and his fingers moving gently through her hair, she felt oddly content as she drifted off.

A screech woke Brandon from a dead sleep. One look at Olivia, blinking awake next to him, told him she hadn't made that sound. She was as startled as he was. So what—

Then the sound came again—*"O-li-via!"*—and he realized what was going on. "Shit! The rehearsal dinner!"

Olivia was already scrambling off the bed, but she didn't have a chance to speak before Noelle started screaming again.

"I know you're in there, damn you!" She banged on the door. "How could you? *How could you do this to me?*"

"What time is it?" Olivia cried.

"Nearly eight."

Her face went pale. "Oh, God! I overslept."

Brandon felt terrible. "I'm sorry. I never intended to fall asleep. I just shut my eyes for a minute."

She rubbed her face as if trying to get her bearings. "We have to go."

Galvanized into action, he hopped out of bed. "You go change. I'll answer the door."

"No, I'll answer. She's so upset there's no telling what she might say."

"Exactly." He gave her a little push. "Better if she says it to me. She can't hurt me, and it might blow off some of the steam. Get ready."

Although reluctant to let him handle her temperamental sister, she seemed to understand the urgency of showing up at the dinner party—where the rest of the wedding party was waiting for them.

"I've got it," he assured her, and she hurried into the bathroom.

"Olivia!" Noelle yelled.

He opened the door before she could knock again.

She immediately stepped back so she could look up at him. "Where's my sister?"

"Getting ready. You can head back. We'll be there as soon as we can."

"Why weren't you there *an hour* ago?"

He stepped out and closed the door so that Olivia wouldn't have to hear this. "We fell asleep, okay? I'm sorry about that—"

"You're not sorry for anything!" She looked a little crazed with her hair falling out of whatever was holding it up. "You're busy banging my sister when it's supposed to be *my* turn!"

Knowing she couldn't have meant that quite the way it sounded, he raised his eyebrows, giving her a chance to clarify.

"To have what I want," she said, her cheeks flushing red. "To have everyone's cooperation. It's *my* wedding. This isn't about you...or her!"

"Then don't make it about us," he said. "Go ahead and enjoy it. We aren't standing in your way."

"Yes, you are! She's my planner! She's supposed to be there taking care of things!"

He lowered his voice, hoping she'd do the same. "The wedding isn't until tomorrow, Noelle. Everything will be fine. Just...calm down, okay? Your sister doesn't need you to flip out right now."

"You're worried about what *she* needs? What about *me*?"

"What about you?" he retorted. "Have you ever stopped to consider how what you've done—what you're doing—might be making *her* feel?"

She narrowed her eyes at his mussed hair and wrinkled clothes. "I *know* what she's been feeling," she said, and stomped away.

Olivia was so self-conscious about entering the ballroom more than an hour late, and with Brandon at her side, she could barely stand it. But she couldn't turn back time. And since Noelle had probably announced that she'd found them together, Olivia saw no benefit in appearing separately.

The instant they stepped through the door, twenty-four sets of eyes turned in their direction. Kyle's family. Her family. Lindsey Manelli, Noelle's maid of honor and best friend. The tight-knit group Kyle had grown up with, including the female members, who were in Noelle's line because she wouldn't have had much of a line without them.

Olivia had expected to attract everyone's attention yet she still felt her stomach muscles tighten. Brandon, on the other hand, seemed to take it in stride. He smiled as if he was completely relaxed and had no reason to be embarrassed. And he kept his hand at the small of her back, encouraging her to follow his lead.

She tried, but her smile faltered when her father pinned her beneath a disapproving stare.

Trying not to allow his disappointment, her sister's angry glare or Kyle's stony expression to attack her confidence, she apologized to the wedding party at large, without providing an excuse for her tardiness. Then she ran through a brief rehearsal just to make sure everyone was aware of how the ceremony should proceed.

Then they were off to the upscale restaurant in the front of the mansion, where Kyle had booked a private room for everyone to have a steak dinner. Noelle had insisted that she could never serve less than the best at *her* wedding. And since Kyle was paying for it, Noelle was getting everything she wanted—the most expensive meal on the menu along with some fancy Napa Valley champagne.

Once they were all seated, the tension eased enough for polite conversation. Everyone joined in except Kyle.

Noelle didn't seem to notice that her groom was upset. Her gaze darted to Brandon every few seconds, even though he didn't pay her the slightest attention. When he did look up, it was to catch Olivia's eye.

Determined to get through the meal as fast as possible, Olivia concentrated on her salad and champagne and tried to block out everything else. But Brandon's mother whispered something to him, and Olivia couldn't help straining to hear what was said.

"Why on earth were you so late? You promised me you'd be on your best behavior!"

"I *am* on my best behavior," he said with a mock scowl that nearly made Olivia laugh. He hadn't answered his mother's question, but when he leaned back and put his arm around her, she seemed so pleased by the loving gesture that she let the rest go.

Smooth, Olivia thought. *Too* smooth. She was going to have to be careful not to fall for him like everyone else.

Chapter Nine

Kyle felt as if the night would never end. He knew he was drinking too much, but he had to do something. Otherwise, he'd get into a public argument with his soon-to-be wife. Noelle was playing games, taunting Olivia wherever and whenever she could. She didn't realize that it made her look jealous and inferior and foolish.

This was the woman he was marrying. But the sense of doom that acknowledgment brought him wasn't the worst of what he was suffering. Not tonight. The worst was watching Brandon and Olivia together. The way they'd walked into the room, united against everyone else. The intimacy of the looks they exchanged across the table. The smiles. They were captivated with each other. He'd never seen his brother so attentive to a woman. He wanted to believe Brandon was just trying to get under his skin, but he knew better. Brandon had his faults. He was competitive and stubborn and determined to live life on his own terms, but he was honest, and he wasn't petty.

Kyle had expected this wedding to be difficult, but it was proving to be almost impossible.

"So have you decided where you'll live?" his future mother-in-law asked.

This had been a subject of much contention. He wanted to stay in the same house he'd been living in for five years. It wasn't big or ostentatious, but it was comfortable and convenient.

Noelle wanted him to buy her a mansion in town. She worked at a dress boutique, making minimum wage, and used the excuse that it was closer to her job.

"We're going to knock down the old Foreman house and build our dream home," Noelle declared.

Kyle gaped at her. Where had *that* come from? She'd been trying to talk him into that plan, but he'd never agreed. "No, we're not," he said. "Noelle will be moving in with me."

"We can't live in that cracker box!" she snapped. "If we build in town, we can have everything just the way we want."

The way *she* wanted. That was all that ever mattered.

He could tell he was making his parents uncomfortable by not respecting her wishes, but the alcohol was interfering with his ability to control the negative thoughts and emotions rising to the surface. "I'm not ready to build in town."

"That's not what you said when we talked about it last," Noelle said, despite the look he gave her, asking her to drop it. "You said you'd think about it."

He shrugged. "I have. The answer's no."

"What I want doesn't count?" Her voice grew shrill. "We're going to stay in that dump just because *you like it*?"

His place was one of the nicest in the area. It wasn't even close to being a "dump." She was just trying to get her own way, like the spoiled child she really was, but before he could say so, someone touched his shoulder.

"Hey, you."

Gail had left her table in the middle of the main dish to rescue him. He knew that as soon as her gaze cut to the waiter filling his glass on the other side.

"What's up?" he said.

"I have a toast I want to do tomorrow," she replied, "but I'd like to check with you to see if what I've got planned is okay. Do you have a minute?"

He glanced around the table at all the faces watching him and managed to conjure up what he hoped was a passable smile. "Of course." He dipped his head toward the rest of them. "Excuse us."

"What about your dinner?" Noelle's mother asked. "Can't you talk about the toast after you finish? You've hardly eaten a thing!"

Kyle put his napkin to the side of his plate. "I'm too excited to eat," he said, even though excitement played no role.

Eager to escape, he followed his friend to a patio that was empty except for a few lingering diners who congregated around a table at one end.

"What's going on?" he murmured.

"That's what I'm wondering," she said, turning to confront him. "I've never seen you drink so much at someone else's rehearsal dinner—and this is your own!"

"I'm fine. I—"

She squeezed his arm. "Kyle, please. If the rest of the gang could've gotten out of that room without making it look too odd, they'd be here with me, trying to talk some sense into you."

He knew where this was going. "She's having my baby, Gail."

She pressed two fingers to each temple. "I know! I understand you feel responsible for that. And I admire how determined you are to do the right thing. But… I can't bear to see you unhappy. We all feel like we're attending your funeral instead of your wedding!"

"It's just extra hard," he said. "With Olivia here."

"I've let my work take over my life, so I'm no expert on relationships," she said. "But…if you won't cancel this, you should at least put it off until you're more confident in your decision."

He laughed. "Are you kidding me? The wedding's tomorrow, Gail. There's no way I can change anything." If he backed out, he feared Noelle would make it impossible for him to ever see his child. "I'm going to be a father. Nothing can take precedence over that."

They were almost out of the room, almost free, when Kyle's father caught up with Brandon and pulled him off to one side. "So what are you doing to keep busy now that the cast is off?" he asked.

Olivia gritted her teeth at being detained. She couldn't wait to leave, to put the rehearsal dinner behind them and return to the peace of Brandon's secluded cabin. She needed to regroup, but she couldn't allow her eagerness to show.

"Just working out every day, trying to get in shape for the season."

Brandon answered Bob's questions politely, but Olivia could tell he was purposely playing up the ski-bum image. He'd already told her that spring and summer were almost as busy as fall and winter. He'd explained that he had to meet with his sponsors, be available to film commercials and participate in photo shoots, most of which required travel to New York or Los Angeles. He also had to appear at various events, and increase his presence on social networking sites. Professional skiing was a business as much as a sport, and the stacks of paperwork on his desk seemed to prove it.

So did the poster samples he'd been sent. One showed him dropping, seemingly without effort, down the face of an alarmingly steep mountain wearing an expensive brand of ski gear. Another captured his smiling face in a pair of Oakley goggles with ice crystals caught in the beard growth along his jaw.

He could've told his stepfather about these things. He could also have mentioned that he was making a tremendous amount of money. Although they hadn't spoken about that aspect, Olivia could tell it was true. But Brandon refused to vie for Bob's approval, and Olivia couldn't help but respect that.

"Can the leg take another season?" This question was spoken with apparent concern, but Olivia heard the subtext. Bob thought Brandon should hang up his skis and get serious about life.

She guessed Brandon interpreted his tone the same way and that made her sad. Brandon was one of the best skiers in the world, yet Bob treated him as if he hadn't accomplished anything.

"Leg's getting stronger all the time," Brandon assured him. "It'll be fine."

Olivia imagined the pain Brandon must've suffered from that injury. Another daunting descent would require courage, but she had no doubt he'd do it. His daring made her smile.

She was still smiling when she realized that Brandon was watching her with a speculative expression. He had somehow guessed that her smile was related to him. His lips quirked slightly as if he was tempted to grin back at her, even though a grin wasn't appropriate to the conversation he was having with the disapproving Bob.

"Well, you've got several months before you go back to Europe. You want to learn what it's like to put in a hard day's work, come on out to the stables," Bob was saying.

Brandon thanked him for the opportunity but begged off, saying he was going backpacking in Nicaragua. That didn't win him any points with Bob, but it made Olivia chuckle. Brandon knew just how to tweak his stepfather's nose without appearing to be impolite.

She turned to hide her mirth and came face-to-face with Brandon's mother. Paige had been talking to Nancy and Ham, who'd just left.

"I'm sorry about how things worked out for you with Kyle," Paige said, almost conspiratorially. "We miss seeing you at the house."

"I miss you, too," Olivia responded, feeling an odd tug for what used to be.

"Brandon's far more of a handful," she responded. "But it's *impossible* not to love him."

Another warning—in case Olivia wasn't already a believer. "We're just friends," she said, but Paige had already started a separate conversation with Cheyenne Christensen, whose mother was suffering from cancer. Olivia didn't think Paige had heard the rejoinder.

"What'd she say?" Brandon had finally broken away from his stepfather.

"She said she loves you."

Taking hold of her elbow, he guided her out. "Was she shaking her head as if it was against her will?" he asked with a laugh.

Olivia had been so eager to get to Brandon's house, but even before they walked through the door she knew she wouldn't be able to unwind the way she'd envisioned. They no longer had to cope with the myriad emotions swirling around the wedding party. Instead, they had to cope with each other, and that was almost more difficult, because every word they'd spoken on the drive back, every accidental touch, felt like foreplay to a sexual encounter she knew she'd be foolish to allow.

It wasn't so unusual for a woman in her situation to want to jump into bed with the next handsome guy. But, oddly enough, this was different. It didn't feel as if Brandon would be a substitute for Kyle. It felt as if *Kyle* had always been a substitute for *Brandon*!

She was fairly certain the rebound experience wasn't supposed to work like that and couldn't figure out why her situation was so different. She and Kyle had only been apart for about three months, and thanks to his betrayal, those three months had been the most miserable of her life. That meant she still loved him, didn't it?

So how could she care more about being with Brandon than she did about being hurt and angry over Kyle's Big Mistake? What he'd done meant they could never be together again.

But that didn't seem to matter so much anymore.

"Would you like some herbal tea?" Brandon asked as she put her purse on the counter.

"What kind do you have?"

"A blend I found in Thailand." He reached into a cupboard to get the box, which he showed her. "You should try it."

She pictured them drinking tea together, talking into the night and eventually ending up in his bed. She wanted that exact scenario so badly she almost chose satisfaction over caution.

Maybe she would have, if not for his mother's words: *It's impossible not to love him.*

She had an inkling that might be true. She'd always been drawn to Brandon, but never more so than in the past two days. She figured it was better to get away while she could. So, after a brief hesitation, she shook her head. "No, thanks. I've got to get up early. I wouldn't want to oversleep the way I did today."

She halfway hoped he'd try to convince her to stay up with him. But he didn't. He told her he understood and added a polite good-night.

Forcing a smile to hide her disappointment, she nodded, but before she turned away, she caught sight of something that held her fast. When he moved, a grimace crossed his face and he shifted to take his weight off the leg he'd broken in his skiing accident.

"Are you okay?" She'd heard him say his doctors had been able to put him back together, that he was healed and already training for the next season.

His expression cleared instantly. He even exerted normal pressure on his leg while putting away the tea. "Of course. Why?"

"I just thought…" She stopped herself. He wouldn't be planning to walk across Nicaragua if his leg was causing him trouble. She must've imagined that he felt pain. "Never mind," she said. "See you in the morning."

Chapter Ten

Something woke Olivia a few hours later. She wasn't sure what—until she listened carefully. Then she realized it was the TV. Although the house was otherwise dark and quiet, she could hear the drone of voices and wondered what Brandon was watching.

It had to be late.

She checked her phone on the nightstand. Sure enough, it was three thirty.

She tried to go back to sleep. It wasn't any of her business what Brandon was doing. But after lying awake for another twenty minutes, she got up to see if he was okay. Maybe he needed someone to cover him and turn off the TV...

He had a television in his bedroom. She'd seen it when they'd napped in there before. But that wasn't where she found him. Perhaps he'd thought he'd keep her awake if he used that one. Or he liked the loft better, because he was there, asleep in a recliner.

He'd changed into an old T-shirt and a pair of basketball shorts. That he'd wanted to get comfortable didn't come as any surprise, but his leg in a brace and buried beneath half a dozen ice packs did.

"Oh, God." She hadn't imagined the flicker of pain on his face earlier. Besides the brace and the ice, she saw a bottle of prescription pain medication on the table beside him. Obviously his leg was still giving him a great deal of trouble.

Her presence and the two words she'd uttered were enough to wake him. He opened his eyes and looked at her. Then he tried to sit up and grab for the remote, but it had fallen out of his hands and onto the floor.

She retrieved it for him, but by then she'd already seen what he probably didn't want her to see. He'd been watching the footage of his own fall. She could see the dark speck he made on the mountain, hear the helicopter from which they were filming and the frantic discussion going on between the cameraman and the pilot. She could also feel the tremendous concern, the sheer urgency of the situation. According to the stopwatch on the screen, whoever held the camera had been filming for two hours and forty-four minutes, but rescuers hadn't yet been able to reach Brandon on that steep slope.

How long did he have to lie there, in a crumpled heap, waiting? She'd never thought about that. She'd seen the same clip as everyone else—the part where he lost control and tumbled like a rag doll down the cliff, hitting rocks and trees along the way—but not this extended version. This wasn't for public consumption. She hadn't even considered how hard it would be for emergency help to get to him or how it must've felt for him to lie there suffering. It was a miracle they'd been able to rescue him at all.

"Are you wondering how you survived?" she asked.

"I'm wondering how I screwed up so badly, how I put myself in that position in the first place."

"You're good at what you do, Brandon, but...anyone can make a mistake. Especially on a slope like that."

He took the remote and snapped off the TV as if he couldn't bear to see any more, and she frowned as she studied his leg. "I hope you're really going backpacking across Nicaragua in two weeks because, if I remember right, I was invited to join you."

"I'll take you next summer." He shifted so he could remove the ice packs on his leg.

"So that invitation—it was just a fake?" Nudging his hands away, she stripped off the packs.

"Sort of. I have to leave town, but I won't be doing any backpacking."

"Where are you going?"

Obviously uncomfortable revealing this information, he cleared his throat. "There's a doctor in Europe. Thinks he can fix my leg." He motioned to a small refrigerator in the corner near the wet bar. "The packs go in there."

Apparently sitting up with his leg in a brace wasn't an unusual occurrence. "You need another operation?" she asked as she opened the fridge.

"At least one," he answered. "In order to regain full range of motion, it might take more."

"And you're not telling anyone because…"

Velcro rasped as he removed the brace and set it beside his chair. "I can't risk losing my sponsors."

She folded her arms. "And you haven't told anyone here at home because you're afraid we might leak the truth to the press?"

"Figured if I'm going to lie, I might as well be consistent among all my friends."

"What about your family?"

"What family?"

"Your mother loves you, Brandon."

"And she loves Bob and Kyle and will soon have a grandbaby. I've made my decision. There's no need to worry her."

How many times had his parents warned him not to take the risks he took? "If I was your mother, I'm pretty sure I'd want to know."

"I've considered that. But if I tell her, I essentially tell my step-father, too, and I don't want to hear him say, 'I told you so.' I especially don't want to put up with having him act as if I deserve this."

She could understand his feelings. She'd heard Bob expound on the subject of Brandon and his choice of career before. At the time, she'd agreed with him. Now she felt…torn. She wanted Brandon to be happy, to see him excel at what he loved. She just didn't want him to lose his life chasing the next adrenaline rush.

Groggy from sleep and possibly the painkiller, he seemed a little out of it, so she helped him to his feet. "Let's get you to bed." He grumbled, but he settled an arm over her shoulders so he could take some of the pressure off his bad leg.

"Back to Nicaragua."

"Are you sorry the trip's off?"

"I'm wondering why you invited me to go at all."

"Wishful thinking."

An adventure like that had sounded nice. It still did.

"And I knew you'd refuse," he added.

He also knew it made a believable cover for the length of time he'd be gone. She had to hand it to him. He was good at hiding the problem. "And if I hadn't?" she asked.

"You could come to Europe with me, travel around while I recuperate—as long as you stop by to see me once in a while."

She could imagine how lonely that would be—to have an operation in a foreign county when all your friends and family thought you were having such a great time they didn't bother to write or call. But, assuming he wasn't any more serious about having her join him in Europe than he'd been about Nicaragua, she let that comment slide. "You made yourself climb these stairs. Maybe if you didn't push yourself so hard, your leg would have a chance to heal on its own."

"Stairs are the least of my worries. I'm going to have to do much more than climb up to my loft if I want to hang on to my career."

He was scared, she realized. Scared that everything he'd been was somehow gone. He had to re-create himself.

She could relate to that. She'd embraced moving to Sacramento, had been eager to have a year to herself to see what she could do to expand her professional aspirations. But then her life had taken the Kyle-Noelle detour and she'd been floundering ever since.

"Would it be so terrible to retire?" Finished navigating the stairs, she guided him into the hall. "Surely you can't expect to ski such dangerous runs forever."

"No, not forever. Just another two or three years. I'm not ready to give it up. When I go out, it'll be on *my* terms."

The conviction in his voice told her that even if his efforts didn't pay off, he'd put up one hell of a fight. "Then I believe you'll make a comeback. If not this season, the next."

He didn't respond. She feared he knew her encouragement was simply that—encouragement.

"For now you need to get some sleep," she said. "Or you won't convince anyone that leg has healed."

They'd reached his room. She hesitated at the entrance, expecting him to continue on himself, but, keeping one arm around her shoulders, he touched her face with the opposite hand.

When she looked up at him, he held her chin so that she couldn't look away as he murmured, "Come to bed with me."

Brandon knew Olivia had every reason in the world to say no. She'd just been through a terrible breakup. She probably wasn't over Kyle. The last thing she needed was to make love with a man who'd soon be leaving, most likely for months.

But he couldn't help trying to capture and hold on to the special quality that made her so difficult to forget.

"Brandon—"

At the distress in her voice, he released her. He wouldn't pressure her. "Never mind, honey. I know it's been a hell of a year for you." Figuring she'd hurry to her own room, he limped to the bed and dropped onto the mattress. His damn leg was aching again.

But then she was there with her clothes off, and the pain disappeared beneath a flood of euphoria.

Olivia supposed she'd known this was coming. Brandon had always been different. Meeting him again had shown her that as much as she'd cared about Kyle, she'd already accepted that their romantic relationship was over.

"That's it, honey," Brandon whispered as she slid her hands up under his T-shirt to run her fingers over the ridge of his pectoral muscles, his nipples, the sprinkling of soft hair that covered his chest. She liked that he was encouraging her to cast her inhibitions aside, to touch and taste him as eagerly as he was touching and tasting her.

When her bare skin first came into contact with his, he sucked air between his teeth and held her still as if he needed a moment to recover. "You've got me so excited I can hardly breathe," he whispered hoarsely.

She loved the power that knowledge gave her. "There's just one problem…"

He gazed up at her. "What is it?"

"I don't want to hurt your leg."

Even the guttural sound of his laugh made her happy. "I don't want you to worry about that," he said. "All I can feel is how badly I want you. Kiss me."

When her mouth met his, Olivia groaned. It felt as if she'd been waiting for this day since the last time he'd kissed her, in high school. Closing her eyes, she parted her lips and welcomed his tongue in her mouth, enjoying the fact that she was in control and he didn't seem to mind.

"You kiss even better than you feel," he told her.

"Good. Because I want to kiss you again."

He rolled her beneath him as the kiss grew wetter and more heated. Then, anchoring her hands to the mattress above her head, he lowered his head.

Olivia gasped when his mouth closed over her breast. She was so wound up, so desperate to release the building tension, she wanted to rake her nails down his back. But she could only arch into him because he was still restraining her hands.

"Ah, you like that?" he murmured as his tongue made arousing circles.

He spent considerable time on her other breast, the sensitive skin on the inside of her arms and her neck before releasing her wrists. Then she was free to touch him wherever she wanted, and she took full advantage of it—until his mouth returned to hers and his fingers found the part of her that wanted him most.

"Brandon…" Her voice caught on his name.

He was so engrossed it took him a second to respond. "What, sweetheart?"

He sounded dazed. She knew she probably sounded the same. Or maybe she sounded desperate. She was certainly *feeling* desperate, craved nothing more than the completion he promised.

"Do you have birth control?" she asked. "Because I… I have nothing."

"I bought some condoms this morning." His mouth was at her

breast again but his fingers…they were torturing her even more sweetly.

"This morning?" she repeated.

He lifted his head long enough to grin at her. "I was thinking positive."

She cocked an eyebrow at him. "Oh, you were."

"Couldn't help hoping."

Catching handfuls of his hair, she laughed as he settled himself between her legs.

"Do it now," she whispered.

He kissed her tenderly. "I've waited a long time for this."

She liked that they'd left the lights on, that she could see him. He was male beauty and athletic grace. "God, I love—"

He hesitated. "What?" he whispered when she stopped.

She'd been about to say, "Everything about you." Those exact words almost came out despite her efforts to hold them back, but she managed a more acceptable substitution. "The way you make love."

He stared down at her. "Thank you. I love the way you make love, too."

That was nice of him, she thought. He sounded so sincere. Then she locked her legs around his hips, drawing him as deep as possible.

Chapter Eleven

Brandon reached for Olivia before he even opened his eyes, but she was no longer in his bed. His hands met with cool, crisp sheets instead. Only a hint of her perfume remained.

He rolled toward the scent, breathing it in, remembering. Then he shoved himself up on his elbows to listen.

Silence. She wasn't showering. She wasn't moving around in the kitchen.

She was gone from more than just his bed.

"Damn," he muttered, disappointed. But at least his leg wasn't painful. The terrible ache that was becoming such a part of his life had disappeared as completely as Olivia had. Of course, given how often they'd made love in the past three or four hours, he had too many biochemicals flowing through his bloodstream to feel anything unpleasant.

He almost drifted back to sleep. But then he began to wonder if she was gone until she ran some errands, until after the wedding, or for good.

Dragging himself out of bed, he tested his leg to see if it would complain when he put pressure on it, breathed a sigh of relief when it didn't and went to check the other bedroom.

"Already?" he grumbled when he saw it.

She'd taken her suitcase with her.

"Are you really with Kyle's brother?" Nancy asked.

Olivia had been so busy this morning pulling together the last-minute details of the wedding that she'd managed to avoid spending any time alone with her mother or her sister. When Nancy and Noelle stopped for lunch, Olivia grabbed a sandwich and moved gratefully on without them.

But now that the chairs, tables and decorations were in place, and the caterers, minister and disc jockey were primed and ready, she only had to make sure everyone was prepared for the photographer at three. So she and her mother were getting a manicure while Noelle was having her hair curled and stacked in an arrangement that could've been featured in *Bride Magazine*.

"No. Brandon and I are just friends," she said, pretending to be preoccupied with her nails so she wouldn't have to look up.

"You're staying with him," her mother pointed out, "instead of us."

The nail tech left to see to a walk-in customer. Olivia wished she'd come back. "He has an extra room, Mom."

"You're saying you slept in it last night?"

Olivia wished she could insist she had. She *should've* stayed in her own bed. She'd been a fool to get up and go find him.

"More or less," she muttered when her mother leaned forward, demanding an answer to where she'd slept.

"More or less?" Nancy echoed. "Oh, no! Noelle was right. She told me the two of you are sleeping together, but I didn't want to believe it. I don't know what's wrong with you girls. You'll do anything to hurt each other."

"What's happened between Brandon and me has nothing to do with her or Kyle."

"Then why are you getting involved with someone so close to both of them?"

"Brandon has never been close to Noelle. He hasn't even been close to Kyle. And I'm not 'getting involved' with him. I admit things got out of hand this weekend. I... I haven't been myself. It's not every day that your sister gets pregnant by the man you thought you'd marry."

Her mother winced, but Olivia could see the nail tech finishing with the other client and wanted to wrap up the conversation before she returned.

"Anyway, it's over," she continued. "I'm heading home after the wedding and trying to forget this weekend ever happened."

"So it's not an ongoing relationship."

She pasted a pleasant expression on her face because the nail tech was walking toward them. "Of course not. Brandon's going backpacking across Nicaragua in two weeks. Then he's got the ski season. Who knows when he'll be back in Whiskey Creek? And I've already moved my business to Sacramento." A plan that had sounded so ideal in the beginning but had, in the end, cost her so much.

The worry lines on her mother's face softened. "That's a relief."

"Why would it matter to you?" Olivia asked.

"Our lives are complicated enough at the moment. I don't like what Noelle has done, but I can't change it, either. At least I know Kyle will make a good husband. That gives me hope that we can all get past the rough start. I'm not sure I'm convinced of Brandon's integrity."

"Maybe he has more integrity than you think."

Her mother had no chance to reply because Noelle suddenly appeared from the other side of the salon. "Well?"

Even Olivia had to admit she looked beautiful. "Kyle will love it," she said.

Pictures seemed to take forever. Noelle had decreed that Kyle was not to see her before the ceremony, so the groom and his men were sequestered in a different area of the mansion than the bride and her ladies. Callie Vanetta, one of Kyle's best friends, owned a photography studio on Sutter Street, near the center of town, and was handling the pictures like the pro she was. First, she photographed Kyle, his best man and other groomsmen, then Callie came to the bridal suite, where she snapped shots of Noelle getting ready with her maid of honor and bridesmaids.

Feeling more like a robot than a human being, Olivia smiled and nodded and offered her fair share of compliments. They toasted the wedding with delicate flutes of champagne, and took pictures of the process. They admired Noelle's veil and jewelry and hair, and took pictures of that. They hugged and laughed and watched Noelle gaze into a giant mirror, and took even more pictures.

As soon as possible, Olivia faded into the background. She wanted this part, which required so much pretending, to be over. But she didn't want the next part—the wedding—to begin. Then she'd have to face Brandon. Although she'd been able to avoid him so far, that wouldn't be the case much longer.

"Olivia, I…"

Olivia turned from the window overlooking the patio where the ceremony would take place to see Callie standing at her elbow.

"I just… I wanted to say I'm sorry," she whispered. "For… what's happened."

Olivia managed a brief smile, but then Noelle, who'd gone into the bathroom, returned and asked if they should take a picture of her by the window, looking down at the altar below.

"Good idea." Olivia squeezed Callie's arm as she moved past, to let her know she was okay. But she felt a little guilty accepting Callie's sympathy, or anyone else's. She knew Callie would be surprised to learn she wasn't brooding over Kyle.

Brandon didn't get to escort Olivia. Noah Rackham was her partner and had been from the beginning. But she was right in front of him. He kept hoping she'd turn and acknowledge him in some way, maybe give him a smile that indicated she'd enjoyed last night as much as he had. But ever since she'd entered the room she'd kept her eyes averted and her attention on what was going on around them—on everything *but* him.

The music swelled as Kyle, followed by the first of the grooms-men and bridesmaids, walked down the aisle. Noah and Olivia were after Eve and Baxter, two more of Kyle's friends. Brandon watched as they moved into the dazzling sunshine, and he waited several beats before stepping "on deck" with Cheyenne Christensen.

"I can't believe he's going through with this," his partner muttered as she slipped a hand through the crook of his arm.

Her words surprised him.

"What did you say?" Brandon asked.

She turned distressed eyes on him. "I feel like someone should stop the wedding."

"And that someone should be…"

"How about you?" she responded, but she grinned when she said it, and he couldn't help chuckling.

"It's too late to save him now," he said.

She ducked her head, presumably so that the guests wouldn't

see her disapproval. "I know." Then they stepped into the sunlight, too, and pandered to the crowd and Callie's camera as they approached the minister, where they separated.

Brandon thought he saw Olivia looking at him as he released Cheyenne. He smiled to see if he could get her to smile back, but she glanced away so quickly he wasn't sure she'd really seen him. He caught Kyle glaring at him a second later so he moved on without missing a beat.

Once the line was assembled, the traditional wedding march blasted from the speakers and Noelle appeared on her father's arm. As she glided toward her waiting groom, Brandon thought maybe he *should* speak up. He would have, if he'd believed it might make a difference.

But Kyle was determined to go to the guillotine, so Brandon kept his mouth shut as the two repeated their vows, kissed and exchanged rings.

The congratulations came next but, in Brandon's opinion, they were rather subdued. *Does anyone think this marriage has a chance?*

Kyle held his bride's hand, but his gaze strayed almost immediately to Olivia, who seemed determined not to look in his direction, either.

As soon as Callie had finished taking pictures, Brandon made his way over to Olivia. "Everything's working out perfectly," he said. "You've done a great job."

When she turned to face him, he again tried to get a read on what she was feeling. But she didn't give him the opportunity. "Thanks," she said, and moved away.

Olivia knew people were keeping a close eye on her, wondering if it was breaking her heart to see Kyle marry her sister. Their pity humiliated her. But she'd expected as much and couldn't focus on it. Not with Brandon in the room. It was all she could do not to head straight over to him, especially since he seemed so confused by her withdrawal. He'd tried, several times, to approach her.

He was kind to show his support. She appreciated his attempts to make this god-awful night a bit better. But she feared that if she spent even two seconds in his company he'd realize he'd been right all along—she wasn't cut out for casual sex. She couldn't say how it had happened, but she'd somehow lost a piece of her heart in that encounter.

So she avoided him at all costs.

"Are you seeing Brandon?"

Cheyenne stood at the candy table next to her. Olivia had been so busy refilling the jars she hadn't noticed her. "No. Of course not." She cleared her throat. "We're just friends."

"Does *he* know that?"

She swallowed. "Pardon?"

"I've never seen him look at a friend the way he looks at you."

Following Cheyenne's line of sight, she saw Brandon leaning against the wall with a drink in one hand. He had a frown on his face, and that didn't change when their eyes met.

She nodded politely, but this time *he* didn't respond. "He's been very…supportive," she said, forcing herself to turn away.

"I've always thought he's not as bad as people make him sound," Cheyenne said. "A lot of that criticism stems from jealousy, don't you agree? People have a hard time accepting someone who soars so high. Someone who dares to break all the rules."

Olivia wondered why Brandon was on his feet and wished he'd sit down and give his leg a rest. "It's great how much he enjoys the things he loves."

"I think he'd like to enjoy you, too." Her lips curved in a conspirator's grin, but before Olivia could say anything, the toasts started and Cheyenne moved back to her table.

The best man, Noah Rackham, spoke first. He talked about the length of his friendship with Kyle and how Kyle's marriage would make their group of friends larger.

Olivia flinched at that. She'd always thought *she'd* be the next official member of their clique. Then Nancy got up and told her new son-in-law how excited she was to have him as part of the family. She related a cute story about Kyle coming to her rescue once when her car wouldn't start. Everyone smiled because it was endearing, and they'd expect nothing less from Kyle, but Nancy didn't add that he'd done it when he was *her* boyfriend, not Noelle's.

As the toasts wore on, Olivia began to see a pattern. Everyone had praise for Kyle, but no one had much to say about Noelle.

Determined to be big enough to overlook the circumstances that had brought them to this point, Olivia retrieved her glass and lifted it high. "I'd also like to offer a toast."

She regretted her impulsiveness when everyone looked at her. A sudden hush swept through the room, attaching more weight to what she was about to say than she wanted. She got the impression that there were people who hoped to see her break down in public, or perhaps berate her sister as Noelle deserved. But Olivia merely wanted everyone to know that she supported the union and was no longer bitter about how this wedding had come to pass.

Stubbornly maintaining a congenial smile, she turned toward the new couple. She wished she could extol her sister's many virtues, but…she couldn't. So she settled for a few simple words to show everyone that she harbored no animosity. "To the bride and groom. I wish you health, happiness, prosperity and…abiding love."

Although everyone else applauded, the despair on Kyle's face made it difficult to drink to her own toast. His expression told her he knew what her words really meant. She'd cut him loose. She thought Noelle would appreciate that, but her sister seemed as crestfallen as Kyle. Maybe, now that Olivia no longer wanted Kyle, Noelle wasn't sure she wanted him, either.

A few others offered toasts, all of them Kyle's friends, except for Noelle's maid of honor. Then the dancing started.

Breathing a sigh of relief that the night was nearly over, Olivia put down her glass and automatically glanced over to where she'd last seen Brandon. But he wasn't there anymore. After a quick search, she caught sight of him, recognized his blond head at the door.

He was leaving.

Chapter Twelve

"Brandon."

Brandon refused to turn when Olivia called his name. He kept walking through the gardens even when she hurried after him and grabbed his hand.

"Brandon, wait. I—"

"What?" he snapped, stopping so suddenly that she had to back up to avoid running into him. "What could you possibly have to say to me after treating me like I don't exist?"

Taken aback by the depth of his anger, she stared at him. She didn't know what to say, how to explain.

"I... I'm sorry," she mumbled and turned before he could see the tears in her eyes. But this time he came after her. He reached her before she could enter the building. And she was pretty sure he cursed when he kissed her.

Brandon had no idea what had happened at the wedding. If Olivia had been confused, or hurt, or embarrassed. But she was in his arms now and that took the sting away, made it easy to forgive her, to chalk her remoteness up to everything she'd been through in the past few months. When her lips gave way beneath his, allowing him to taste the warm wetness of her mouth, he couldn't even remember why he'd been mad.

"There you are," he breathed as her arms circled his neck. "I've missed you."

She smiled against his mouth. "I've missed you, too."

It didn't matter that it had only been a day. He meant what he'd said, and he could tell she did, too. Eager to take anything she was willing to give him, he groaned as she ground her hips against his. He knew what she wanted. He wanted the same thing.

It would've made more sense to take her home, but he was rattled enough by her earlier behavior to fear she'd change her mind again if he waited. So he pulled her into the shelter of some trees, where they had a degree of privacy.

"You're all I've thought about," he admitted, framing her face with his hands.

"Funny you should say that. You're all I've thought about, too," she said, and then they were kissing again and straining to get closer and she started to remove his belt.

Olivia knew what she was doing was crazy. She'd never behaved like this before—but she'd never felt like this before, either. Instead of stopping him when he slipped a hand inside her dress, she encouraged him, shifting so he could reach what he wanted to touch. Only the fear that what they were doing might cause him to injure his leg gave her pause.

"Don't hurt yourself," she murmured.

"I'm fine," he whispered. "All I need is you."

"But your leg…"

"I'm being careful," he said, but he didn't seem to be keeping that promise when he put on a condom and lifted her up against the building.

Sheer excitement crashed into frantic need for an incredible few minutes, obliterating every bit of pent-up longing. She could hear the music, smell the roses, but all she could feel was Brandon moving inside her.

Afterward, his heart pounded hard and fast beneath her ear and his chest rose and fell as he struggled to catch his breath.

"I've never done it at a wedding before," he told her with a chuckle.

She tilted her head back to look up at him. "I've never done it *anywhere* in public."

Lowering her gently to the ground, he kissed her temple. "I'm a bad influence."

"No. It was my fault as much as yours."

He straightened his clothes while she straightened hers. Then he offered her his hand. "Let's get out of here, go home."

She shook her head.

"Do you have to stay for a while? I hope not. I want more of you."

"I'm sorry, but—" she bit her lip "—this is goodbye, Brandon. I'm not going back to your place."

His eyebrows drew together. "What are you talking about?"

He wasn't used to being denied. But she knew it was better to leave him wanting more. To end on a positive memory…

"I've got my life and you've got yours. I don't even live here."

"So? You're not far. Why not enjoy each other for as long as we can?"

She wanted to walk away while she still had the strength to do it with some dignity. He was leaving the country in two weeks, anyway. "Because you were right."

"About…"

"I'm not capable of casual."

He lifted her chin with one finger. "What if—" he started, but another voice interrupted.

"Olivia? Olivia!"

Noelle was looking for her.

"Where are you?" her sister cried.

"Damn," she whispered and began to step out of the trees, but he tugged her back.

"I'm not ready to let you go."

She wasn't sure if he was referring to this moment or their relationship in general. But it didn't matter either way. "It'll be easier now than later," she said. Then she slipped out.

Hoping to rejoin the wedding without bringing attention to herself, Olivia drew a deep breath and smoothed her hair. But Noelle saw her as soon as she entered the room and came straight for her.

"Where have you *been*?" her sister demanded. "Everyone's been asking about you."

Olivia struggled to appear serene, but the intensity of what she'd just experienced had left her shaken. "Outside, getting some fresh air."

Her sister's eyes narrowed. Had she noticed Olivia's flushed face and Brandon's recent departure and put the two together? "Doing what?"

"Nothing." At the suspicion in Noelle's voice, she couldn't help turning to see if Brandon was behind her, but he wasn't.

Noelle raised one hand to pluck a leaf from her hair. "At my wedding, Olivia? At my wedding?"

Olivia told herself to cross the room and say goodbye. But she couldn't bring herself to stay another second. She'd given this weekend all she had. And still she felt as though she'd failed more than she'd succeeded. "I'm leaving," she said. "I hope you enjoy your honeymoon."

"Wait! Who's going to clean up?" Noelle called, but Olivia ignored her. She walked faster and faster until she was outside, running.

When she reached her car, she got in, locked the doors and peeled out of the lot.

It wasn't until she was almost at her apartment that she realized she'd received a text nearly half an hour earlier. It was from Brandon: I wish you'd change your mind.

Olivia never came back. And she didn't call him. He told himself to move on without her. He'd known all along that he wasn't the kind of man she needed. And right now he had a battle of epic proportions on his hands if he expected to get back on a pair of skis. He didn't need to be involved with a woman who could distract him.

Everything he told himself was logical and true, but that didn't make her any easier to forget.

Friday, when his parents invited him to dinner, he accepted immediately and was grateful for the diversion—until Kyle and Noelle showed up. They must've returned early. They were supposed to be on their honeymoon until Sunday night.

"Did you have a wonderful time?" his mother asked as Bob let them in.

"It was—" Noelle sent Kyle a sulky look "—fine."

"Fine?" Paige blinked in confusion. "You went to Napa Valley. There isn't a more beautiful place on earth."

Noelle lifted her nose in the air. "There was nothing wrong with the scenery. It was Kyle. He insisted on working the whole time we were gone."

"I have a company to run," he explained. "I had to take a few calls. Nothing big."

"Maybe it wasn't big to you." Noelle regarded Brandon with an accusatory air, but he had no idea how she could blame him for anything. "You weren't the one who was always waiting," she snapped at Kyle.

Kyle seemed embarrassed, which was, no doubt, Noelle's intent. "I gave you plenty of attention," he grumbled, and surprised Brandon by appearing relieved to see him. "How's the leg?"

Brandon hadn't heard that question in a while. Only Olivia knew he was still having problems with it. But the pain it caused him had been getting harder and harder to hide. "Fine. It's been fine since I got the cast off."

Fortunately Kyle didn't question that. "Great. When do you go to Nicaragua?"

Paige drew Noelle into the kitchen while Brandon answered. "Next Friday."

Kyle shot a look at his father, who was turning off the TV. "I wish I could go with you," he said in a low voice.

Brandon scowled at him. "Damn it, Kyle."

He didn't say anything. He just pinched the bridge of his nose as if the past week had been one of the hardest he'd ever endured.

"I wish you weren't so damn noble," Brandon muttered.

"It wasn't my nobility that got me into this mess."

Brandon chuckled as Bob came back toward them.

"What?" He looked between them.

Kyle answered. "Nothing," he said, but he didn't seem bothered that his father could overhear when he asked, "How's Olivia?"

An image of her, naked beneath him, popped into Brandon's mind, making the craving he felt for her that much worse. "I wouldn't know."

Kyle studied him for a moment. "If you care about her, don't let her go." He sounded jealous but resigned to the idea. "She's crazy about you. I could tell."

Brandon was so shocked that Kyle would encourage him, he couldn't decide how to respond. Fortunately his mother saved him the trouble by entering the room, carrying a hot casserole. Noelle was right behind her with some rolls.

"Come on over and sit down," she said. "Dinner's served."

Olivia had almost called Brandon a million times. She wanted to see him again. But she knew that if he was leaving in a week there was no point. He'd go on his way and forget about her. She didn't need to grow even more attached to him.

But it had been a long, lonely week since the wedding. It didn't help that Kyle texted her on Sunday: Brandon seemed lost at dinner Friday.

There was no context to let her decipher his meaning or his intent. She planned to ignore it but ultimately wrote back: What does that have to do with me?

Everything, came the reply.

Aren't you supposed to be on your honeymoon? she typed.

Work brought me back early.

A few seconds later, he added a Thank God that almost made her laugh. She knew, in a way no one else probably did, what he was talking about. Noelle was not an easy person to take for long periods of time.

I refuse to feel sorry for you, she texted back.

He followed up with a wink, and that brought a smile to her lips. "Poor Kyle." She was just glad she hadn't heard from her sister. She was also glad that it was wedding season and she'd signed three new clients. The added work was keeping her busy, giving her a good excuse not to drive back to Whiskey Creek—even though, when she stopped working for five seconds, that was exactly where her heart wanted to take her.

Chapter Thirteen

Kyle, of all people, called to say goodbye. "Do you have every-thing? Do you need a ride to the airport?" he asked.

Brandon glanced at the luggage he'd packed. He'd hired a car to take him to Sacramento. He was meeting his agent, Scott Jones, for lunch before heading to the airport. To pay a driver to come all the way out to Whiskey Creek was expensive, but he couldn't let any of his friends or family see that he wasn't taking a backpack.

"I'm covered," he replied. "Thanks, though."

"Your plane leaves at five?"

He grimaced as he shifted. His leg was giving him so much trouble today. It was getting worse all the time. "Five thirty."

After this small talk, there was a slight pause. "Okay. Have a nice trip."

Brandon stopped Kyle before he could hang up. "You thought you'd offer me a ride because…"

"When she was here for the wedding, Olivia told me something I've decided might be true."

He hadn't realized Olivia and Kyle had had much chance to talk, or were even on speaking terms. That toast at the wedding had been so generous it had blown Brandon away. He couldn't imagine many other women being able to forgive so quickly that they could wish a sister well despite the hurt she'd caused. "What did Olivia say?"

"That I should try talking to you now and then. That I might be missing out on having a great brother."

A fresh pang of longing shot through Brandon. He hadn't talked to Olivia since their encounter in the gardens during the wedding, but his desire to hear her voice hadn't diminished. If anything it had grown stronger. "She did?"

"I told you how much she admires you."

"I remember. I'm still not sure why you bothered to do that."

"I missed out. Doesn't mean you have to," he said and hung up.

Brandon stared at his phone. He wanted to call Olivia one more time, to at least be able to say goodbye. But a honk let him know the car had arrived.

Today Brandon was leaving for Europe and his surgery. Olivia had received a text from him a few days ago telling her he'd like to stop in to say goodbye. She wanted to say goodbye to him, too, but she knew it would be too difficult to see him again, knowing what lay ahead.

She sighed as she clicked on one YouTube clip of him after another. He was truly an impressive skier. She loved watching him plunge down those treacherous mountains. There was an inherent thrill in seeing someone who mattered so much to her do something so magical. But she also cringed with each new descent. She knew he was addicted to the adrenaline, and if he continued, he might not survive.

Her phone rang just as she was trying to make herself go to the office. She had work to do, work that was piling up because she couldn't seem to quit thinking about Brandon.

For a split second, she thought maybe it was him on the phone. But it wasn't. This was Noelle. Her sister was trying to reach her for the first time since the wedding.

Unable to deal with Noelle on this of all days, she set her phone aside. But a minute later, she heard the buzz of an incoming text.

"What do you want?" she grumbled and checked her messages.

Brandon's off on his Nicaragua trip for God knows how long. He probably won't even remember your name when he gets back, her sister had written.

Noelle couldn't seem to help herself. She just had to be spiteful.

Olivia nearly responded with some sarcastic remark. But her mother had told her Noelle was having a tough time adjusting to married life. Apparently stealing Kyle hadn't brought her the happiness she'd thought it would. So, instead of unleashing all the hurtful things she was dying to say, Olivia wrote, I wish Brandon the best.

Then she went to get showered. Noelle was right on one account. Brandon would forget her soon enough.

* * *

Lunch with Scott was tense. His agent was the only one, besides Olivia, who knew that Brandon's leg wasn't healing properly, the one who'd arranged the operation to fix it. He had a vested interest in seeing Brandon succeed, so he clearly wasn't happy when Brandon came toward him, unable to walk without a slight limp.

"It's worse?" he said.

"A lot worse." He hated to hear himself say that, but there it was.

Scott cursed, looked away, then forced a smile. "Dr. Shapiro will take care of you. He's the best leg man in the world. A real miracle-worker."

Brandon nodded and listened as Scott detailed what they'd accomplish next season. Neither one of them admitted that, if the operation didn't work, his career was finished.

By the time the waitress brought the check, Brandon was eager for lunch to be over. He'd thought seeing Scott would be encouraging, but he found that their visit had depressed him instead. It was the worry in Scott's eyes.

"When do you have to be at the airport?" Scott asked.

Brandon glanced at his watch. "Half an hour. We'd better go."

They rode in silence. There wasn't much more to say. Brandon had a rough few weeks ahead of him, with uncertainty his only companion.

They were in line at the ticket counter when he received a text from Olivia.

Before you go, I just want you to know that I've never felt about anyone else the way I feel about you. You own my heart, Brandon. I think you have since prom. So please, be safe. I want to see you on the slopes next fall.

"What is it?" Although Scott had been getting anxious to leave, he was watching Brandon now, too curious to be distracted by the passing time.

"A friend," he replied, but he realized almost as soon as those words came out of his mouth that she was much more than a friend. He'd never felt about anyone else the way he felt about her, either.

"I can help you here, sir." The gal at the ticket counter smiled, expecting him to approach. But he couldn't move.

"Brandon?" Scott had already dragged his luggage to the scale.

"I can't do this," he said, remaining right where he was.

Scott's eyes nearly popped out of his head. "*What?* Are you crazy?"

The reason behind the fear that had been gripping his stomach for days suddenly became clear. It wasn't only his career he was afraid of losing. "I have to see someone."

"I have no idea what you're talking about," Scott said. "See who?"

Waving the family behind him to the counter in his place, Brandon stepped out of line.

His shocked agent hurried over with his bags. "What are you doing?" he whispered. "If you miss this plane, you'll miss your operation. And I'm not sure when we'll be able to reschedule."

"I can't leave her," he said simply.

"Can't leave *who*, for crying out loud?" Scott jerked on his tie, trying to loosen it. "You have to get on this plane! Do you want to ski next season or not?"

He wanted to ski. But that was no longer *all* he wanted. "Drive me back to Sacramento or I'll take a cab," he said, and wrenched his suitcases from Scott's hands.

Olivia felt much better after texting Brandon. She knew she'd probably never see him again—unless it was to bump into him occasionally while visiting Whiskey Creek. But at least she'd finally had the guts to be honest with him about her feelings. It wasn't as if she expected anything in return. She'd spoken the truth so he would know how hard she'd be praying for his health and well-being while he was gone. That was all. He needed someone to know, someone to care.

Now she'd given him that.

She was packing her briefcase with swatches and magazines—she had to meet another bride at River City Resort Club & Spa tomorrow morning—when she heard the buzzer that indicated someone had walked into the small anteroom outside her office. She didn't have any employees, couldn't afford payroll, so she called out, "Welcome to Weddings by Olivia. I'll be right there."

"Could you hurry?" came the response. "I've got a plane to catch."

Brandon! Olivia's heart jumped into her throat as she scrambled around her desk.

When she reached the reception area, she saw him standing just inside the door with an exasperated-looking man wearing what appeared to be an expensive suit.

"What...what are you doing here?" she asked, glancing between them.

"I couldn't do it," Brandon said. "I couldn't leave without you."

Was she hearing him right? "But your...your operation!"

"It can wait."

"Not if he wants to ski next season, it can't," the man he'd brought with him cut in. "But he can still make it if he's on the next plane."

"When does it leave?" she asked.

"In three hours."

"I'll only go if you go with me," Brandon said. "Do I have any hope of talking you into that?"

"I—" Her mind whirled as she thought of her apartment, her business.

"Come here, honey," Brandon said, reaching for her.

He didn't have to ask twice. She walked right into his arms and pressed her body against his, so grateful to see him, to touch him, her chest ached at the prospect of letting go.

He'd come back. For her.

"I think what we feel deserves a chance," he explained, his voice low in her ear. "I don't want to walk away from it."

"I'd like to be there for the operation." She wanted nothing more than to watch over him, keep him safe. "But I have clients to take care of and rent to pay—"

The other man made a show of tapping his watch. "Maybe you could join him in a week or two."

"Olivia, meet Scott Jones, my agent," Brandon said. "You don't have to listen to anything he says. Personally I'm finding that quite liberating."

Now she understood why this other person was so upset. Brandon was risking his career by coming here.

"You could make it for the recovery," Scott said. "That's the most important part, anyway."

Not to her. She wanted to be there to support Brandon through the whole thing. She wanted to go with him now.

She could refer her clients to another planner she knew in River City. That wasn't the tough part. The tough part was paying her rent without that income…

"He's right," Brandon said. "I'm being selfish. I've just missed you so much. You can come later."

She considered the money in her savings account. She'd put that away to get her through difficult times, had promised herself she wouldn't touch it except in an emergency.

Was she willing to spend it on love?

Everyone she knew would probably tell her she was being foolish, reckless. If Brandon recovered, he'd return to his career. But when she was with Kyle, and even long before that, she'd been so responsible, methodical, cautious—and that hadn't saved her from heartbreak. If Brandon could risk his career for her, she supposed she could risk her career for him.

"I'll throw some clothes in a bag. The rest I can handle via the internet," she said, and smiled happily as his arms tightened around her and he buried his face in her neck.

"I'll make you glad you did," he promised.

Epilogue

"So what happened?" Lorianna leaned forward, her hair now dry and her coffee long cold. "What was wrong with Brandon's leg? I mean, I've seen footage of the accident. I knew his injuries took him out of the sport. But why didn't his leg heal? What did the doctor find?"

Olivia tightened her ponytail, then turned her mug of tea in a slow circle. She was thinking about how lucky she was to have found Brandon.

Maybe letting go of her resentment over what Noelle had done wasn't completely outside the realm of possibility. Noelle had behaved badly and often behaved badly still, but she was so caught up in fulfilling her own needs that she seemed almost incapable of considering the needs of those around her. She definitely didn't understand that the way she approached life would never bring her the satisfaction she craved. Look where she was. Not only had she lost Kyle, she'd tried to get together with several other men since, none of whom were interested in more than a quick fling. She was working as a day clerk at a gift shop, moonlighting as a waitress at Sexy Sadie's and living at home. She didn't even have any good friends. The type of people she associated with came and went.

Weren't the natural consequences of her actions punishment enough? Why did Olivia feel Noelle had to be remorseful in order to obtain forgiveness?

Maybe she was using Noelle's behavior as an excuse, Olivia realized. It was easier to move on without someone like that in her life. But they *were* sisters.

"Olivia? You still with me?" Lorianna prompted.

Olivia looked up. "Oh, sorry. You asked…"

"What was wrong with Brandon's leg."

"It was a bone infection," she said. "Dr. Shapiro wasn't sure how the doctors here missed that, considering it was so extensive. He had to scrape away the infected area and drain a couple of abscesses. But, thanks to his efforts, followed by some heavy antibiotic therapy, Brandon recovered completely. He has no pain now."

Lines appeared on her friend's forehead. "So it wasn't his injury that took him out of skiing?"

"Not really. He could've come back for one or two more seasons. He considered it."

"Why didn't he?"

A sense of warmth, of well-being, passed through her. "He wanted something different by then."

Lorianna's lips curved upward for probably the first time since she'd arrived in Whiskey Creek. "He wanted *you*, a family."

Olivia's hand went to her stomach. "Yes."

"I bet Scott was upset to hear that news," Lorianna said with a laugh. "I don't know him well. Jeff had a different agent when he was skiing. But any sports agent who repped an athlete like Brandon wouldn't want him to quit too soon."

"Scott was definitely disappointed."

"But Brandon didn't change his mind."

"No."

Lorianna pushed her cup toward the center of the table. "How did you feel about his decision?"

"Torn. If he was going to give up skiing, I didn't want him to regret it, or blame me later. But I also didn't want him to take the same risks he'd been taking."

Lorianna bit her lip. "And? *Has* he missed it?"

Olivia went over the past three years in her mind, examining those days, as she often did, for any dissatisfaction on his part. "I'm sure he has. But he's never focused on that loss. He got involved in opening the store and giving ski lessons. He even started his own winter camps for kids, and he still skis for fun. He seems to be…content." And that made her content, as well.

After that, they both seemed to get lost in their thoughts, and the silence stretched out.

Several minutes later, Lorianna spoke again. "So that man who came to the door—your ex-boyfriend—he's also your brother-in-law?"

"Can you believe that?"

"I guess stranger things have happened. But it can't be comfortable to see him at family gatherings."

"It's getting easier. I believe he's glad I'm happy."

"Is he happy?"

"I think he'd like to find someone and settle down."

"He's a handsome man. I can't imagine that'll pose a problem—once he gets over you."

"I hope you're right. I'd like him to have what I have."

Lorianna pulled the top of her robe more tightly closed. "So what are you going to do?"

Olivia got up to set their cups in the sink. "About what?"

"Noelle. Isn't she the person you need to forgive? Because it sounds like you've forgiven Kyle."

"I'm not quite sure how to handle my sister," she admitted. "What would you do if you were me? Should I let the past go?"

Lorianna toyed with her belt. "That's hard to say. She doesn't deserve it."

"Same thing Kyle said. But your husband probably doesn't deserve it, either," Olivia pointed out.

"At least *he* claims he's sorry," she responded.

"*Claims?* You don't believe it?"

She stared down at her hands. "Actually, I do. He was in tears when he told me what he'd done. I've never seen him cry like that."

Olivia leaned against the counter. "So…what does that mean?"

"It means, once I recover from the disappointment, I'll try to rebuild, give him another chance."

After what she'd been through herself, Olivia had a small inkling of what Lorianna must be feeling. "That won't be easy," she said as she rinsed the cups and put them in the dishwasher.

"No. But your story about Kyle made me realize that I don't want to throw away what we have over one mistake."

After wiping off the counter, Olivia went over and plugged in the Christmas tree lights. She couldn't say if Lorianna was doing the right thing. Only time would tell whether Jeff was capable of appreciating her forgiveness for the gift it was. But as Olivia stood back and looked at all the twinkling lights, her heart lifted as if it had suddenly divested itself of a huge burden.

She was confident she'd arrived at her decision, too.

"You're *sure* we have to do this?" Brandon raised one eyebrow as they stood on the doorstep of her mother's house. Olivia was holding a casserole dish, while he was loaded down with the presents she'd purchased and wrapped.

"Not entirely," she replied. "But it's Christmas, right? I want to give a more meaningful gift than a new purse or...or a shirt."

That didn't seem to change his mind. "This is more of a sacrifice than I think you should be required to make."

"Anything that doesn't require a sacrifice isn't much of a gift. Remember that O. Henry story?"

"Sure. But when has Noelle ever sacrificed for anyone?"

"Don't confuse me," she said. "My decision can't be contingent on that."

He winked at her. "Okay. I won't argue. I'm just happy you're the kind of person you are."

"We're going to have a baby. We want to have good relations with both our families, don't we?"

"Personally? I like things the way they are, but you mean enough to me that I'm willing to do anything—even if it involves your sister."

Her mother opened the door before she could respond. "Olivia! Brandon! What are you two doing here?"

"We came over to surprise you," Olivia said.

Her mother smoothed the apron covering her black polyester slacks and red sweater. She wore Christmas tree earrings that blinked, with a matching brooch. "I was just doing some holiday baking. Smells like you've been doing the same."

"I made some hot crab dip for your dinner tonight."

"That cheesy one?" she asked with apparent enthusiasm.

Olivia nodded.

"I love that!"

"I know." She smiled, but she'd already warmed the dip and the heat was beginning to seep through her hot-pad holders. "Are you going to let us in?"

"Of course. I just—" Nancy lowered her voice "—Noelle's home tonight."

For a moment, Olivia's customary reaction to the prospect of seeing her sister nearly got the better of her, but she quickly beat back those negative feelings. "That's okay. We thought maybe we could all have dinner together for a change."

Her mother's gaze shifted disbelievingly from her to Brandon and back again.

"It's true," he said. "But she gets all the credit. I tried to talk her out of it."

He was teasing, trying to lighten the mood, but they all understood that it was basically true.

"Has Kyle talked to you?" her mother asked.

"He came by, yes," Olivia replied.

"Then I wish I'd gone to him sooner."

Olivia wasn't sure she would've been ready before now. But there was no time to respond. Her father spoke up from where he sat on the couch, watching TV. "Well, are you going to let them in, Nancy? Or are you going to make them stand out in the cold all night?"

At that, her mother stepped out of the way, and Olivia hurried inside to put the hot casserole dish on the stove, where it couldn't burn the countertop. She'd originally planned to have a talk with her family, to finally sit them down and hash out the past. After that, she'd imagined embracing Noelle and telling her she no longer held anything against her. But the coziness of her parents' home, and the fact that Noelle, when she walked out from the bedroom area in back, acted pleasantly surprised but didn't question their presence, made Olivia change her mind. Why go into all of that again? Why cause fresh tears by dredging up those negative emotions?

"How're things at the shop?" her father asked Brandon.

"Sales are strong, considering that we haven't had a lot of snow this year," he replied, and sat down with Ham while Nancy drew her and Noelle into the kitchen.

"Come see the pies I made this morning," she told them, as excited as though it was already Christmas morning.

If Noelle had already seen what her mother had baked, she didn't say so. Like Olivia, she admired the pies, which were sitting off to one side so they wouldn't be in the way of other preparations.

"They look and smell wonderful," Olivia said.

"Maybe someday I'll learn how to cook." Noelle sounded somewhat wistful, which reminded Olivia of everything they'd been missing out on since they'd stopped having much to do with each other.

"We could set aside a few hours and have Mom teach us both," she suggested.

Nancy's smile couldn't have stretched any wider. "There's a real knack to it, but I could show you."

"I don't know when I'd be able to do that." Noelle sounded genuinely disappointed. "I have to work so many shifts during the next two weeks."

"You'll have Christmas off, won't you?" Olivia asked. The boutique would be closed—Olivia knew that much—but Sexy Sadie's stayed open year-round.

"No, but people should be in a good mood that night." She shrugged. "Maybe I'll get some decent tips."

Olivia studied her.

"What?" Noelle sounded slightly defensive, as if she was expecting a comment—but Olivia smiled.

"I like the way you just turned that into a positive."

Noelle pressed a hand to her chest. "You like something about *me*?"

Olivia remembered how cute Noelle had been as a young girl,

how enthusiastic she'd been about every aspect of life. "I like a lot of things about you," she said. And then, even though this hug wasn't the one she'd planned in her mind, she pulled her sister close. When she let go, Noelle looked absolutely stunned. "What was *that* for?"

"We're sisters," Olivia said simply. "And it's Christmas."

Their mother blinked as if holding back tears, but then a buzzer went off and she rushed to the oven. While her attention was elsewhere, Noelle lowered her voice. "I'm sorry. I don't know why I did what I did to…to you and Kyle. I don't know why I do half the things I do."

Olivia patted her arm. "It's okay," she said and, somehow, she meant it.

"This is going to be quite a Christmas," her mother said, joining them again. "I don't remember a time I've felt so optimistic."

With a laugh, Olivia slipped an arm around her mother's shoulders. "Merry Christmas."

* * * * *

HARLEQUIN
Reader Service

Enjoyed your book?

Try the perfect subscription for Romance readers and get more great books like this delivered right to your door.

See why over 10+ million readers have tried Harlequin Reader Service.

Start with a Free Welcome Collection with free books and a gift—valued over $20.

Choose any series in print or ebook. See website for details and order today:

TryReaderService.com/subscriptions